"*Dactyl Hill Squad* is an engaging, lively adventure with a heroine I wish I were, in a world I didn't want to leave." —Jesmyn Ward, two-time National Book Award–winning author of *Sing, Unburied, Sing*

"This incredible story brings history to life with power, honesty, and fun." —Laurie Halse Anderson, *New York Times* bestselling author of *Chains*

"Kids, the Civil War, and dinosaurs—action doesn't get any better than this!" —Tamora Pierce, *New York Times* bestselling author of *The Song of the Lioness*

"A crackling fantasy adventure full of thrilling scenes." —James McPherson, Pulitzer Prize–winning author of *Battle Cry of Freedom*

Praise and Awards for

FREEDOM FIRE

A Publishers Weekly Best of Summer Reading

"An unforgettable historical, high-octane adventure." —Dav Pilkey, author/illustrator of the Dog Man series

★ "Blisteringly paced, thought- provoking adventure." —*Kirkus Reviews*, starred review

★ "Intelligent, rousing, and abundantly diverse, this is every bit as satisfying as the first installment." —*Publishers Weekly*, starred review

"Older has middle-graders' number with this dino-charged series. Stampedes are likely!" —*Booklist*

Praise for

THUNDER RUN

"Older infuses what could have been a basic romp with depth, using a critical social justice lens to examine the past while also embedding in it representation that we can aspire to in the future." —*Kirkus Reviews*

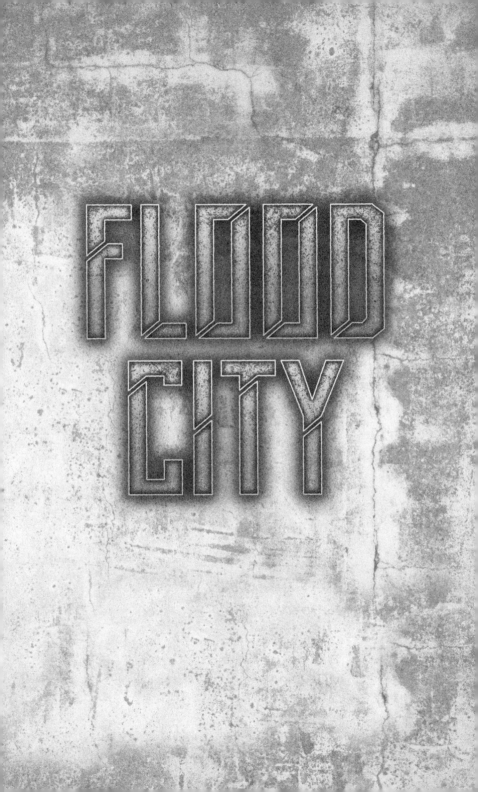

DANIEL JOSÉ OLDER

SCHOLASTIC PRESS / NEW YORK

Library of Congress Cataloging-in-Publication Data

Names: Older, Daniel José, author.
Title: Flood City / Daniel José Older.
Description: First edition. | New York : Scholastic Press, 2021. |
Summary: Flood City is the only habitable place left on the drowned Earth, but it is also a battleground between the Star Guard who have controlled the city for decades and the Chemical Barons in their spaceships who once ruled the planet, want it back, and are now preparing to destroy it; the future will depend on Max, his sister Yala of Flood City, and Ato, a young Chemical Baron who just wants to keep his twin brother alive and not hurt anyone—and somehow these natural enemies will have to work together to save Earth.
Identifiers: LCCN 2020028676 (print) | LCCN 2020028677 (ebook) |
ISBN 9781338111125 (hardcover) | ISBN 9781338111149 (ebook)
Subjects: LCSH: Dystopias—Juvenile fiction. | Brothers and sisters—Juvenile fiction. | Twins—Juvenile fiction. | Government, Resistance to—Juvenile fiction. | Friendship—Juvenile fiction. | Science fiction. | Adventure stories. | CYAC: Science fiction. | Brothers and sisters—Fiction. | Twins—Fiction. | Friendship—Fiction. | Government, Resistance to—Fiction. | Adventure and adventurers—Fiction. | LCGFT: Science fiction. | Action and adventure fiction.
Classification: LCC PZ7.1.O45 Fl 2021 (print) | LCC PZ7.1.O45 (ebook) | DDC 813.6 [Fic]—dc23

1 2020

Printed in the U.S.A.   23

First edition, February 2021

Book design by Kay Petronio

FOR ERICKA AND SKYLA

PART ONE

FLOOD CITY CITIZENS!!!

TODAY IS FLOOD CITY DAY!

A MUNICIPALITY OF THE
INTERGALACTIC STAR GUARD
CONGLOMERATE

FESTIVITIES WILL COMMENCE TONIGHT AT THE MUSIC HALL

The Flood City Orchestra will play the *Founders' Suite*. Mrs. DeAngelo's class will perform the choreography. Mr. Sanpedro's dougies will be available. The Star Guard has generously agreed to donate extra ration packets to facilitate our celebration. Come mark the anniversary of Flood City's founding with your fellow citizens! Check today's *Flood City Gazette* for full schedule and details.*

* All Flood City citizens are reminded to stay alert at all times for Chemical Baron and/or iguanagull attacks when participating in events. Attendance constitutes recognition and implied acceptance of risks and dangers associated with being in crowded areas. The Star Guard's participation in said event is limited to the granting of permission for use of space, the use of printing tech for the purposes of this propaganda, and the temporary waiver of daily ration limits. Star Guard participation does not indicate the Star Guard's approval of any political messaging or their openness to arbitration in the event of a tragedy, which hopefully won't happen. And if it did, it would be terrible. But you still couldn't hold the Star Guard legally responsible. Thanks.

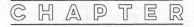
Max Salazar and his older sister, Yala, burst out of their twentieth-floor apartment and sped into the still-gray sky over Flood City. Side by side, they plummeted toward the jagged ground. The wind screamed against their ears, sent Yala's locs flying out behind her, and made Max's stomach turn somersaults. The broken buildings around them sped past, faster and faster, until everything blurred into one soggy gray-brown smudge. Then (finally) Yala yelled, "Now!" and zipped out of sight with an explosion of fire and smoke. Max pushed both his heels down inside his jetboots, waiting for that heart-stopping jolt as the rocket engines propelled him skyward.

Nothing happened.

Uh-oh.

The ground flew up toward Max like an angry monster. He pushed his heels down again and felt the ignition pedals drop uselessly against the boot soles.

"Max!" Yala yelled from far up above. Max could already make out the mountains of scrap metal between the crumbling buildings. A peaceful stream wandered amidst the detritus beneath him. He dug his heels in again, this time getting a shallow sputtering. It was better than nothing. If he could get ignited, he still might be able to . . .

FWOOOOOM!!!

The jetboots exploded to life. Max jolted forward, bounced off a tire mountain, and zipped just inches over a pile of razor-sharp metal shards before speeding back up, up, up, past Yala's bemused face and higher than their apartment building, straight into the early morning sky and way above Flood City, which glimmered and shone below. There was the cliff at the far edge that separated their neighborhood from the other areas. Beyond it, the main downtown section had already begun to bustle, and past that lay the open plaza outside the Music Hall where the pageant would happen that night. A little ways below it, the front end of a huge ocean liner stuck straight up into the air, marking Barge Annex. Off in the distance, Max could just make out the Tumbled Together Towers.

He took it all in for a single sweet moment, then let himself drift back down to where his sister hovered, looking unimpressed.

"Close call, space cadet," Yala said. "You forget to take off the ignition lock?"

"Maybe."

Yala had programmed Max's jetboots to bypass the ignition lock if he pressed down on the heel pedals a few times in a row. It wasn't the first time that had come in handy. She rolled her eyes at him and then blasted off.

Sometimes Yala would sneak out of their house and just sit in the tunnel late at night to let her thoughts wander. Today though, her mind was cramped around a secret, and even the fresh ocean air in her favorite hideaway wasn't enough to cheer her up. Max was so absentminded. Another near-death experience for the records. And what was he going to do when she was gone?

"Yala! Wait up!" Max flitted into the circular tunnel that gaped out of the rock wall across from the fifteenth floor of their building. His flickering headlight made him look like a dizzy firefly as he veered too close to the wall. Yala had already glided in and clicked on her headlight. It was still early, so no one else was around. The darkness was peaceful. Occasional drip-drops accompanied the shushing waves not far away.

"Hurry up, slowpoke!" Yala called over her shoulder. Before Max had time to let the calmness of the passageway seep in, the bright lights of downtown Flood City were dancing toward him. He zipped out and was instantly surrounded by the daily ebb and flow of jetbooted commuters bustling off to work. The smell of Mr. Sanpedro's freshly baked goods filled the air just outside the tunnel, and sure enough, a sizable crowd had gathered around the window to get their morning snacks. Mr. Sanpedro ran his bakery from inside a half-destroyed train car that jutted out of the rocky slope.

"Yo, I want some dougies," Yala said as Max floated up beside her.

"I don't know," Max panted. "That line is pretty long."

"I don't think I can take another day of these ration packs."

Max eyed the little gray package that dangled from his knapsack. Inside was the blandest of bland food ever: stale bread with some sickly gray pudding on it and a bag of flaky cracker things. It was the same meal the Star Guard provided to every Flood City household, day after day after day since they'd stopped the Chemical Baron attack and taken over the one city left on Earth. Just thinking about the ration pack made Max want to barf his guts out.

No one knew how Mr. Sanpedro did what he did, but if you brought him your ration, he'd hand it over to his team of hunterfly helpers and a few minutes later they'd send it back up transformed into a delicious, steamy hot pastry called a dougie. It even had gobs of thick, sweet sauce dripping off it.

It was worth the long line, but they were already running late. Max looked out toward the ocean, past the Tumbled Together Towers, to where Saint Solomon's Hospital hovered over the ocean. "Mom's shift is ending soon and I don't want to miss her."

Yala shrugged. "I guess since the pageant's tonight we probably shouldn't—"

"I don't wanna talk about the—" Max didn't finish because he was too busy ducking out of the way. Something blurred past his head and smashed into the rock wall behind him. "What the—?"

"Tinibu!" Yala yelled.

A small orange head with a long beak appeared from the brand-new hole in the mountainside. With two tiny hands, the creature adjusted the ornately carved mask on his face, shook off a cloud of dust, and then popped fully out.

"Jeez, Tinibu, you almost knocked my head off," Max said, brushing debris off the little hunterfly.

"What are you doing up so early anyway?" Yala asked. "You usually don't leave the house till long after we do."

Tinibu flitted his wings and nodded his head in the direction of the bakery.

"Right," Yala said. "For the big concert tonight, of course! Mr. Sanpedro asked for extra hunterflies to help him out with deliveries and baking so he could prepare for the feast. What's wrong, Max?"

Max had turned an uneasy shade of green at the mention of the concert. It would be his first time playing lead in the horn section. What was worse, the whole entire city would be watching. Even worse than that, Djinna, the holographer's daughter, was leading the percussion ensemble. She'd probably be right next to him in fact, and she'd know every single time he messed up. Max's tummy squirmed like it was trying to break loose and wander freely around his body. "I'm fine."

Yala rolled her eyes and turned back to Tinibu. "Yo, can you hook us up? We trying to make it to Mom's hospital before her shift ends."

Tinibu twittered irritably.

"I know, I know . . . but Max's all nervous about the show tonight . . ."

"I am not!"

"And doesn't wanna wait in line."

The hunterfly raised an eyebrow at Max, made a clicking noise with his tongue, and then flashed off to the bakery.

"Great," Max groaned. "Now I'm gonna wake up tomorrow with half my hair shaved off or something."

"You didn't wanna wait and I wanted dougies. This way, everybody gets what they want and I get to see you with a ridiculous haircut. Now c'mon. Tinibu will catch up to us."

Yala sped off into the crisscrossing jetboot traffic. Max followed, grumbling. Jetboot repair shops and odds-and-ends bodegas were opening up for business in the sloping rock walls and sea-soaked buildings around them. Iron grates grumbled and clanked back to their resting spots to reveal storefront windows glowing with the first rays of sun.

Old Man Cortinas hovered out in front of his barbershop. He waved at Yala and Max. "Hey, kids!" he yelled, a mischievous grin stretching beneath his big mustache. "You ready for the show tonight, Max?"

Max's tummy did a cartwheel.

"Hi, Mr. C," Yala yelled, gliding easily out of the way as a group of chattering kindergartners fluttered past behind their teacher. "He's—"

"I'm fine!" Max said. "I can't wait!"

"Right." Old Man Cortinas nodded. "You'll be fine!" He took a sip from his tiny coffee cup and chuckled.

Around a corner and down a narrow alleyway, the hustle and bustle of downtown Flood City was only a vague murmur beneath the gnashing ocean waves. Yala had taken them along Max's least favorite shortcut. "You said you were in a hurry," she reasoned, springing along the winding corridor.

"But, Yala . . . so close to the Electric Ghost Yard. I don't know . . ."

The Electric Ghost Yard was a no-man's-land: a mess of tangled electronic cabling spread across an abandoned lot. The Chemical Barons had dumped the wiring as they fled to space after the first Flood City uprising. Everyone said that the cables harbored errant souls of people from the days before the Floods. Rumors or not, the place was creepy. It lay in the shadow of a tall, crumbly row of brownstones. Flashes of blue electrical light crackled between the wires, which seemed to writhe like a slo-mo worm pile.

Max gazed farther down the dark alleyway. He could just make out where the building wall gave way to a jangled barbwire fence. He could hear the snapping currents. The wind brought in a nauseating whiff of burning rubber and something else . . . something that maybe had been alive once, but was now just charred ickiness.

"Chicken?" Yala said.

"No, I just value my life is all. Unlike some people."

"You know what'd be even faster? If we just flew directly *over* the—"

"No! Are you nuts, Yala?"

No one flew over the Electric Ghost Yard. Even the toughest Flood City folks, the ones who scoffed at all the creepy stories, the ones who'd happily zip straight off into an oncoming typhoon to help fortify the city—even they weren't *that* nuts.

"Suit yourself." Yala shrugged. "Around it is." She sped off.

Max put a palm on his forehead. "How do I let you— Hey, wait up!"

As Max dashed after his sister, something on the alley wall moved ever so slightly. It was practically invisible, a large dark stain on a brick area between tattered posters and exposed pipes. Its motion was languid, could've been mistaken for the shadow of some cloth wafting in a gentle breeze. Two long white slits opened along the shape and squinted toward where Max and Yala buzzed around the edge of the Electric Ghost Yard. A crease folded through the middle of the shadow, its edges turned upward into a smile.

Somewhere in the sky far above Flood City, a cloud cruiser hovered silently. It was long and gray, its sleek body designed for speed and camouflage in the thick haze of pollution that had covered Earth since before the Floods. Four laser cannons glared out from its lower hull; each sent tiny red beams of light dancing through the cloud banks.

The lasers circled endlessly, leaving faded ghost lights in their wake. If any one of them picked up the slightest motion, even a passing butterfly or iguanagull, all four would immediately focus on that spot and the cannons would begin charging up. It was beautiful and creepy at the same time, Ato thought, gazing out the window at the swirling vigil.

Everyone else was asleep, zonked out after a long night of planning their surveillance run, and besides the slow drifting of gray-brown clouds, the lasers were the only things moving. The mission was a few hours away still—Mephim's maps and charts calculating every last detail were splattered haphazardly across the table—but for some reason Ato felt a terror rising up inside of him every time he thought about it.

It's not like it was his first run. Even though Ato and his twin brother, Get, were only twelve and by far the youngest Barons in the ruling Chemical Dynasty, they'd been on more than their fair share of missions. The first few were terrifying: flack from the Star Guard ground guns exploding all around the cloud cruiser, that rising nauseous feeling coupled with the utter helplessness of being in a ship that someone else was driving and not being able to see anything that was going on, *and* being only twelve. But once the booming and rattling died down and both brothers were still alive and intact, they were flushed with the thrill of having survived such an ordeal. All they wanted was to do it again. Ato still remembered that exhilaration coursing through his body, the look in his brother's wide eyes, Mephim gazing proudly from the commander's chair.

In the past few months, missions had become a routine part of life for Ato and Get, like dodging Star Guard potshots was just another thing that happened in the day. It still rattled Ato, but at least the regularity had steeled him a little to the constant thought of death.

An urgent beeping from one of the control panels pulled Ato from his reverie. The laser seekers had picked up an unusual movement in the sky around them.

Ato glanced out the window. The gray pollution clouds hung in the air like droopy old whales. Nothing seemed to be moving and the lasers were nowhere in sight. He crossed to the other end of the cruiser—nearly tripping over a half-empty coffee mug someone had left on the floor during their planning session the night before—and peered out into the clouds. There it was: a single iguanagull coasting along just a few feet away. Ato could make out its large scaly head, that light green swath of skin flapping along its neck, and the gray feathers lining its wings. The four laser seekers had grouped on its midsection. Ato could imagine the cannons beneath him aiming hungrily at the creature, waiting for the push of a button to unleash their fire.

The control panel lapsed into a calmer beep now that the target had been identified. A red button flashed on and off. Ato stared at it. The iguanagull's razor-sharp claws could tear straight through the cruiser's metal armor, but it would take a whole flock of them to do any serious damage. One by itself was hardly a threat.

"What's goin' on, Ato?" It was Get, still in his pajamas, his brown hair sleep tussled and his eyes groggy. The laser alarm must've woken him. "Oh, an iguanagull?" He gazed out the window at it. "Ugly, huh? Well, go 'head, blast it."

"It's not doing anything, Get, just gliding along. Besides, iguanagulls are supposed to be able to intercommunicate telepathically, and once you blast one, then the whole flock'll—"

"It's just a birdlizard, Ato. They don't read minds." He reached over his brother and pushed the flashing red button.

"Get!" Ato yelled. "No!"

The ship let out a whirring sound and then lurched as an explosion of light thundered out. The iguanagull disappeared in a puff of smoke. For a moment, Ato and Get just stared at the empty space in the clouds where the creature had been. Gray and white feathers floated peacefully through the air and then zipped off on a current of early morning wind.

"Well," Get said, "back to bed I go." He started off toward the sleeping quarters. "Next time don't be such a—"

A distant cawing cut him off. Another scream answered it, this time much closer. The two brothers looked at each other. Suddenly the air was full of iguanagull screeches. The seeker lasers dashed back and forth through the cloud bank. Red panic lights flashed on and off inside the cruiser.

"It's an attack!" Ato screamed.

From somewhere above their heads came the horrific sound of metal being shredded by claws.

CHAPTER

"You comin', bro?"

Max putted along toward where Yala hovered on the path, giving the barbwire fence a wide berth. He could hear the angry electric hum and snapping of currents on the other side. The air around the Electric Ghost Yard was always thick with the feeling that something terrible had just happened or was about to go horribly wrong. You couldn't even inhale fully because the tiny particles floating around would irritate your throat and make you cough.

Just beyond the fence, the sea of black-and-gray wires squirmed in slow motion. A fizzle of blue light erupted a few feet away from Max, making him dodge sideways in surprise. He gathered himself, caught his breath, and sped forward, waving his hand at Yala to assure her he was okay.

Max looked anxiously ahead. His heart was thundering in his chest and his breathing was shallow. At this rate, he figured, he might just drop dead halfway through the alleyway even if they didn't get jumped by some angry digital phantom. And of course, Yala just gallivanted on ahead like it was another stroll through the park.

Even the upcoming Flood City pageant was less frightening than the crackling sounds (were they coming more and more frequently now?), so Max tried to concentrate on his feezlehorn part. He knew it by heart from hearing the same bit year after year. The Star Guard only let the Flood City Orchestra play one performance, once a year, and it had to be done exactly the same every single time. It was pretty tedious really, and if Max didn't love music so much, he'd have probably quit by now. But even with the same boring notes, Max got that jolt of excitement every time he put the horn to his lips and felt the rest of the orchestra fall into place around him. There was no feeling like it. And he'd certainly never expected to play lead.

Then came the day a few weeks back when Tinibu had passed him a small scrap of paper asking him to stop by Old Man Cortinas's barbershop when he had a chance. "You know," Cortinas had said later that afternoon as he snip-snipped at Mateo the Bricklayer's few remaining hairs, "now that Jorge has gone off and joined the Star Guard, we'll need someone to lead the horn section this year."

Somewhere deep inside Max, the notion that he might one day play lead sparked to life, but he quickly shushed it away as utterly ridiculous. "I suppose so," Max said. "Maybe Deezer? He's been pretty on point recently."

Cortinas and Mateo both chuckled. Those two always seemed like they were in on some big joke that no one else got, and today was no exception. "No, m'ijo," Cortinas finally said. "I mean you. I want you to take over for Jorge."

YES! a voice inside Max yelled. But he shook his head. "I couldn't." Cortinas stopped clipping and looked sternly at Max. "I . . . I'm so young," Max insisted. "And there's others . . . who are more prepared. I wouldn't want to . . . thank you though . . . but . . ."

To Max's horror, Mateo burst out laughing. Why did he always have to make light of everyone else's messes? Cortinas quieted the bricklayer with a stern hand on his shoulder. "I wasn't asking your permission, young man," the barber said. "I was telling you that that is your new job in the orchestra. Period. Finito. End of story."

"But I . . ."

"If you think you're not ready for it, then you better get studying, joven."

Mateo started laughing again.

"Max! Watch out!" Yala's voice blurted out.

Lost in his memories, Max had strayed too close to the Electric Ghost Yard. A blast of blue static zapped out through the fence and smashed into him. Max felt like his whole body was on fire as he smacked against the wall on the other side of the alley and then landed in a heap on the ground.

When he looked up, the angry blue current was flashing

along the fence just across from him. It formed a screaming face momentarily and then shattered into a web of crackling lines. Sparkly tentacles stretched through the barbwire toward Max, stopping just short of his jetboots. Max pushed himself as far back against the wall as he could and pulled his feet in.

Yala sped toward him. She was carrying an old tire that she'd picked out of the alley debris. She was too close to the fence though, easily within range of the angry ghost.

"Yala!" Max yelled, but it was too late: The blue light was already dashing up through the wiring to attack. Still accelerating forward on her jetboots, Yala held the tire up between her and the Electric Ghost Yard. She hurled it at the fence just as the phantom of blue light burst out toward her. Instead of a terrible explosion, there was only a dull fizzle as the tire withstood the full electric force of the ghost and then fell to the ground with a thud. A tiny voice screamed in the air around them.

Max blinked at the smoking tire.

"You alright, man?" Yala asked.

"I think so." He looked down at his body, which strangers had always told him was a few sizes too big—one of their mom's fellow doctors had lectured him about weight gain and body mass when he was just eight—but he knew was just the right size, was round in just the right ways, and that padding had managed to protect him from getting too hurt so far, which was no small task considering how many heights he'd plummeted from. Today was no exception: Sure, he'd been zapped by one of the feared electric ghosts, but nothing seemed to be fried or broken. He wiggled his arms and legs to make sure they still worked. "Just a little shook up."

"I bet."

"Thanks for saving me. Again . . ."

"Here, take my hand. We gotta move fast now. There's gonna be more where that one came from."

"What's that?" Max pointed into the sky. Something was floating toward them.

"I don't know," Yala said. "But there's another."

"Weird."

"Feathers," Yala said. "Iguanagull feathers from the look of 'em." There were hundreds of them. They drifted down like giant gray snowflakes over the Electric Ghost Yard. "Uh-oh."

"What?" Max followed his sister's gaze up to the murky cloud bank above them. Bursts of laser fire were exploding like red lightning through the gray sky.

THE FLOOD CITY GAZETTE

HAPPY FLOOD CITY DAY, CITIZENS!

RATIONS REPORT

The Star Guard has generously waived the daily ration limit in honor of Flood City Day. Mr. Sanpedro will remain open into the night to accommodate the revelers and has brought in extra hunterfly assistants. Eat up!!

THE DAILY TIDE

Low tide today will be at **0431**.

High tide will be at **2114**.

Please *avoid the city edges during high tide, as conditions can worsen suddenly.*

IGUANAGULL AHOY!

Star Guard peacekeepers at the Tumbled Together Towers report moderate levels of iguanagull sightings. Stay safe and keep your eyes in the sky!

THE BOOO'CAST

Reported spectral/electromagnetic activity levels have been high as of late by the Electric Ghost Yard. Please keep your distance from this area at all times!

THE VAPORS & ABANDONED OCEAN LINER REPORT

We have nothing to report.

CHEMICAL BARONS

Even though it's been years since the Star Guard sent the Chemical Barons scurrying for their lives out of Flood City, they could return at any time. Intelligence reports from Star Guard allies indicate the Barons are still plotting an attack. Let's keep them away! Stay vigilant, stay alive! Report any signs of enemy aircraft or unusual activity to your nearest Star Guard peacekeeper.

CHAPTER

ArchBaron Mephim sat in the commander's chair, a picture of calmness in the center of utter chaos. His narrow, pale face scanned slowly back and forth. Ato watched the ArchBaron's blue eyes squint ever so slightly as they took in all the information exploding around them. Ato wondered if he would ever be able to stay that calm in the midst of a battle, even if it was just against iguanagulls. It seemed like no matter how many times he went on missions, some part of his body rebelled against the rest of it and refused to keep cool.

"Man the roof cannons," Mephim said, "and prepare to reinforce the shields on my order."

Liutenant Oso, the crew commander, stepped away from Mephim's side and addressed the four soldiers at the gunner controls. "Tamin, take the roof cannons. Sala, you work the shields. Go!"

The horrible scraping noises were getting louder. The iguanagulls must've penetrated part of the main hull already, Ato guessed. He looked over at Get, who was cowering shamefaced in a corner, trying to be as tiny and out of the way as possible.

"Aren't we going to get out of here?" Get said.

"If we use our power engines," Mephim explained in a voice so soft it might've been a whisper, "we will blow our cover and the Star Guard will capture us. As it is, we are at risk using our cannons, but there is no other choice. We're almost over the water anyway, so the debris won't be as noticeable. Won't be much longer though."

Much longer till what? Ato wondered, but he kept his mouth shut.

A large computer terminal lowered from the ceiling. It had a seat attached to it with two handlebars stretching out from the main screen. Ato jumped into the seat and the screen blipped to life. A panoramic view of the cloudy sky unfolded on the computers, overlaid by swirling grids and letters.

"Watch carefully, boys," Mephim said. "This is important."

The cruiser shuddered as the iguanagulls continued their fierce assault on its defenses. Ato could hear their screeching get louder with each passing second.

"Guns ready?" Mephim whispered.

Lieutenant Oso towered over where Ato was seated at the gunner terminal. Ato nodded up at him.

"Guns ready, ArchBaron," Oso said.

"Ignite electrified shield power."

"Shields go!" Oso yelled.

Sala pushed a series of buttons on the control panel she was seated at. The ship whirred and shook. Then the noise was unbearable. All the iguanagulls must have screamed at the exact same time as torrents of electrical shield power zapped through their bodies. The gunner terminal computer screens were suddenly filled with flapping and falling creatures.

"Nice!" Get yelled. "That was awesome!"

"Fire at will," Mephim said. "Destroy them all."

"Fire!" Oso commanded.

Ato leaned into his terminals and began squeezing off cannon shots with the triggers on either end of the handlebars. The digital images squirmed, fluttered, and exploded across the screen.

Ato watched with rising uneasiness as the creatures fell one by one past the cruiser windows. He knew the Barons were only doing what they had to in order to survive and accomplish their mission, but still . . . something didn't feel right. Of course, Mephim was his teacher, the man their loving parents had entrusted with raising him and his brother to be true Warrior Barons. And of course, Mephim's skill and calmness were to be admired. Ato couldn't put his finger on it, but as much as he looked up to Mephim, he was also terrified by his tall, cloaked mentor. Besides, he had never seen an iguanagull, and he'd wanted to get a closer look.

The laser cannon blasts continued around him. "Sir," Oso said, "we have eliminated ninety-two percent of the targets."

Tamin let out a joyful grunt.

"Make that ninety-five," Oso added.

"Hmm," Mephim said, placing his hands together beneath his chin and closing his eyes. "I see."

Two smaller iguanagulls dashed across Tamin's screen. He thrust his handlebars to the side, trailing the target circle just behind them, and then cut upward. One of the creatures curved up, directly into the gun sights, and Tamin leaned into the triggers, releasing a spray of cannon fire. Everyone heard the cawing as the wounded iguanagull tumbled out of the sky.

"I believe," Oso said, "that we have virtually . . ."

Mephim's eyes sprang open. "Don't say it!"

". . . accomplished this—what?"

"You insolent brute!" Mephim yelled, rising to his full height, his red robes swooshing around him as if blown by a spontaneous draft of wind. "How dare you?" He raised an arm as if he was about to strike Oso but then caught himself. For a second, no one moved. The computers blipped away their coordinate readings, oblivious to the sudden outburst.

Ato had never seen Mephim lose his cool. There were always rumors, he remembered now, that the ArchBaron was particularly superstitious, but Mephim never seemed like the type to go for old wives' tales.

"Never—" Mephim started at a yell and stopped himself. He tried again, quieter this time. "Never talk about a battle like it's won before it's even over. Never. Or I will have you demoted and beheaded. Is that clear?"

Oso nodded. Rather than look ashamed though, his face was

tight with anger. He was almost as tall as Mephim and had about two hundred pounds of pure muscle on him, not to mention being a top crew commander in the Chemical Baron cloud cruiser covert expeditions fleet, but here he was being hollered at like a child. And in front of his crew, making it a double embarrassment. Ato took note of the lieutenant's face and stored it away for later. He'd never seen a crew member show outright disdain for an ArchBaron before.

"Now," Mephim said, settling back into his spinning chair, "have we destroyed all of the . . ."

The overhead lights flickered on and off and then the tearing metal sound came back. This time it was coming from only a few feet above them. Somewhere in the ventilation shafts, Ato figured. The iguanagull must've gotten in before they'd activated the electroshields.

A claw burst through the ceiling and sent a cascade of debris down on the crew. Get ran forward, his small spray cannon pointed upward toward the screeching iguanagull.

"Back," Oso said, grabbing at the boy. "And put the shooter away! If you let off a shot, you could hit a mainline and then we'd all be toast."

"Back off me!" Get dodged the burly lieutenant's grip and raised his hand cannon up toward the ceiling, just in time to see the iguanagull bearing down on him in a torrent of falling plaster and metal. Get screamed, falling backward, but the creature never reached him. Mephim had snatched it out of the air. In one fluid motion, the ArchBaron wrapped his long fingers around the thing's neck and snapped it. There was a clicking noise, then a horrible tearing. The iguanagull went limp. Everyone stared at Mephim with shock.

"Let's get out of here," he said, dropping the feathery body to the ground. A pool of thick, dark blood spread from the empty stump of its neck. Ato watched in horror as Mephim tucked the still twitching iguanagull head into some unseen pocket of his robes. "The Star Guard will be here soon and we need to assess the damage and prepare for tonight's surveillance run."

The shadow crept along steadily behind Max and Yala. He had watched with interest as the girl once again saved her brother from imminent disaster. He slithered along the wall after them as they raced through the shower of iguanagull feathers. He stayed just far enough behind so as not to be noticed, but close enough that he wouldn't lose them. It was tricky, tracking young people, because they were unpredictable—their chaotic movements didn't follow that drab routine that most adults fell into. And that's what made it all the more fun.

Now they had stopped again and were discussing something beneath the Tumbled Together Towers. The shadow paused behind a rust-encrusted steam pipe. Most likely, they would speak for another two minutes or so, and then jet off across the harbor to their mom's hospital. Everything was, more or less, moving according to plan. He peeked out, just to make sure, and jolted back with surprise. The kids were gone. Impossible! If they'd headed toward the water as expected, he would be able to see them on the other side of the Towers. But there was no sign of them whatsoever.

The shadow was about to rush out into the open but caught himself. If they were gone, it meant they'd either been snatched up, which seemed unlikely, or were somehow onto him. That was also highly unlikely, but there'd been no sounds of struggle, and it had only been a couple of seconds. No, ridiculous though it was, they must've gotten wise to their pursuer. Which meant they'd hidden in an attempt to flush him out into the open. The shadow flattened himself even farther behind the pipe and quickly slid off to begin searching.

Max hated having to stay perfectly still. He was not the patient type and didn't care much for tension either. His heart thump-thumped away in his ears. His belly did a ridiculous little dance. Sweat glistened on his forehead. His muscles were getting sore from not moving. Still, he kept his body firmly pressed against the tower wall and gazed down at the dockyards twenty-six stories below him.

"We're being followed," Yala had said as they stopped beneath the Tumbled Together Towers. "I don't know what it is, but I know it's there."

"How?" Max had said, the panic rising in his voice.

Yala had put a finger to her lips. "Doesn't matter now. Just do what I say. When I count to three, accelerate straight up. Flatten against the ocean side of the tower. Don't move. Wait ten minutes and then head straight for Saint Solomon's. Don't stop for nothing. Don't look back. Just go. I'll meet you there."

"What're you gonna—"

The finger had gone back to the lips and Max shushed. "Just go. Now."

He'd shot up into the air so fast he hadn't had a chance to even see which way his sister went. When he'd looked down, the spot they had just been standing in was empty.

Now all he wanted to do was get off this wall and zip to the hospital where his mom would be waiting with open arms. But nothing was ever that easy in Flood City. To distract himself, he opened the door in his mind that let the music in. It was as simple as flicking a switch: Suddenly the ricocheting clacks and thumps of the drums and the swirling horns came flooding into his brain. His aching muscles became a distant tingle, barely noticeable compared to the thundering rhythms.

BLOOM BA DUM! Djinna's balooga drum rumbled. That was the biggest one in the set, almost twice as tall as Max. Then the timbaleos would rattle along over the dying vibrations from the balooga. Ortega, Jesus, and Mateo played those with expert precision when they weren't chatting it up outside Old Man Cortinas's barbershop. The cymbals would shimmer in next, dazzling and slick. Jasmine was the cymbalist; she somehow always managed to have a completely calm and cool expression on her face, even while the rest of the group was sweating through some extra-complex section.

Max could hear it all as perfectly clear as if it were happening right in front of him. He could foresee what would come next in the music, where the song wanted to go, who would have a difficult part coming up, who would have to play louder or softer and when. The horn section was about to start, but something was distracting him, something wasn't right. He opened his eyes (he hadn't even realized that he'd shut them) and almost slipped off the wall from shock.

The humongous, light blue faces of two Star Guard patrollers were staring at him from a few feet away. The giants were a species called the snell and came from a planet light-years from Earth that no one could pronounce the name of. They'd been the ones, under the fierce leadership of Star Guard commander Bartrum Uk, who'd helped fight off the Chemical Barons all those years ago, and they'd stuck around ever since. The Star Guard giants were known to be pretty foul tempered though, often locking up Flood City folks for no reason at all or cutting off food rations just to prove a point.

"What you doing up on this building wall, boy?" the taller giant said.

"You know it's against regulations to linger on a wall side like that. Particularly the Tumbled Together Towers."

"I was putting up a banner," Max said.

The taller Star Guard raised a blue eyebrow. "What kind of banner, son?"

"A banner about how great the mighty Star Guard is, of course."

"Really?" the shorter one said, looking genuinely surprised.

"On Flood City Day? Aren't you celebrating the anniversary with the rest of them?"

"Why live in the past, I always say!" Max managed to blurt without choking on the lie. "You guys give us our provisions and keep us safe from the Chemical Barons. I just think a little appreciation is in order, don't you?"

The giants looked slightly taken aback. Max was pretty sure they were about to let him go when there was a fizzling sound and suddenly Commander Bartrum Uk himself appeared between the two Star Guards. He was a tiny fellow who looked even smaller next to the giants he commanded. No one knew if he had legs, because he was always stuffed into a mini-hovercraft from which his torso and large head protruded like an angry mushroom. His skin was a sickly blue green, and he wore a very uncomfortable-looking red-and-gold uniform that seemed to hold his slimy body in place.

"What is this about?" the regional commander of the Star Guard demanded. He buzzed up close to Max and stuck out his saliva-covered bottom lip in disapproval. "What's going on? Why are you breaking legislation and lingering near the Tumbled Together Towers, eh?"

One of the giants raised his huge arm. "He was putting up a banner, sir, in favor of the Star Guard."

Max cringed inside. His excuse sounded even more implausible coming from the big blue guy's mouth. Commander Bartrum Uk squinted at Max. "Where's your banner, son?"

"The one I was gonna put up?"

"Yes, the one you were going to put up." Little flecks of Uk saliva splattered across Max's face.

"It blew away."

"Really?"

"It did. On a gust of wind."

"I see."

The commander seemed to be burning holes into Max's face with those squinty little eyes. Then he turned to the giants. "This one seems ripe for the Star Guard, don't you think, Captain Gorus?"

Max restrained a shudder of fear. Joining the Star Guard was almost as bad as being thrown in the brig. No one knew what exactly happened to young people who were recruited, but there were horrible rumors. Basically, it meant shipping off to get blown up by the Chemical Barons on a faraway asteroid or being the equivalent of the blue giants on some other poor planet that couldn't protect itself.

"I dunno, Commander," the captain muttered. "Maybe."

Bartrum Uk stared down Max for another couple of seconds. Max felt like the strange little creature was memorizing his face somehow, putting it in a mental file cabinet for the next time they met. One thing was sure—he wasn't buying the goofy banner story.

"Alright, carry on," Bartrum Uk said finally. "Find your . . . banner. Or whatever. We have more urgent business to attend to than vagrant children. That is all. Long live the Star Guard."

"Long live the Star Guard," Max said, trying not to sound grudging about it. He powered up his jetboots and rocketed off. What secrets were those blue giants keeping? And where had Yala disappeared to? And who or what had she seen following them?

He sped past the docks and out over the crashing waves toward their mom's hospital.

CHAPTER

Yala dashed across an alleyway and threw herself against a brick wall. She had tried to catch a glimpse as she flashed past, thought she might've seen something move but wasn't sure. She could tell she wasn't as on point as usual. The weight of being about to leave and, even worse, having to tell her family about her decision was taking up so much room in her mind she couldn't think straight.

Something was definitely moving in the alley. Worse, it was coming toward her. Whatever it was, it was extremely deft at being stealthy. If there was one thing Yala felt completely confident about, it was her ability to outmaneuver any follower. Growing up in the messy, danger-ridden Flood City streets had given her a sharp ear. She could hear the wing flap of an attacking iguanagull long before it ever swooped out of the sky. She could distinguish between various models of jetboots as they approached. Outsmarting the oversize, clumsy Star Guard was never a problem. Best of all, she knew the city inside out, so when something did come at her, she always had a tunnel or hideaway to disappear into.

But this was completely different. She'd barely caught onto her follower earlier, only happened to catch a fleeting glimpse of it as she tossed the tire at the electric ghost. It was a shadowy figure peeking around a corner, barely visible at all, and then it was gone. She hadn't mentioned anything to Max until they were close enough to the hospital that she figured he'd be able to make it alone if they split up.

Yala couldn't even tell how she knew it was there. The thing wasn't making any noise; it was more like a feeling she had. Like the molecules of air that it swept aside were sending tiny wind gust warnings to her. She shivered.

The half-sunken rust-covered ocean liner loomed overhead. The boat was one of the first pieces of floating sea debris to form what would one day become Flood City. It was huge and cast a constant shadow over the windy labyrinth of alleyways in the weird shadowy neighborhood known as Barge Annex. Yala often headed there to get away from patrolling Star Guards or pesky scavengers, even though it was strictly forbidden by her elders. The seemingly endless maze of alleys and tunnels was a perfect way to disappear.

Her follower was only a few feet away now, and moving fast. She eased off the ignition pedals on her jetboots, letting herself slide slowly toward the ground. The uneven brick wall scraped against her back. She thought about Max, imagined him making it safely to the hospital, hugging their mom. Then she started to worry about how he would get on without her around. *Put it out of your head, Yala. This isn't the time for that. You gotta worry about keeping your own self alive right now.* She slipped onto the uneven crevice where two buildings had settled into each other: a mess of shattered brick and mortar that didn't make for easy movement. Up ahead, it narrowed into a jagged crawl space that probably led to some scavenger den or creature's nest, but it would do for a temporary hiding place. Yala wanted to see just what exactly was trailing her. If she had to retreat deeper in, so be it, but hopefully her pursuer would go past without noticing her. Hopefully.

She waited, her eyes glued to the alleyway. She knew there wouldn't be footsteps, but surely the thing would make some noise as it approached. Again her mind wandered back to Max. He was so impossible sometimes, so easily distracted. She could only hope . . . It wasn't a noise, but the sudden intense whiff of some kind of cologne snapped Yala back to alertness. She glanced over and had to force herself not to gasp. It was a vapor.

There had been one along with the original crew of Flood City Founders, but since then nobody one had ever seen one except for a few old-timers. Of course, there were stories—eerie tales of a whole secret race of mist people, sneaking back and forth through the alleyways of Barge Annex in the service of whatever strange engine urged them all forward. Babies disappearing, a sudden surge of iguanagulls, or the dearth of edible fish—Flood City folk could chalk up any number of natural disasters and petty calamities to the vapors' meddling ways. But Yala never really thought she'd see one.

The vapor could've just been a large puff of smoke, but then it stopped, right in front of where Yala was hiding. Two long, cloudy arms unfolded from either side and then a wide smile crescented across its front.

"Hey, Yala," the vapor said, chuckling and opening its disturbingly human eyes.

In the dim officer's cabin on the cloud cruiser, Mephim sat with his fingers interlaced. How was it that everything could go exactly as planned and still be an utter disaster? He rummaged through the events of the last few days, from the debacle at Corinth to the iguanagull swarm. The crew was repairing the damaged areas on the ship and they would probably still be able to complete their mission, but something nagged at the edge of Mephim's mind. There was trouble brewing somewhere, right underneath his nose, but he couldn't quite put his finger on what it was.

He let his hands drop to his lap and touched something solid folded within his cloak. Of course—the iguanagull. Mephim pulled out the scaly, blood-crusted head and held it with one hand in front of his face. The jaw was frozen open in an expression of terror. The sightless eyes gazed off to either side from beneath folds of green flesh. A few tattered feathers adorned the base of the neck. Mephim smiled. It was an unusual stroke of luck in an otherwise grim scenario—an uninvited guest and a gift. It would be perfect for a test run, the ArchBaron thought. He closed his eyes. Perhaps Oso's big mouth was a blessing in disguise.

A quiet beeping interrupted Mephim's reverie, and he quickly stashed the head back in his robes. "Enter," he said, and the cabin door slid open with an electric whir. It was the boy, Ato.

"Good day, ArchBaron." Ato bowed slightly.

"Good day, young Baron. What do you want?"

"I was wondering, sir, since the ship's almost repaired, and we have some free time, if I might have a look at the iguanagull head you . . . procured earlier."

Mephim struggled to suppress the violent stirring inside of him. "Why do you want it?"

"Just to study, sir. I've always wanted to get a look at one up close. And it seemed like a rare opportunity."

They stared at each other for a few seconds. Mephim had the unpleasant feeling that everything he thought was plain as day to this young boy. "It's gone," he said. "I threw it out the waste hatch as soon as I returned to my quarters. Think no more of it; it's a hideous, useless beast."

Mephim could see in the boy's eyes that he wasn't buying a word of it.

"That's too bad," Ato said, without losing eye contact. "I would've liked to . . . Oh well." He took some steps back and then turned and walked out of the room.

_____

Ato had known it'd be a long shot getting the head to study. He'd expected disappointment. What he hadn't counted on was all that weirdness from Mephim. It had felt like the air was thick with the ArchBaron's discomfort, like he could taste it. Ato felt, more than saw or heard, that Mephim had been lying to him about throwing the thing away. He was certain of it.

The ArchBaron had always kept such an enigmatic air about him, never allowing anyone to see his emotions or fears. He was just Mephim: steady, ferocious, and direct—a warrior at heart. But today, he'd lost his cool, killed an animal with his bare hands, and blatantly lied. It was true: Ato wasn't the only one who experienced a certain uneasiness when the ArchBaron came around. But everyone assumed that was simply the discomfort of being near such a competent, focused commander, a man who had seen his share of murder and mayhem. It just went with the territory. But Ato was beginning to think there was something else going on besides all that, something much more sinister.

He strolled onto the bridge, where Oso was overseeing the last few repairs to the internal wiring. "Almost good?" Ato asked.

"Hardly," grunted Oso. "Those monsters worked us over pretty bad. That one that got in chewed through half our gunnery wiring on the left upper channel. The guys on the outside tore some sizable holes into our metal outershields. One of the cannons is gone."

"Dang," Ato sighed.

"Dang indeed." The lieutenant leaned over to glare at one of the gun station monitors. He pushed a button on his headset. "To the left, Sala! The left!" He looked back at Ato. "And what's worse? Mephim is still gonna want us on this maneuver tonight."

"Really?"

"Of course! Like we don't have enough problems. The ship's a mess. The Star Guard might know we're here by now, which would mean they'll be ready for us. God knows what'all armaments the Flood City folks have up their sleeve. Plus it's their anniversary celebration, so that's never a good look. I just don't like the whole thing."

No one had ever spoken so honestly about a mission to Ato before. And it was all true, of course.

"Why are we surveilling them, anyway?"

Oso shrugged. "Orders. You know the higher-ups all want to get back to Earth more than anything, and they see Flood City as the only way to do it. And supposedly these guys on the ground have some plan to team up, the Star Guard and the Flood City folks, and strike at the Baron base fleet. So we're here to make sure that doesn't happen."

"I thought the Flood City people couldn't stand the Star Guard."

Oso sighed. "Well, depends who you ask. At this point, if Mephim says we move, we move, because we're soldiers. Understand?"

Ato nodded, but he thought Oso sounded more like he was trying to convince himself than anyone else.

"Did he give you the birdlizard head to study?"

Ato was taken aback. He hadn't mentioned that to anyone, not even Get. "Huh?"

"I saw you looking at that thing when it dropped. And I

43

remember back on Corinth, when you couldn't take your eyes offa them star spiders. Gotta thing 'bout animals, I see. Nothing wrong with that. We need to understand the things better anyway, if we gonna live near 'em. Can't just go blowing 'em outta the sky every time they get near us."

"Yes," Ato said, flabbergasted that Oso had just perfectly summarized everything he'd been thinking for the past two weeks. "Totally."

"Anyway," Oso said, gazing at the monitor again, "did you get it?"

"No. He said he tossed it out the waste hatch."

"That's weird," Oso said. "Then why'd he bother keeping it in the first place?"

"That's what I was trying to figure out."

"The left, Sala, even more to the left!" Oso yelled suddenly. "It'll be a miracle if this piece of junk makes it to tonight, let alone past that. Say, maybe they didn't toss the body yet. Did you try and track it down?"

Ato perked up. He hadn't thought of that. "Great idea!" he yelled, and ran off down the hall.

When the Floods first crashed across Earth and the Chemical Barons escaped into space, a tiny group of survivors holed up in a star cruiser. They were mostly children; the cruiser had been about to set off on an intergalactic field trip with almost an entire school on board. Instead of trying to breach the Barons' blockade, the faculty and crew decided to remain just above the surface of the waters, scouring the planet for land.

They didn't find any, of course. For miles and miles, all that was left was the crashed-together mess of buildings that had risen up around what was now the Music Hall. The Founders, mostly kids at the time—like Max and Yala's parents and Dr. Maceo—along with Old Man Cortinas, set up camp and eventually converted their original star cruiser into Saint Solomon's Hospital.

It hung above the churning water a little ways off the shore. Max zipped over the waves in record time and into the emergency hold. This had been the main hull of the starship, and during those months when they'd been lost at sea, the Founders had used it to hold council meetings. Now the hull was full of stretchers, beeping machines, fluid tanks, and moaning sick people. Nurses and doctors worked their way between beds tending to various illnesses and injuries, making notes on charts and adjusting infusions.

Surely Yala had gotten here already. She was the faster one by far and presumably hadn't been held up by the glowering Star Guard or whatever it was that'd been following them. Max didn't see her among the bustling emergency hold, but he did spot his mom turning into one of the side corridors.

"Mom!" Max called, taking off after her.

"Hey, little man," Dr. Sarita said. She was smiling, but her face told of another exhausting night at the hospital.

"You almost done with your shift?"

"Twenty more minutes. Where's your sister?"

"She hasn't shown up yet?" Max tried not to look panicked.

"Uh-uh. What happened?"

What didn't happen? It'd been a perilous morning, even by Flood City standards. But the main thing was that something had been following them, according to Yala, and she'd insisted they split up. Max tried to explain as briefly as possible.

"She didn't say what it was following you?" Dr. Sarita, her eyebrows arched, had entered commando mom mode, there was no doubt about it.

Max shook his head.

"I don't like it. I don't like it at all."

One of the other doctors, a tall, happy fellow named Sebastian, poked his head around the corner. "Bed three is calling for you, Dr. S. Hey, Mr. Max." Sebastian grinned. "Come to visit us?"

"Seb," Dr. Sarita cut in before Max could answer. "Watch my patients for a sec. I gotta make a holocall." She stormed down the hallway, Max scurrying along behind her, and ducked into a wooden booth. Inside, a holodeck blinked to life as she tapped a few numbers into its keypad. Blue light spread across the circular deck and then a tiny 3-D image of Old Man Cortinas materialized.

"What's goin' on, Doc?" the shuddering hologram asked.

"Good afternoon, Mr. C," Dr. Sarita said. Max could hear his mom straining to calm her voice just as he had earlier. "You haven't seen Yala by any chance, have you?"

"Earlier today she sped past with Max, but not since then. She gone missing?"

Dr. Sarita nodded.

"Not like her," Mr. C grumbled. "I'll send Mateo to see what he can find."

"Thank you, Mr. C."

The old man turned to something that wasn't being transmitted over the holodeck and waved his arm. Then the call was cut off and he blipped out of existence completely.

"Where's Tinibu?" Dr. Sarita asked, turning to Max.

"He zipped off too."

Dr. Sarita exhaled sharply, rolling her eyes. "What's the use of having a hunterfly around if they just disappear when you need them most?"

They were heading quickly down the corridor again. "Now what?" Max asked.

"We're leaving." They slid between stretchers, ducked around IV lines, and avoided a passing X-ray machine. "Just gotta make one quick stop." They reached the far side of the emergency hold. Dr. Sarita tapped once on a doorway and then cracked it open. Max glimpsed the sullen face of Dr. Niska, the hospital supervisor, looking up from his desk.

"Yes, Dr. Sarita?" Dr. Niska did not look thrilled about being interrupted.

"I have to leave a little early."

"Getting ready for tonight's festivities?"

"No." Dr. Sarita's words were sharp. "Yala's missing and Max and I are going to look for her. The paperwork will be on your desk tomorrow."

"And your patients?"

Max recognized the expression his mom made when she was about to unload a bucket of curses, but instead she took a deep breath and said, "Seb will manage for the last twenty minutes of my shift."

Niska grunted, but Dr. Sarita had already turned and headed off across the emergency hold. Max rushed after her.

CHAPTER

Ato walked quickly through the main corridor of the cloud cruiser, past the cramped living quarters to the engine room. Inside, Tog Apix was hunched over some contraption that sent up occasional spark bursts and clicked and clattered.

"What are you doing?" Ato asked, trying to sound casual.

Tog raised his old, gnarly face from the table and squinted at Ato. "Repairs. What'dya want?"

"The . . . um . . . iguanagull body, the one that ArchBaron Mephim . . ."

"What about it?"

"Did you incinerate it?"

"'Bout to. It's in the trash canister."

Ato felt a little thrill of excitement as he hurried toward the large metal bin.

"Why you want it?" Tog said. He waddled over to a drawer, fiddled with some wires inside it, and then returned to his project.

"No reason. Just curious." Ato removed the lid and immediately wished he hadn't. The stench of several days' worth of cloud cruiser refuse wafted directly into his face.

Tog slammed down his wrench. "Ay! Some of us are trying to work here!" He stood.

Ato gazed into the pile of food peelings, crumpled plastic containers, slop scrapings, and shiny mulch lumps. "Ugh!"

"Shut that lid!" Tog started across the room, scowling.

Ato held his breath and reached his hand into the muck. Nothing that felt like an iguanagull. He pushed some blue-gray stained rags over to one side, trying to ignore the lurching feeling in his stomach.

"Shut it, I said!" Tog hollered.

"Just . . . one . . ." Ato threw his hand in deeper, all the way to the elbow, grasping frantically for anything solid, anything that might be . . . There! His fingers closed around a cool, scaly shape. He pulled and out came the headless iguanagull corpse. "Got it!" Ato yelled. He grabbed a plastic bag from the top and then jumped away from the trash bin just as Tog reached it and slammed the lid closed.

"Get outta my engine room!"

Ato was already gone.

CHAPTER

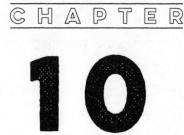

10

"Where we going, Mom?"

They'd just rocketed over the stretch of ocean from Saint Solomon's, and Dr. Sarita had veered sharply off toward the far edge of town. Max hurried after her, blasting with awkward little jolts to stay on course. "Yala was heading downtown when we separated."

"C'mon," Dr. Sarita said sharply. "There's a better way to find her."

There wasn't much on this side of Flood City: crumpled old warehouses huddled together, lurching in odd directions from sea-soaked piles of debris. It was so close to the edge of the ocean that when the tide came in, foamy waves would flood the abandoned buildings up to the roofs. The air was always wet and misty, like a low-hanging rain cloud that would never leave. Because of all this, virtually the only building that was inhabited at all was the ancient church steeple that shot up into the sky, the tallest structure around by far.

Max gasped. "The holographer's tower! Brilliant, Mom!"

Dr. Sarita turned her head just enough to show a satisfied grin and then zipped off between the crumbling buildings and crashing waves.

Max's excitement turned sharply into dread. If they were going to the holographer's tower, it meant they would probably see the holographer's daughter, Djinna, and that was enough to make Max slow his jetboots and hover awkwardly in the air for a few seconds.

"You comin'?"

Max gave a half-hearted push on his foot pedal, thrusting himself toward the tower, which now seemed even taller than he remembered it. All his worries about Yala now had the company of all his terror at seeing Djinna.

It wasn't enough to say that the holographer's daughter played in the drum squad of the Flood City Orchestra. She *was* the drum squad. Max still remembered the first day she showed up at practice. He'd seen her before at school of course, but she was just another girl who didn't seem to notice him. Then she stepped up in front of the class on that first day, took a deep breath, and unleashed an astonishing barrage of sharp, rhythmic clacks against her snare drum. Everyone in the room perked up. When she brought in the gigantic booming balooga drum with a few reverberating smacks, people were transfixed. The rhythm swam along wildly for a few measures, the snare cracking at breathtaking speed, and then suddenly the whole thing just glided effortlessly into some kind of easy swing. Djinna hadn't even broken a sweat, just stood there with a slight frown on her face like she was trying to work out a complicated math problem. She rounded the whole thing off with a crescendo of balooga smashes and some final clacks on the snare. The entire room jumped to their feet to applaud when she was done.

Max couldn't move. He wasn't even sure if he was breathing. Everything had changed from that moment on. He suddenly was so very happy that he played the horn; not just played it, in fact, that sometimes it was the only thing that made sense to him. That he spoke that language. A language not so far removed from the one Djinna had just serenaded his ears with. Music. Max spoke music, with his hands, his lungs, his whole body. It made sense to him. And so did Djinna. She was speaking to him right then and there. And he was understanding. It wasn't anything he could ever translate into words, but that was the whole point.

Then of course Splink had said, "That was pretty cool," and blown the whole moment to shreds. Splink, who was tall, skinny, and ridiculously outgoing, always managed to mess up important moments with some wisecrack or pointless summary. He wasn't even in the band, just happened to be sitting in on the session, and still he felt the need to jump in.

Djinna joined the orchestra but try though he might, Max had never been able to work out the right words to say to her. He eventually gave up, tired of his lurchy stomach and sweaty palms. He'd just speak to her with the notes he played, and one day she'd get the message. Then he could stop worrying.

But now . . . now he was about to be in her house. With his mom. Without any time to prepare, to overthink things, to worry. That wouldn't do at all.

"Max." Dr. Sarita hovered outside the entrance window of the holographer's tower, her finger on the buzzer.

"Maybe I'll just wait outside," Max mumbled.

"Don't be ridiculous! It's wet out here. And besides, don't you go to school with Dr. Maceo's daughter?"

Max gulped hard and nodded.

"Well, perfect, see? You two can hang out while we look at the holomap." She turned back to the window and pushed the buzzer. A tiny version of Djinna materialized in front of the panel, startling Max half to death.

"Hello?" The mini-Djinna looked curiously into what must've been a holodeck somewhere inside. "Oh, hey, Dr. Salazar!" She waved at the camera, her face breaking into a wide smile. Max realized he'd never seen her smile before. It wasn't that she walked around glowering all the time; she just didn't throw her grin out first. Even through the staticky hologram, Max could tell it was a big smile, free and uninhibited. A smile that meant it. He sighed.

"Max with you?" Djinna's tinny voice said.

"He is," replied Dr. Sarita. "And we need to trouble your father for a moment, if that's alright. I'll explain upstairs."

"Here, lemme buzz you in."

Djinna pushed a button. The door growled mechanically and then swung open.

Just before they walked in, Max heard another voice over the intercom. "Who is it, Djinna?" He stopped short in his tracks, staring at the little 3-D Djinna. He knew that voice. Then a tiny Splink appeared behind Djinna, his hands grabbing her shoulders, his face squinting down toward the monitor. "Oh, hey, Max!"

Dr. Sarita and Max powered down their jetboots and started up the winding staircase that disappeared into the darkness. "So, Max," Dr. Sarita said. Max didn't have to see his mom's face to know she had on that mischievous grin of hers. "Djinna."

"I don't wanna talk about it, Mom. Seriously."

"Okay."

"Obviously it doesn't matter anyway," he mumbled. Actually, he really did want to talk about it, but not right then and definitely not right there and *definitely* not with his mom.

"Okay, Max."

"All I'm saying is . . ." A tiny fizzling shape was floating toward them from the darkness. "Um . . ."

Dr. Sarita looked up. "Oh!" As it got closer, the shape turned out to be a very small woman, or was it a bird? Some kind of bird-woman with brightly colored feathers and a shimmering glow around her. She was sending off sparks in all directions like an angry firecracker. And she was smiling. "Must be . . ."

"Welcome to the tower of Dr. Maceo, Flood City holographer extraordinaire." The sparkling birdlady curtsied. "I'll escort you to the doctor."

"Must be one of his holograms," Dr. Sarita whispered.

Max nodded, his eyes wide in the shimmering light. It looked so real, nothing like the fuzzy projections he was used to.

They followed her up the winding stairwell and then stopped suddenly when a horrible growling sound burst out from somewhere above. The whole tower trembled and then something green and gigantic plunged toward them. *It's just a hologram,* Max told himself. *It's just a hologram!* But somehow he didn't believe it. It was so alive, this monster plummeting at full speed down the empty column in the middle of the tower. *Don't run!*

Max watched in horror as the thing opened its mouth wide. He saw speckles of bloody saliva glinting on its razor-sharp teeth. It growled again, just a few feet away now, and Max could feel its rage reverberate through his whole body. He nearly toppled over backward as the creature whisked past and evaporated into thin air.

"Helloooo? Dr. Sarita?" called a timid voice from the top of the stairs. "Sorry 'bout that! Security system acts up sometimes, you know!"

CHAPTER

Yala had taken a few steps backward into the crawl space when it occurred to her that the vapor had called her by her name. He simply floated there grinning while she scrambled to get as far away as she could without taking her eyes off him. It wasn't going well. The jagged tunnel was tighter than she'd thought, and while she would have probably been able to squeeze through if she was going headfirst, backing in was more of a problem.

"Yala," the vapor said. "Let's get this over with . . ."

How would you even go about attacking such a thing? Yala wondered. The only solid part seemed to be the mouth and eyes, and that didn't leave much to go on.

"I'm not here to hurt you." The smile dissipated into thoughtfully pursed lips. "Or Max, for that matter."

"I don't believe you."

"Of course not. I'm a vapor. Probably the first one you've seen."

Yala nodded, still racking her brain for some kind of attack but coming up short again and again.

"I know about your plan."

That's when everything stopped. Yala hadn't told a single person about leaving tomorrow. Not a soul. She'd tumbled it through her mind a hundred thousand times, sitting alone in the tunnel outside their house or lying in bed while Max snored loudly nearby. She'd held raging arguments with herself about it. Gone back and forth until she was dizzy, but she'd never spoken a word of it out loud. "How?"

"We vapors have a way of keeping our ears to the ground."

"That's not a good enough answer."

"It's all you're gonna get. For now, anyway."

"What do you want?"

"Just a word with you, Yala. You can stay where you are if you feel safer."

Yala allowed her body to untense a tiny little bit. The vapor was creepy, but somehow, he seemed to be genuinely uninterested in hurting her. "I don't like being followed."

"Understood. My apologies. The work I do requires a certain amount of . . . discretion." A slight bow. "My name is Biaque."

"You can't stop me from . . ." He had said he knew her plan, but he hadn't said what it was. Yala wasn't about to be bluffed into giving it up. She let her voice trail off.

"I have no intention of convincing you not to join the Star Guard," Biaque said. "In fact, I'm here to ask you to do exactly that."

Yala raised an eyebrow at the vapor. "Really?" She was about to ask why when she noticed Tinibu flashing toward them. Perhaps she was saved, although she wasn't sure from what yet. Biaque saw her gaze and, rather than turn around, his eyes and mouth simply vanished into the cloudy form and, presumably, materialized on the other side. Yala shuddered.

The tiny hunterfly slowed to a glide a few feet in front of Biaque and nodded at him. Yala gazed in amazement. They knew each other. Biaque nodded back and then his features surfaced toward Yala again.

"You know Tinibu?" she gasped.

Biaque smiled. "We go way back."

Tinibu hopped into the crevice, nuzzled Yala a few times, and then perched happily on a jagged rock ledge. He pulled a greasy paper bag full of dougies out of his little satchel and started munching away, not bothering to take them out of the bag first. "Then I guess you can't be altogether evil," Yala muttered. She was dying to get out of that uncomfortable position anyway. If the vapor had wanted to hurt her, he'd already had plenty of opportunities. She crawled out and stood beside where Biaque hovered, looking him up and down suspiciously.

The vapor smiled. "Let's take a stroll."

CHAPTER

Finally alone in his room, Ato laid the plastic bag on his desk with a heavy thud. He reached in, grabbed a handful of cold, scaly flesh, and pulled out the iguanagull's headless body. The thick dark blood had congealed in dry clumps around the hole at the end of its neck. It wasn't too gooey, but a horrendous odor issued out as soon as it was free of the bag.

Ato spread the plastic out and laid the creature flat on its belly. The muscular arms and legs had already begun to stiffen some, and they stuck out at odd angles. Tremendous white feathers sprouted thickly from a membrane stretched from the forearms to the pelvis. The long arms ended in three curved claws, and Ato could see instantly how they'd be sharp enough to cut through steel. A spiky ridge ran the length of the iguanagull's spine, sharp waves that peaked midway down its back and shrank toward the tail.

Iguanagulls. Ato squinted to remember his bio textbook's exact phrasing. *A regressive mutation resulting from the quickening caused by environmental changes in the atmosphere.* Something like that. *The combining of two or more once-related species into a brand-new one.*

A ferocious one at that, Ato thought. But what on earth could Mephim have wanted with its head?

He ran his fingers idly along the scaly back, feeling the ridges of its muscles and the gentle protrusions where its ribs were. Then he grabbed it with both hands and, with some effort, flipped the creature onto its back. The underside was smoother and a lighter shade of green. Being as careful as possible, Ato held the iguana-gull's arm with one hand and uncurled one of its claws with the other. Something was odd about the inner edge of those sword-like talons. He ever-so-carefully stuck his finger into the curve of one and then pulled it back out. His eyes went wide and his mouth dropped open.

"Come, come," twittered Dr. Maceo, a tall, dark-skinned man with a shiny bald head. "Ignore the nonsense." His chuckle sounded oddly urgent, like he was in a hurry to get the laughter out of his throat. "I've been meaning to fix the bugs in that security system for ages. Djinna always gets mad at me for it, of course. How are you, Dr. Sarita? It's been far too long, you know."

Dr. Sarita smiled, panting her way up the last few stairs, and then wrapped Dr. Maceo in a warm embrace. Of course, Max remembered, they had been on the original starship together as kids.

"And you!" Dr. Maceo directed his terrific smile, apparently a family trait, to Max. "Excited about the performance tonight? Djinna can't stop talking about it!"

Max nodded, hoping he wasn't expected to hug anybody. "Yes, sir."

Dr. Maceo led them into a high-ceilinged room with scientific charts and crude sketches covering the stone walls. To Max's relief, neither Djinna nor Splink were anywhere to be seen.

Dr. Maceo ushered them onto an old couch and began fiddling with a rusty coffee maker. "What brings you by so suddenly?"

"Yala's gone missing," Dr. Sarita said. Dr. Maceo stopped what he was doing and looked up. "She was with Max this morning, and they got separated somewhere near the Tumbled Together Towers."

"That's awful, Dr. Sarita."

"I was wondering about the holomap . . ."

"Ah! The holomap!" Dr. Maceo said, and then he looked puzzled. "Hmmmm." His hands went back to fiddling with the coffeepot, but his gaze was elsewhere. "Interesting. I've never tried it for such a thing, Dr. Sarita. You know it's only in the very early stages and all that."

"Of course."

"But I wonder . . . The Star Guard's holoscope coverage is by no means comprehensive, nor is it quite up to date yet. That is, there'd be a time lapse, of course."

"Of course."

"And our pirating systems are only rudimentary. We've just been able to hack their account recently. Still . . ." As he spoke, Dr. Maceo filled the little metal pot with Star Guard ration coffee grounds and poured water into the basin. Then he screwed the upper canister on and set it to boil on a portable burner. "It's worth a try," he said very slowly. "Yes! It's worth a try!"

Dr. Sarita stood up in excitement and Max jumped up beside her. "Indeed it is!" she said.

"Max," Dr. Maceo said, "would you kindly go upstairs and ask Djinna to power up the holomap?"

Max nodded and headed up the spiral staircase. He poked his head up into the loft area, trying not to hold his breath. Well, they weren't kissing at least: They sat across from each other at a table, each immersed in a different book.

"Hey, Max!" Djinna said, standing.

"Hey, Djinna." Max managed to find a smile for her, but he was sure it looked contrived. "You excited about tonight?"

Ugh, small talk! Why did he bother?

Djinna nodded enthusiastically. "Can't wait." She was never this animated at rehearsals. *Maybe it's because her true love is here*, Max thought. But Splink seemed so corny compared to her; it didn't make sense. "We were about to go up on the roof to see what Krestlefax has to say, you wanna come?"

That sounded horribly awkward and Max would definitely be a super-extra third wheel. "Sure." He shrugged. "Oh, and your dad told me to tell you to power up the holomap."

Djinna looked surprised and then walked quickly over to a long, shiny table in the middle of the room and flicked on a switch.

"You never showed me the holomap!" Splink moaned. The table hummed to life, sending a blue glow toward the ceiling.

"Cuz it's not really done. Dad's still tinkering with it. Something really serious must be going on for him to show it to your mom. Everything okay, Max?"

"Yala's gone missing," Max said.

"Oh, that's terrible!" Djinna put a hand on Max's shoulder.

"She's probably okay though," he added quickly. "But you know . . . things being what they are"—he was pretty sure none of his words made any sense, but he kept talking anyway—"and all that. Just being sure."

"Of course." Djinna nodded, frowning.

Splink said, "That sucks, kid, I'm sorry."

Max shrugged, 'cause what do you say back to that?

"I'm powering up the holomap, Daddy," Djinna called into the trapdoor. "We're going up to the cupola while it charges."

One by one they climbed a ladder into the dark rafters and then through a metal gate and out into the chilly fresh air. They stood on a walkway that circled the pointy, shingled roof of the tower. It was a cloudy day with sprinkles of rain splattering here and there. Flood City lay concealed mostly in mist. A few taller buildings poked out of the fog; there was the ocean liner marking Barge Alley and the apartment complex Max and Yala lived in, partially hidden behind the great rock wall. The sea spread all around them, those gray waves stretching out into the white sky.

"You know I'm leaving tomorrow," Splink said.

Max had never seen him look so serious. "No. Where you going?"

"Star Guard Academy, obviously. Our transport leaves at sunrise."

Max was at a loss for words. "Wow."

"Kinda awesome, right? Gonna fight the Barons. Blow up some spaceships."

It sounded horrible. Plus, Max seriously doubted that's what he'd be doing. Scrubbing some toilets and getting blown to bits was more like it. "Awesome."

"I think it's horrible," Djinna volunteered. "I hate the Star Guard."

Max felt a surge of excitement. He put away the big smile that was trying to come out and instead nodded solemnly. Most people in Flood City couldn't stand the Star Guard, but it wasn't the kind of thing you spoke about openly.

"I mean, I'm not crazy about them either, to be honest," Splink said. Max thought he sounded like he was trying a little too hard, or maybe he just wasn't used to speaking earnestly. "But I wanna get rid of the Barons and that's the only way I know to do it."

Djinna shrugged. That wasn't the response Splink was looking for, and he went in for a kiss. Max quickly turned his head away and then gave a shout. The last bird left on the planet flew out of a cloud directly toward him. It was enormous and covered in brown and gray tattered feathers.

"Krestlefax!" Djinna yelled. "You made it back!"

The old bird circled the tower once, regarding them with its sharp eyes and long beak, and then alighted on the old weather vane at the top of the cupola. Djinna started climbing the slanted rooftop.

"Be careful," Max said, but hoped she hadn't heard him. Splink leapt after Djinna and then Max climbed up carefully, trying hard not to think about what would happen if he slid and flopped over the railing and off into the empty sky . . .

"You've been far this time, Krestlefax," Djinna was cooing as she ran her hand along the huge bird's wing feathers. Krestlefax nodded. "You have learned about the future?"

Another nod. The bird sat proudly, his back erect like a military general, eyes set and stern.

"What can you tell us, old one?"

"WAR!" cawed the ancient bird. *"WAR!"*

CHAPTER

Ato closed his eyes and tried to block out the stench of dead iguana-gull. His bio tutor, an old vapor named Kistle, had always said: *When you want to unravel a mystery, you follow it right to the roots. Otherwise don't bother.* He'd say it and then sip thought-fully at his coffee, his eyes elsewhere, and the words would send Ato into an excited reverie about all the mysteries he could unravel as an interstellar zoologist. He imagined himself spe-lunking through craters, diving to the bottom of gelatinous moon oceans, discovering new species of space worms on asteroids. It didn't matter that Kistle was ancient and had most of his other pupils snoring; his lectures always had Ato riveted.

Ato looked at the strange substance he'd scraped from the iguanagull's talon. Soil. It couldn't be . . . but if it was . . . He squinted at it, his mind reeling at the implications. It wasn't just grime or grease. This was a for real clump of brown soil. The kind you used to be able to plant things in, back when there was land on Earth. This meant that somewhere out there, somehow, there was again!

If only he had a . . .

Someone pounded on the metal door.

"Ato!" Get yelled. "Open up, man!"

Ato dropped the soil in a tiny plastic tube he kept for his little bio samples and pocketed it. Then he scrambled to bag up the iguanagull. "Coming! Hang on!"

"Open up!"

Some yellowish fluid puddled on the desk, but otherwise there was no sign of the creature. It would have to do. Ato braced himself and then in one quick motion pushed the open button and bustled past his brother into the corridor, holding the plastic bag low against his body.

"Hey!" Get yelled after him. "What's the deal, bro?"

"Nothing," Ato called.

"Ugh! What's that smell? What were you doing in here?"

Ato kept moving around the corner and then threw himself against the wall, his heart pounding. Why was everything so tense all of a sudden? He hadn't been thrilled to go on this mission, but he'd accepted it as part of his duties as a young Baron. Everything had seemed fine, at least manageable, until the iguanagull attack this morning, and then Mephim had lost his temper, shown a side of himself few people had ever seen, and the whole ship seemed to be anxious and out of sorts. Maybe they were just worried about the attack tonight, what with the depleted shields and all.

Or maybe something else was going on. Ato headed quickly

down the corridor. He'd have to get rid of the iguanagull body, much as he hated to. There was simply no way to keep it without being found out. He headed back to the engine room, fast-walking around a series of corners, and then stopped suddenly at the door. There were hushed voices coming from inside, and one of them was definitely Mephim.

"Almost, my lord, almost," Tog Apix was saying.

"How much longer?"

Ato slipped soundlessly inside, clutching the plastic bag close to his body so it wouldn't rustle, and ducked behind a clacking furnace.

"Should be ready by tonight."

"*Should* be?" Mephim hissed.

Ato could just make out the two figures huddled over something in the far corner. Whatever it was, it had a strong enough glow to light up the otherwise dim engine room.

"Will be, ArchBaron. Will be."

"It better be, Tog. Or I will find a new engineer. Are we clear?"

"Yes, ArchBaron."

"Come, let us prepare."

With a whir and a click, the room returned to its normal gloominess. Ato held his breath as Mephim swept past with Tog stumbling along in his wake. He waited till their footsteps faded and then crept out, dropped the iguanagull in the waste basin, and made for the corner of the room where the two men had been standing.

There was a mechanical compartment built into the wall. It was so drab and unimportant looking, Ato would never have thought twice about it if he hadn't just seen the light that had burst out. He punched the base fleet security code into a little keypad, and the compartment swung open easily. The room filled with that strange glow once more. Ato had to shield his eyes at first. He pulled a pair of goggles from the wall and put them on. Inside the compartment, a round metallic capsule sat on a pedestal. It had a little window in the center, which the light poured out of. Ato peered a little closer and could just make out a white gem the size of a fist. A skull-faced hazardous materials sign was printed on the container over some numbers and symbols. He recognized it immediately from chem class: weaponized uranium.

There were rumors the Baron leaders had salvaged some as they fled the flooding on Earth, but Ato had figured it was just chatter. Here it was, though, real and glowing.

Mephim was getting ready to nuke Flood City.

"Let me ask you this," Biaque said.

Yala looked at the vapor floating beside her as she buzzed slowly along the edge of the half-sunken ocean liner. She nodded.

"Why?"

It was such a simple question. Just one word! But it'd kept Yala up nights on end with no answer. There was the easy explanation of course: Once she finished Star Guard Academy, the soldier's stipend would guarantee her mom and Max a life of relative comfort. But there was something else too. Something deeper. She knew it was the right choice. There was no question of that. And therefore, she also knew she would do it, because once she knew something was right, it was as good as done. The problem was, she had no idea why it made any sense at all. She made a show of thinking it over, knowing she wouldn't come up with any new answers, and then shrugged. "I dunno really."

To her surprise, Biaque nodded, arching his eyebrows in thought. "Hmm. Do you want to protect the noble alien overlords?"

She couldn't stifle her laughter in time, and it burst out in an awkward guffaw. "No! Never . . . Not that. I hate the . . . I don't like that they . . . are here." Words didn't seem to be doing it. And explaining herself had never been Yala's strong point. "I just feel like I need some purpose. Something bigger than this." She gestured to the crumbling ruins around her.

Biaque hmmed. They'd sailed above the gigantic boat and could see down into all the debris-filled crevices and shattered building tops surrounding it. Folks darted back and forth through the alleys and into windows carrying their daily provisions, chatting in small circles about the celebrations later. "I love it here," Yala said, letting herself down on the tip of the ocean liner. Tinibu zipped up past her, did a loop-de-loop in the air, and then disappeared into the ship. "I really do. It's my home. And I wouldn't trade it for any other. Even with all the mess and trouble and everything else."

Biaque nodded. Yala found him to be a shockingly good listener, considering that fifteen minutes ago she thought he was coming for her life. There was something undeniably genuine about how those oh-so-human eyes regarded her. She'd never felt so comfortable confiding in someone.

"The thing is," she went on. "I know . . . I feel like . . . there's many challenges ahead. Beyond even the daily struggle, making sure Max doesn't dash himself against the rocks or get lost in the

Electric Ghost Yard . . . something else. Something much worse. I don't know why. Just feels like clouds are gathering. That feeling right before a storm and I . . ." Her voice trailed off. She'd felt this way for a long time, she realized, but never put words to it. "I want to be ready."

Biaque's eyes narrowed like he was trying to see something far, far away. "And joining the Star Guard is the best way you know how." His voice was quiet, almost a whisper.

"Yes."

"Even though it seems to go against everything you believe."

"Exactly."

"Well . . ." He shook his head thoughtfully. "You know that we vapors are gifted with a certain amount of . . . shall we say, foresight?"

"People say you can see the future. It's true?"

He shrugged. "In a way, yes. It's not precise as all that, more like snippets. I don't know everything that will happen, and anyway, our choices do matter. Nothing is set in stone . . ."

"But?"

"But, yes. War is coming to Flood City, and you must be prepared, Yala. I've known your family for a long, long time, you know."

"I didn't . . . Wait." Something seemed to click into place in Yala's mind. "You were the vapor on the *Gallant*, weren't you?" The *Gallant* was the lumbering transport ship meant to ferry schoolkids out into the far reaches of the universe for field trips.

Biaque nodded. "Indeed."

Yala had so many questions, she didn't know where to begin. They must've shown on her face, because Biaque shook his head and said, "There'll be time for all that later. For now, I will just say this: You're right."

"About what?"

"Everything," Biaque said. He smiled, but his eyes were full of sadness. "Everything."

They were quiet for a long time.

"Max!" Dr. Sarita's voice called from below. "Come down, the holo-map is ready!"

Djinna, Max, and Splink exchanged nervous glances. "Comin'!" Max yelled.

"Is that all you can tell us, Krestlefax?" Djinna urged. "Nothing more?"

The bird sat motionless, staring out into the gray sky. Max started making his way down the roof. Above him, Djinna and Splink spoke quietly to each other.

"The feeds from the Star Guard's holocams are normally fuzzy, and wildly inaccurate," Dr. Maceo was saying as Max let himself down from the ladder. "But still, it's not bad." A miniature Flood City sprawled across the holodeck. Besides being blue and staticky, it was a startlingly perfect 3-D map.

"But they can't have holocams everywhere," Max said, walking a circle around it. "How can it be so complete?"

"Well, it cheats some of course," Dr. Maceo said with another chuckle. "But you'd be amazed how thoroughly watched even the backstreets of Flood City are. Plus, there are several hovering holocams making rounds through the air at any given time. You've seen them, I'm sure. They look like metal globes about the size of a basketball with little lenses all over them."

"Right!" Max said. "I hate those things."

Flickering images skittered around the alleyways and plazas of Flood City, and if you looked at them real close, you could make out features, sometimes recognize people. Max was impressed that his mom had thought to come here rather than scour the streets all night looking for Yala. "You think we'll see her?"

"If she's anywhere outside, she'll be on the map," Dr. Maceo said. "That is, if she was outside approximately twenty-seven minutes ago, she'll be on the map. Heh-heh."

"This won't be easy," Dr. Sarita said, sticking her head directly into a cluster of buildings to get a better look.

"I'll ask Djinna and Splink to help," Dr. Maceo said.

Max found himself so transfixed by the holomap he barely noticed Djinna and Splink and the heavy cloud that had fallen over everything after Krestlefax's grim prediction. The little figures blipped along in jerky, rhythmic bursts as the feed caught up to itself. If he squinted and got real close, Max could even make out facial expressions and tiny gestures that were individual to each person. He found Old Man Cortinas outside the barbershop, chatting as always with Mateo and Tecla. There was Del, the jetboot mechanic, helping a little girl into her first pair.

Hunterflies slid back and forth through the sky, just blurry blips over the holomap. The line outside the bakery wound all the way to the middle of Flood City Plaza, and Max imagined he could see the hungry patrons chatting with one another, gossiping about their day, planning festivities for the night ahead. Some looked skyward, wondering no doubt about when the next attack would come. Max smiled, forgetting for a second that his sister was lost somewhere in there.

"There she is!" yelled Djinna. "I think that's her." Dr. Sarita made it to her first, followed by Max.

"Where?" Dr. Sarita demanded.

"Right there," Djinna said. "On the tip of the ocean liner."

"What's that thing next to her?" Max asked.

Dr. Sarita looked very pale suddenly. "Oh my . . ."

"What, Mom?" Max said. "What is it?"

"Let's go. Now."

They said brisk goodbyes to the Maceos and Splink and then launched off into the midafternoon sky. Max had never seen his mom move so quickly across Flood City. He asked her what was wrong, but she just grunted and zipped faster.

"How do you know she'll be home?"

"I don't. Hurry up."

They zipped around a corner, Max taking it a little wide and almost crashing into a hovering streetlight, and careened up along the sheer cliff face and into the tunnel.

"Mom! What's going on?"

But then they were home, speeding up the twenty flights to their cramped three-bedroom apartment, and there was Yala, sitting calmly at the kitchen table next to what looked like a puff of smoke with eyes and a mouth.

"Biaque," Dr. Sarita said to the smoke once she'd landed and powered down her jetboots.

Max raised his eyebrows. He was only barely adjusting to the fact that his sister was sitting at the kitchen table with a vapor and now it turned out his mom was on a first-name basis with said vapor? Too much.

The vapor nodded. "Dr. Sarita." There was a pause—a very thick pause during which four sets of eyes looked curiously back and forth at one another and then Dr. Sarita simply walked across the room and wrapped her arms around Biaque, burying her head in his cushiony cloud.

Max's mouth fell open.

"It is you," Dr. Sarita whispered.

Biaque nodded. "Of course! Did you expect someone else?"

"I didn't know! It's been so long! Years . . ." She took a step back, understanding dawning across her face. "Oh," Dr. Sarita said, and looked at Yala. "It's time?"

"I have something to tell you both," Yala said. It was as serious as Max had ever seen her look, and Yala was a pretty straight-faced girl. "I'm leaving tomorrow morning—"

Dr. Sarita nodded her head, her forehead creased. "Biaque told me this would probably happen, a long, long time ago."

"Told you what would probably happen?" Max asked. "Where you going?"

"—at the break of day."

The break of day. That's when Splink . . .

"No!" Max gasped. "What? Why?"

Yala scrunched up her face and sniffled. "It's hard to explain, Max. It's just something I have to do."

"But the . . ." Max tried not to imagine life without Yala around. "And the . . . How could you?"

"I'm sorry, Max. You know I'll miss you. And I'll write every day."

Max had no more words. It was all too much. He took a deep breath and looked out the window at the afternoon sky over Flood City. "Okay," he said finally. "I have a concert to get ready for." He walked out of the room.

THE FLOOD CITY GAZETTE

SPECIAL ALERT EDITION!!

STAY ALERT AT THE FESTIVITIES TONIGHT!!

Several unusual red flashes were reported in the eastern cloudscapes earlier this morning. These are unconfirmed sightings and we don't know the source of them, but there is a POSSIBILITY, REPEAT, ONLY A POSSIBILITY, that they are laser cannons. Additional reports mentioned a preponderance of feathers floating down from the skies nearby, but this also has not been confirmed. City authorities deployed holocams to investigate but the cloud cover was too thick to determine anything useful. Remember to keep your eyes on the sky.

Ato headed toward the bridge, his mind reeling. Mephim had always been a little creepy, it was true, but this ... this was something different altogether. How many people must be down there? Several thousand at least. And sure, they were rebels and in league with Star Guard, armed to the teeth and vicious according to the intelligence reports, but to obliterate the entire city? Only a madman would do such a thing.

He rounded a corner and stopped. He felt dizzy, like all the different things that had just happened were weighing down his head, clogging his thought channels. Who would rip off an iguanagull's head with his bare hands and hide it away? Had Mephim always been evil or did something happen?

At the other end of the hall, the flight deck was alive with blips and commands. The crew was checking the system over to make sure everything was ready for their scouting mission tonight. Ato started walking again, very slowly. He didn't like what was going on one bit. A klaxon burst out over the quiet drone of the engines, and the corridor turned bright red with alarm lights.

"Battle stations," ArchBaron Mephim's staticky voice growled over the intercom. "Prepare for the intelligence run on Flood City."

Old Man Cortinas stepped into the empty auditorium and let out a long sigh. Besides the music itself, this was one of his most treasured moments of any concert. The place was so quiet, but he could feel the anticipation hanging in the air, like the walls themselves were anxiously awaiting all of Flood City to bustle in. He shuffled down the center aisle, enjoying the echoing clanks of his jetboots against the linoleum floor. The musicians' chairs were set up in a half-moon around the Hole, just like they were supposed to be. Cortinas walked right to the edge and peered into that endless emptiness. No one was allowed this close to the Hole except on Flood City Day, when the orchestra played a special commemorative concert to celebrate their survival and honor all the drowned ancestors whose bodies lay somewhere beneath the sea.

The old man nodded at the depths, sighed, and then laid down the suitcase he'd brought with him and popped open the clasps.

To all outward appearances, the case was just a regular instrument carrier. Cortinas was, after all, an old man, and what else would an old man be carrying around but music paper and his horn? Inside, of course, it was a whole different story: The slicer X3900 with laser-vision sighting and a magnum push attachment sat cozily in its foam bedding. Just beside it, in a separate hollow space, was the detachable rocket launcher.

Cortinas smiled. "Hello, baby girl."

He lifted the weapon out of its case with all the tenderness of a loving father and ran a cloth over its sleek body. Then he sat down, cradling the slicer in his lap, and picked up the shorter, thicker attachment. With a satisfying click-clack the two pieces became one, and Cortinas grinned even wider. He perched the thing on his shoulder and pointed it at the ceiling. There had been reports earlier about red flashes in the clouds above Flood City. Laser fire. "Maybe this year," he whispered. "C'mon, Barons. We're waiting for you."

Max normally had a rumbly tummy before his performances. Even speaking up in class gave him the shivers. But tonight he felt nothing. In the morning, his sister would be gone, whisked off to join the Star Guard. She'd be subjected to untold horrors, probably never to be seen again. What else could possibly matter more? He entered the grandiose and dilapidated auditorium building from the back, making his way straight for the dressing rooms.

How could she? And why? The useless questions kept charging through Max's head like a flock of squawking iguanagulls.

He knew there was no answer he could understand, didn't even think she fully knew why she was doing it, but still—the questions remained. He undressed quickly, glad to have arrived a few minutes early and have the room all to himself, and pulled on his fancy trousers.

Max looked in the full-length mirror and a wave of guilt cascaded over him. What right did he have to demand his sister do anything? So what if she wanted to run off and join the Star Guard? Let her. It'd be a fine opportunity for him to take care of himself for once, and not have her meddling with him all the time. Fine. So be it. Then he sighed and pulled on the button-up shirt with a growl.

Whatever. Yala would do what she wanted. Hopefully it wouldn't get her killed. He nudged his pre-tied tie over his head and adjusted it. Hopefully it wouldn't get him killed either. Then he remembered the ancient bird's one-word prophecy: *WAR!* Now fully dressed, Max frowned at himself.

"Yo, Max," Deezer said, walking into the dressing room. "What it do?"

"Ugh," Max said.

"That good?"

Deezer and Max had known each other since they were tiny. He played the second feezlehorn in the orchestra. They weren't exactly best friends, but they shared an easy familiarity.

"Yala's joining the Star Guard tomorrow," Max muttered.

"Oh," Deezer said, suddenly solemn.

Max smacked his forehead. "C'mon, man! You're supposed to cheer me up! It's not like she's dead."

"No. She'll be fine." Deezer started to get changed.

"Thanks," said Max with a roll of his eyes. "Thanks a lot."

He walked out of the dressing room and down the hall to the main auditorium, where he found Old Man Cortinas asleep on a fold-out chair, cradling his tattered instrument case like a baby.

CHAPTER
19

"Alright, everyone," Chief Gunner Sak yelled. "Listen up!"

The general hubbub on the bridge died down. Everyone turned to look at Sak.

"We're turning off the cloaking device in five."

That wasn't right, Ato thought. They were supposed to stay under cover! Otherwise . . .

Lieutenant Oso raised his hand. "Chief Gunner Sak."

Sak shot him an irritated glance. "Hm?"

"This is an intelligence mission. If we decloak—"

"That is a direct order."

"I realize that, Sak—"

"Chief Gunner Sak."

"The order comes from me," Mephim said, sweeping into the room. "Do you have a problem with the mission and chain of command, Lieutenant Oso?"

Oso clenched his lips. "No, ArchBaron."

Ato felt like the whole ship was made out of glass suddenly. Was Mephim even going to mention the nuke? Apparently not. And why was everything so tense all of a sudden? It wasn't uncommon to see some back and forth about tactics, especially between Oso and Sak. But something was different now.

"Um . . ." Ato said, standing. He'd jumped up without being completely sure of what he was going to say—anything to break the tension between Mephim and Oso. "What is the plan if we get shot down?"

Mephim didn't stop glaring at Oso. "The plan is don't get killed. We're well out of range of backup support. It is a top-secret mission. Most of the Barons don't even know we're here or why. That is the risk of this work—if you don't like it, you shouldn't have come."

"No, I don't mean—"

"So, if we get shot down, Ato"—Mephim was still locking eyes with Oso, but he hissed Ato's name so fiercely it felt like a threat—"we may well never be heard from again. Not many of you will blend."

And it was true—from what Ato had read, most of the folks who'd been left behind on Flood City were black and brown. Everyone on the cloud cruiser and most of the people on the Baron base fleet were white like him. The official Baron histories seemed a little touchy about those demographics, most preferring not to mention them at all; the rest glossed over them pretty quickly.

"Anyway," Mephim said, glowering, "Flood City doesn't take

kindly to Barons showing up near its cultural institutions, especially on the one and only holiday. So we'll probably take fire if we uncloak, correct?"

Everyone on the crew looked back and forth at one another. Ato felt a lump in the pit of his stomach.

"Correct?" the ArchBaron growled.

"Sir, yes, sir!" yelled most of them. Ato just blinked. What was about to happen?

"Then we better lay down some preemptive fire, hm?"

"Yes, ArchBaron," Sak said, snapping a salute.

Mephim nodded and sat back down. "Now," he said, steepling his fingers, "we have continuing cloud cover; let us approach the target. Charge up your cannons, and turn off the cloaking device."

Max watched the Flood City pageant drift along around him. He sat in the same spot as always, nestled smack in the middle of the horn ensemble, the Hole a gaping chasm at his back. The hunterfly conjunto hovered in perfect formation to his left. Past them were the string players. On his right stood Djinna, just visible past her monster balooga drum. But Max barely registered her. Normally at this point in the performance he'd be shaking with nervousness. His stomach would be growling. He'd be a mess. Then the main orchestra section would come in and he'd catch his rhythm and things would fall into place; his nervousness would give way to the moment.

Tonight though, everything was different. Max still couldn't shake the feeling that he'd never see his sister again. He tried to tell himself it would all be fine, she had to live her life, but that empty feeling in the pit of his stomach remained.

Around him, the pageant swaggered on as always: Cheerful

five- and six-year-olds ran onstage, giggling and clutching a luminous stretch of blue fabric—the Great Flood. Max had been thrilled to graduate out of this agonizing stage of the performance and become a musician's apprentice. A few older kids, already working hard to project that air of perpetual whateverness, strutted on carrying the same giant papier-mâché starship they used every year. They held it over the giggling waves and the crowd broke into applause right on cue. It was the *Gallant*.

Then, to much hooting and hollering, a group of kids representing the crew of the *Gallant* marched onto the stage. They made a big show of seeing the audience—an overused metaphor for discovering Flood City that still teared up some of the elders. It was all pretty corny, but everyone loved it and the whole crowd was on their feet and clapping. Max always used to try to pick out which kid was supposed to be his mom, but it was useless of course—the little actors weren't doing a one-to-one representation. The only ones you could really tell apart were one kid with a big fake mustache that was obviously meant to be Cortinas, and another wearing a sheet over his head to make him look like the one vapor who'd accompanied the survivors on their journey after the Floods. The thought of any vapors, even one of the Founders, made Max grimace and retreat deeper into his shell.

As if in response to Max's foul mood, the orchestra swung dramatically into the sinister, minor key procession part that was the cue for the Chemical Barons to attack. A couple of ten-year-olds entered from the left wearing cardboard Baron uniforms. The crowd booed accordingly. Max hit each note with precision but otherwise felt only tired and empty. The Chemical Baron kids made a show of chasing people around and generally being terrible before a bunch of older kids with blue face paint came running in on stilts. The Star Guard. No one cheered. Cortinas, Max imagined, was cringing like he did every year. There was no mention of the Flood City rebels, the group Cortinas had formed to fight off the Barons. Just big blue giants, saving Flood City from total destruction, year after year, always under the watchful eye of Bartrum Uk, who always hovered somewhere in the back shadows of the auditorium.

The Chemical Barons finally retreated into the wings with exaggerated gasping and stomping. Flood City was free. Sort of. The little kids all took big bows and paraded off the stage, laughing and shoving one another.

Now that the reenactment portion of the show was winding down, it was time for the music to enter full swing—the orchestra's moment to shine. Here's where Max's stomach knotting would reach its agonizing peak, his pulse would get fast and thready, and his breath would come up short. But none of that was happening. All he felt was empty.

The music jangled along as it did every year—an easy kind of strut, each section clacking perfectly into place, all the pieces falling together like an expertly built machine, but Max was distracted. Or maybe bored. Both. Either way, he just wasn't feeling it. He managed to stay in line, let out each note just in time, but his mind filled with images of Yala getting blown up or lost in an asteroid belt or sucked into a black hole. And then there would be funeral arrangements to deal with and their mom would never be the same and everyone would shake their heads sadly as the casket passed.

Something nagged at Max's subconscious and he looked up. People were staring at the rhythm section. Something was wrong. Or different. It was Djinna. Max couldn't put his finger on it, but something she was doing with that balooga was off. Well, it was off in the sense that it had never been done before. Only just slightly—each note was playfully waiting till you didn't think it'd come and then jumping in, somehow right on time. It made Max want to move his hips and shuffle his feet. He looked out across the audience. Some folks were hemming and hawing uneasily, but most had started bobbing their heads in time with the music.

Djinna was doing something brand-new. She looked terribly sad and determined at the same time, but there was some kind of joyful glow coming off her too. At least, Max thought so—like the simple awesomeness of shuffling that rhythm up was spreading over her in a cloud. He thought maybe they were meant to be together and then he remembered stinking Splink and how she was probably playing with him in mind. And that reminded him of the Star Guard Academy and Yala about to be gone and the gloom came over him again.

"Max!" Deezer hissed. Max looked up. He hadn't missed anything, but his solo was coming up. Max glanced at Old Man Cortinas, who winked at him with that mischievous grin and then hit a high note on his horn that cued the percussion ensemble to rev up to Max's entrance point. Djinna and Jasmine launched into a series of crashes and booms, and Fast Eddie sent the bell clattering along underneath.

Max closed his eyes. He put his lips on the feezlehorn, waited a beat after the moment he was supposed to enter, just long enough for people to get antsy, and then blew. He didn't know what note he was hitting, didn't care really, he just let the sadness and anger and fear pour out of his mouth and into the music. The note sounded right, yes, but more importantly it *felt* right. It resonated deep down inside him somewhere. He blew again, the same note but stronger this time and longer. It was all wrong, totally against the script, the history, the whole thing, and it made Max unbelievably giddy. He let out a series of blasts in between the downbeats, sliding partway up the scale and back down again, hit another long, satisfying note and relished the way the drums trolloped along underneath him.

And then the drums stopped. Max opened his eyes. Not a single person was moving in the whole Music Hall. The band had stopped playing, the eight-year-old flood dancers had all paused mid-twirl. Everyone was gaping at this strange new music being born out of nowhere from Max's horn. Trellis, the conductor, shifted uncomfortably in his seat. Max looked at Old Man Cortinas, who was looking expectantly at the percussion ensemble. Max followed his gaze and his eyes met with Djinna's. She was smiling. She nodded slightly, then picked up her sticks and cracked them across the surface of her balooga. The deep bursts of sound organized into a rhythm, but it was a new one, faster and more explosive than anything they'd played before. Djinna closed her eyes and settled into the rhythm, her head nodding as each measure found its way back to the first.

Max felt a smile erupt inside of him. The sadness of Yala leaving was still there, but now it was mixed with something else—a jittery kind of pride. He put his lips back on the horn and let this new joyful sadness soar out in each note. Cortinas poked one of the eight-year-olds, and they all started boogying across the stage to Djinna and Max's new song.

For a few perfect seconds, it was just Max's horn and Djinna's drums and the twirling kids and nothing else. Max let his melody swirl along the rhythm and then splattered his notes in between it. A clack-clacking beneath Djinna's booming let Max know that Fast Eddie had jumped in. One by one, the whole Flood City Orchestra recovered from their surprise and picked up their instruments and joined in the new song. The little flood dancers were laughing and making up all kinds of new moves to go along with the music.

That's when Max noticed the iguanagulls.

There were just a few at first. They circled the upper rafters of the Music Hall. Then more and more began swooping in through the open windows, and eventually the whole dome was a swarming mass of green feathery creatures. People in the audience gasped and pointed. The orchestra wavered, unsure whether to keep playing or make a run for it, but Cortinas glanced sharply at them and waved his arm to continue.

Max hated iguanagulls. They hadn't been known to eat anybody in years, but the thought of those giant prehistoric-looking beasts lurking in the sky gave him the creeps. And now they were just a few dozen feet above him, circling and cawing away? If he hadn't been so thoroughly excited by the new direction of the music, he'd have probably taken off. He felt some responsibility though. Whatever it was had come directly from him and Djinna, had been born of their sorrow, and he wasn't about to run out on it just because some birdlizards wanted to crash the party.

The iguanagulls settled into the rafters, perching in little clumps along the outer rim of the dome and glaring down at the Flood City Orchestra with their big beady eyes. Meanwhile, the brand-new music rattled on. The rest of the rhythm section had followed Djinna's lead and jumped in, filling out into a rumbling and joyful accompaniment that shuffled alongside Max's horn bursts. The hunterflies, after some conferring in their mysterious little buzz language, laid down a perfectly tuned drone beneath it all. Soon the string section joined in and the audience was on their feet, clapping and screaming along.

And then things began exploding.

CHAPTER

"Fire!" Mephim hollered. His voice had become increasingly shrill with each scream and now he sounded almost maniacal. Ato narrowed his eyes at the ArchBaron. Then his stomach seemed to float up above his head as Oso steered the cloud cruiser into a sharp dive toward Flood City.

"All our initial stun bombs are deployed," Chief Gunner Sak yelled over the roaring engines.

"Very good," Mephim said, suddenly calm again. "Prepare your blasters. Shields up full."

Sala punched a few buttons on her control panel. "Shields up full."

"This is it!" Get whispered. "We're going in." He swiveled his chair around to the visiscreen.

Ato felt nauseous. Everything seemed wrong. Why were they attacking? That wasn't the mission! And did anyone else besides Tog and Mephim know about the nuke? Were they going to drop it or keep it for a just-in-case measure? He peered over his twin brother's shoulder and watched Flood City spin toward them dizzyingly fast on the visiscreen.

"Watch carefully, young Barons," Mephim said in his calm voice. "And learn." He turned back to the crew. "Resistance?"

"Negative enemy fire, sir," Sak reported. "And the streets appear to be empty."

Mephim's smile stretched all the way across his face. He closed his eyes. "Excellent."

"We are in direct firing range of the auditorium, ArchBaron."

"I want a barrage of scattered cannon fire across the rooftop on my command."

"Awaiting your command, ArchBaron."

The cloud cruiser lurched sharply to the right. Ato was flung hard against his seat belt. Get, who had stood up with excitement, flew back into his chair with a grunt. Mephim stumbled a few steps and grabbed a handrail to steady himself. "What was that?" he demanded. Lights flickered on and off and the klaxon burst out overhead.

"Enemy fire!" Sak yelled. "And more incoming!" He had barely finished speaking when the ship trembled again. Everything went dark for a few seconds and all Ato saw were the hundred flashing lights of Flood City spinning around him. The ship lights flickered back on and the crew began shouting back and forth.

"Silence!" Mephim yelled, climbing back onto his seat. "Get ahold of yourselves, soldiers!" The shouting dissolved into scattered grumbles of fear. "What do we know?"

"Wasn't Star Guard," Oso reported. "Probably rebels on rooftops with some kind of antiaircraft artillery."

"Status report?" Mephim glowered.

Sak looked at some screens. "We've sustained two direct hits. Massive engine damage, and shields are at thirty percent."

"Impossible!"

"We can't take much more. One hit, maybe two, and we're toast, ArchBaron."

Ato looked at Mephim's face. It was twisted with rage. He seemed to be struggling fiercely within himself over something. Both his fists were clenched. "Very well," the ArchBaron finally said, taking a long stride from his commander's chair. "Continue evasive maneuvers but stay in the vicinity of the target. I'll sort this out myself." He stormed out of the room.

Before Ato realized what he was doing, he'd launched himself out of his chair and taken off down the hall after Mephim. He didn't know what he was going to do, but he couldn't let the ArchBaron drop a nuke on a city full of innocent people. He crept along the corridor, peering around corners, and then rushed toward the engine room.

Giant chunks of plaster fell from the ceiling. People were screaming, crying, rushing toward the exits. Max was paralyzed for a
moment, staring at the chaos around him. The building shook
with another explosion and part of the ceiling collapsed in on
itself. Mountains of dust shot up into the air. There was more
screaming. Then Max could see the starry night sky through the
new hole in the auditorium ceiling and hear the menacing hum of
the cloud cruiser somewhere nearby.

"Max!"

Everything moved in some strange underwater rhythm, far
too slowly.

"Max!"

It was Djinna. She was running toward him. A cloud of dust
billowed up around her.

"We gotta get outta here!" Djinna yelled.

The other musicians were scattering toward the exits. Max

grabbed his horn, his mind finally catching up with itself. His knees felt weak and he realized he was terrified.

"Which way?"

There was a deafening roar, and they both looked up to see the Chemical Barons' ship hovering over the gaping hole it had opened in the Music Hall.

"We can't try to cross to the exits," Djinna yelled. "We'll never make it!"

Laser cannons spiraled in quick circles on the underside of the ship.

"The back exit," Max said. "Through the dressing rooms."

But even as he spoke, the cannons blasted a bright red line of fire directly into the wall behind Max and Djinna, reducing it to a pile of rubble. They ran toward the edge of the auditorium as the dust cloud exploded around them. Max was pretty sure he was about to die.

"Here," Djinna said, and collapsed against a wall. Max stopped beside her, gasping for air. Every breath dragged another flood of debris into his lungs. "I don't think the . . ." She stopped talking suddenly.

Max followed her eyes to the center of the auditorium, where Old Man Cortinas was hoisting a slicer X3900 onto his shoulder.

"Mr. C!" Max yelled.

The old man squeezed the trigger, and a flash of light burst into the sky and slammed against the cloud cruiser. Max and Djinna cringed and huddled close to each other as more plaster poured down from the ceiling. When Max looked up, Cortinas was rushing toward them with astonishing speed. Max had no idea the old guy could move that fast! He was beside them in seconds, and then another burst of cannon fire shredded the row of chairs where he'd just been standing.

"You have to get out of here!" Cortinas yelled.

Max nodded. That much was a no-brainer. But how?

"My troops have set up escape routes along some of the covered passageways leading to downtown. You should be safe if you can make it outside."

"Your troops?" Max gaped. Cortinas was just some geezer who cut hair and played the horn. Sure he'd been on the original starship, but nowadays? At his most adventurous he moved at a mild shuffle and usually looked like he might just take a nap at any given moment. Was it all a ruse?

"No time to explain," Cortinas said with a chuckle. "But I'll tell you this much: Things are about to get very hairy in Flood City."

Another blast from the laser cannons. The cruiser had adjusted slightly and the attacks were swinging closer and closer. The air was thick with dust and falling debris and some horrible burning smell. Outside, Max could hear scattered machine-gun fire coming from the roof; probably Cortinas's troops launching their counterattack. And things were *about* to get hairy?

Great.

Yala hurdled over crumbled rock piles, dashed between scattering concertgoers, dodged a stray laser blast, and finally ducked safely behind a shattered wall.

"Not bad," Biaque commented, floating up beside her.

Yala grunted her thanks. "You sure Mom's safe?" she said once she'd caught her breath.

"Safe as she can be for now," Biaque said. "I'm more worried about your brother. Come on, we don't have much time."

Yala peered over the wall, still panting, and then vaulted it and dashed into the open area in front of the Music Hall. The Barons' cloud cruiser had spun out of sight, and there was a temporary reprieve in the fighting. She glanced from side to side but didn't see Max anywhere. He'd either already escaped or he was somewhere inside. The motor of the cloud cruiser started getting louder and then the ship appeared over the auditorium roof like an angry mechanical sun, laser beams blazing. Yala bolted for the double doors that led into the mezzanine and threw herself inside.

"Yala!" Old Man Cortinas came running toward her. He had something long and fierce looking slung balanced on his shoulder, and he was covered in dust. Yala ran over and hugged the old barber. Her hand came away bloody.

"You're injured!"

Cortinas smirked. "A scratch. Never you mind."

"Have you seen my brother?"

"He was one of the last to get out," Cortinas said. "With Djinna. I just sent them back through the dressing rooms because the cruiser was directly over the—"

"Duck!" Yala shoved Cortinas as hard as she could as a laser blast flashed down and exploded next to them.

"Saint Juniper!" Cortinas yelled, hunching up his shoulders. "I have had it with that darn thing!"

Yala helped him up. Her heart had been racing for so long now that she barely even noticed it anymore. What was one more brush with death? She coughed, out of breath, and then eased herself against the wall and onto the floor, safely out of range of the lasers. Little blue dots were blossoming in front of her eyes.

Cortinas stopped fussing with his shoulder cannon for a second and looked at Yala. "You okay?"

She nodded. "Just need a second to catch my breath."

"Good," the old man growled. "Because I have to go finish this once and for all."

———

The corridor leading to the engine room was empty. That was good, because Ato didn't want anyone to see what he was about to do. Not that he was even completely sure what his next move was. He just knew he needed to do something, and fast. It was ludicrous really, and against everything he'd been taught, but somehow nothing had ever been clearer.

Ato peeked his head into the engine room, heard Mephim's frantic voice, and ducked behind the same furnace he'd used to hide earlier that day. "I don't care if we're too close!" Mephim growled. "That's not an issue! Are you disobeying a direct order?"

"No, ArchBaron." Tog's voice was weepy. "Just informing you of the consequences of—"

"I know the consequences, imbecile! I'm a Chemical ArchBaron. Now initiate the launch sequence. Target the auditorium. NOW!"

A few blips and hums sounded. The ship rocked back and forth and then came the rat-a-tat-tat of small arms fire crashing against the shields. The dim engine room lights flickered a few times, and then a digital voice announced that the weapons launch would begin in ten seconds.

Nine.

Ato crept out from his hiding place and saw Mephim and Tog huddled over the glowing warhead.

Eight.

There was a large red button on the panel in front of them. He knew if he could hit it, the launch sequence would abort and buy him a little more time. After that he had no idea what he'd do.

Seven.

It was now or never.

Six.

Ato sprang at Mephim, catching him around the waist and pile-driving him forward against the panel. The ArchBaron was quicker than Ato had imagined; he spun his body even as he toppled forward, swiping at Ato with his fists.

Five.

They clambered against the panel, a tangle of thrusting arms and legs, and suddenly Ato found himself staring directly into Mephim's eyes. An expression of shock came over the ArchBaron's face.

Four.

Ato punched him as hard as he could and reached up onto the panel, slapping randomly until he saw the red button.

Three.

He hit it just as Tog Apix jumped on him from behind. They both fell forward on top of Mephim.

Launch sequence aborted. Thank you.

"What have you done?" shrieked Mephim. His long arms were clawing at Ato, but there was too much going on for him to get any good swipes in. "What have you . . . ?" The lights went out again as the ship sustained another blast from the rebels' missile. Then Sak's voice blurted over the loudspeaker: "Shields are at zero power! We can't take another hit!"

CHAPTER
24

Old Man Cortinas jumped up into the air and then landed with a grunt. "No!" he yelled as his jetboots sputtered. A plume of smoke rose from the left one. "This is not the time!"

"Can I help?" Yala said.

Cortinas whirled around and eyed her. The slicer was strong enough to obliterate the cloud cruiser's shields with a single blast. Another explosion rocked the Music Hall. Dust and debris cascaded around them, but it all seemed far away somehow. Cortinas nodded and held the slicer out to her.

She put her hands on it. Cortinas didn't let go. "The trigger is touchy," he said, strangely calm. "And the kickback ferocious."

"Okay," Yala said. She tried to unclench her body. This was it. This was what she was about to walk into: war. Deep within her, a tiny voice cried out in fear. She would take lives. She might die horribly. She built a wall around it and nodded at Cortinas.

"Aim for the hull. The blast will shatter what's left of their shields and probably rupture the main engine valves. Anything less than a direct hit will just be a mere annoyance though, and then their laser cannons will turn you to dust. In fact, they might anyway."

Another explosion. Outside, people were screaming.

"Do you understand?" Cortinas asked.

"I do," Yala said. Her fingers itched for the slicer. Her whole body knew what to do. She'd practiced jetboot combat tactics a hundred times over the open water just outside the city, spun through endless flips and dodges carrying whatever weapon-size chunks of debris she could find. She was ready.

"Godspeed," Cortinas said. He let go of the slicer.

Yala looked up. The nose of the cruiser edged into view, peeking like an angry giant through the gaping hole in the Music Hall ceiling. Laser fire blazed around it. Yala took a deep breath, hoisted the slicer onto her shoulder, then jumped into the air and took off.

It took a second to find her balance—the slicer turned out to be heavier than she'd thought, and she veered dangerously close to the balcony before correcting her course.

And then she was out in the open sky.

For a chaotic second, everything around Yala was a whirl of flashing lights and explosions. She spun, saw the massive cruiser looming directly overhead, and adjusted the slicer. *Anything less than a direct hit*, Cortinas had said. She centered the sights on the hull and squeezed the trigger. The explosion burst out sooner than she'd expected—it threw her back, and she only barely managed to keep hold of the slicer as she tumbled into a free fall toward the Music Hall rooftop.

Had she hit? The world was still a spinning jumble of lights when the concussion registered, a dull, ear-shattering THUD that seemed to swallow up every other sound. Yala glimpsed the faint glow around the cruiser shatter into a billion tiny particles and then vanish as fire tore through the main hull. A cheer went up around her: the rebels who had been firing from the rooftops.

Still reeling from the kickback, Yala let herself fall backward into the Music Hall as the Barons' ship began to veer toward the ground.

Perfecto.

CHAPTER 25

Max and Djinna made their way through the rubble backstage. The winding passageways were barely recognizable through all the smoke and debris, but eventually Max saw the men's room door. Was this really happening? This was the door he'd gone through almost every year of his life, and now he was dodging laser beams to get to it.

"Max!"

He whirled around and saw Djinna staring at a pile of rubble a little farther down the hall. He was about to ask her what it was, but her face stopped him. Then he saw it: a pale hand sticking out from the crumbling plaster and stone. They both ran forward and tore at the rubble until they could see the arm, then the face. It was Deezer. He was dead.

Max stood up, panting and sweating. His arms were covered in dust and grit. His friend was lying dead at his feet. And explosions were still popping off all around him. Djinna looked up. "We have to get out of here."

He didn't want to leave Deezer like that, but there was nothing they could do. He didn't even feel scared anymore. The sadness he'd expected seemed a million miles away. He just felt empty. "Alright," Max said quietly. "Let's go."

Djinna took his hand, and they started back toward the dressing rooms. "We can try to come back when it's safe."

Max nodded. He wondered if he'd ever feel safe again.

Outside, people were rushing around and screaming. The cloud cruiser loomed overhead, smoke pouring off it as Cortinas's gunners took rooftop potshots. Max looked for his mom and sister amidst the bustling throngs of Flood City folks. It was dark though and he could barely tell one from the other.

"I think they're directing people into that alleyway," Djinna said. And it was true: Some order was beginning to take shape from the rush of bodies. Max saw a few guys from the barbershop hovering a little above the crowd in their jetboots, waving people toward a narrow opening.

He looked at Djinna. She wore a tight frown, her eyebrows creased with determination. "Your dad?" Max said quietly.

Djinna shook her head. She was covered in dust and shaking but still looked so alive in the flickering blasts of the firefight. "He had to take care of some holograph issue," she said. "It killed him to miss the pageant, but I guess really it saved him."

Max nodded. "And Splink?"

She shrugged. "I dunno. We had an argument earlier tonight after he said he wasn't sure if he could make it to the show. Because he had to get ready for deployment tomorrow."

A strange mix of giddiness and concern flitted through Max's brain. He tried to ignore it.

"So he's probably fine." Djinna didn't sound too thrilled about it.

"You ready to make a run for it?" Max said. The cloud cruiser had swerved out of sight for the moment, but they could hear its damaged engines gurgling somewhere nearby.

"Let's do it."

They broke out across the open area. A few scattered people still ran back and forth, looking for loved ones, but most of Flood City had disappeared into various alleyways. It was a good thing Dr. Maceo was fixing the hologram transmitters, because there would surely be lots of chatter tonight. They'd made it about halfway across the square when the sky lit up. A bright red flare shot out from the Music Hall roof, sizzled over their heads, and smashed into the side of the cloud cruiser. The ship trembled, heaved forward, and then plummeted toward Flood City in a flaming mass of metal.

It was headed directly for Max and Djinna.

THE FLOOD CITY GAZETTE

WE ARE UNDER ATTACK BY WHAT IS BELIEVED TO BE A CLASS A CHEMICAL BARON CLOUD CRUISER. UNKNOWN NUMBER OF CASUALTIES, UNKNOWN NUMBER OF ASSAILANTS. INITIATE EMERGENCY RESPONSE PROTOCOLS IMMEDIATELY, WHICH IS TO SAY RUUUUN!!!!! FIND COVER! GET AWAY FROM THE CENTRAL PLAZA!!! A COUNTERATTACK FROM THE STAR GUARD IS IN PROGRESS. HAVE NO FEAR, FLOOD CITY. THIS TOO SHALL PASS!!

There was nowhere to run. The cloud cruiser was simply too big to escape; it was like trying to get away from a giant flaming building dropping out of the sky. Max felt his knees go weak. He grabbed Djinna's hand, both of them knowing full well they weren't going to make it, and together they kept running anyway.

Max could feel the air around him get hot as the thing barreled closer and then, very suddenly, everything went quiet and he was thrown backward and landed hard on something round and unforgiving. Djinna was beside him, looking just as confused as he was. They seemed to be inside some kind of bubble. The fighting was still raging on all sides, the cloud cruiser was still bursting toward them, but somehow they were safe. Or trapped.

Before Max could figure out which, the cloud cruiser smashed down over them and the bubble they were in went flying into the air. Max and Djinna somersaulted forward, smashing against the far edge, and then spun back. Max was vaguely aware of the city lights, the flashing laser fire, the flaming cloud cruiser, all spinning wildly around him. He thought he was going to be sick. Then they were plummeting, suddenly weightless—that charming feeling of impending death once again. Max closed his eyes, too terrified to bother vomiting, and with a magnificent jolt they smashed down into an alleyway and rolled to a stop.

"Wow!" Max said when the world slowed its frantic carouseling some.

Djinna was lying beside him. "Are we dead?"

"Nope. And I'm pretty sure I didn't puke."

"Good news. What happened?"

Max looked around. "I have no idea. Apparently a bubble ate us and then jumped into the sky."

And just like that, the bubble slurped out of existence and the vapor who'd been in Max's kitchen was hovering over them.

Max gaped at him. "You!" The same vapor who had played some mysterious role in Yala signing up for the Star Guard . . . and just saved Max's life. "You." Max had too many conflicting emotions to put any sentences together, so he just laid his head back down and concentrated on not puking.

"Biaque," said the vapor. "At your service."

Djinna sprang to her feet. "That was you . . . around us?"

Biaque nodded.

"You're a . . . a vapor!"

Another nod. "We have some tricks up our sleeves."

"But you were solid! And . . . round!"

"Well, our fibers are not a set consistency. That is, we have the ability to—"

"You saved our lives!"

He was about to shrug, but Djinna got to him first and wrapped her arms around his strange little nebular body. "Thank you!"

Max stood and nodded at the vapor. "Yeah, thank you." He wasn't sure what to do with his body—couldn't quite bring himself to hug Biaque—so he just stood there fidgeting. "For saving us."

Biaque swiped the air. "De nada. The least I could do. And there's many more I couldn't save. Come, young ones, we must be getting back. They'll be needing help at the crash site, I imagine."

They dusted themselves off and started down the circling alleyway toward the auditorium. Biaque went first, bobbling along like some strange little cloud and emitting a dim glow so he'd be easy to follow.

"Yala?" Max said, falling into stride beside the vapor.

"She was safe last I saw her. We returned to the auditorium to look for you."

Max swallowed hard. If anything had happened to her while she was trying to help him . . . he didn't know what he'd do.

"She's very good at surviving, your sister," Biaque said.

"I know."

"And I know, not everything feels like it makes much sense right now."

"Try nothing at all."

"Right. Take this, Max." Biaque put a piece of crinkled paper in Max's hand.

"What is it?"

"The number for the holodeck at the ocean liner. It's where most of us vapors hang out—you can usually find me there. If you ever need anything, *anything*, find me there."

Something about Biaque's words sounded like a warning, but Max was too worn out to decipher what it might be. "Thanks, Biaque."

They rounded a corner and saw the cloud cruiser sticking out of a pile of concrete that had once been a building. Scattered flames danced across its surface. Djinna walked up next to them, shaking her head.

"Good thing most people were out in the street," she said.

Max didn't know what to say.

Biaque floated toward the wreck. "Let's go find your sister."

Cortinas walked through the crowd of gaping bystanders. His rebel troops were trickling in from their battle positions, converging on the downed cloud cruiser with their weapons drawn. "Did anyone get out?" Cortinas asked a middle-aged woman who was just staring straight ahead with her mouth open.

She nodded without taking her eyes off the wreck. "A few people. They scattered almost as soon as it touched down."

Cortinas whirled around and made eye contact with Tecla, his first lieutenant. He nodded at her, and she tapped two of the closest rebels and dashed off with them. Then he turned back to the woman. "How many? How many got out?"

She just shook her head. Cortinas growled and advanced on the ship. The flames were mostly dying on their own, and the basic structure of the thing was intact. The whole crew may have survived. The old barber grabbed a handhold and heaved himself onto the top of the cruiser. Then he unslung his slicer from his shoulder and leveled it at an open escape hatch. They'd have streamed out from there. This was a very high-level mission, so there had to have been at least one, maybe two, ArchBarons on board. He tightened his grip on the slicer and was about to step into the hatch when someone's head appeared from within.

"Easy, old man!"

Cortinas lowered his slicer and exhaled. "Mateo! What are you doing in there? I almost blew you away, you ridiculous little man." He offered a hand to his comrade and lifted him out of the cruiser.

"I saw the guys jet off as soon as the thing landed, but they were gone quick. Just evaporated into the city. So I figured I'd see who stayed behind."

"Anyone down there?"

Mateo scowled. "No one alive. A couple of bodies. It's pretty messy."

Cortinas made a hand motion, and several of his troops swarmed onto the cruiser and disappeared down the hatch. "Thanks, Mateo. Did you happen to see which way they escaped to?"

"Like I said, they scattered in all directions. Just jetted off real quick, there was no chasing 'em."

"Any ArchBarons?"

"Probably, yeah," Mateo said. "One had a long flowing robe though. Looked irritated to no end. The rest pretty much seemed like grunts. And two youngsters that looked exactly the same."

"Twins?"

"Or a real weird coincidence. But they left separately. One first, all by himself, and then the other went with the flowy fellow and a small band of gunners."

Cortinas nodded. "Alright. I'm going after them." He launched into the air and nearly smashed into the towering Star Guard captain who had just rounded the corner.

"Ah, Cortinas," Captain Gorus said. "Just the man I was looking for. What's the commotion?"

"If you have to ask me that," Cortinas snarled, "then you don't need to know."

Captain Gorus's smile faded fast. "Now look here, sir, we came to help as soon as we were alerted of the surprise attack."

"Fine. You're late. And I'm busy. Now if you'll excuse me . . ." Cortinas jetted up, but the captain put out a hand, blocking his way.

"Not so fast, Cortinas. The Star Guard is imposing a general curfew in response to this attack. We ask that you report immediately to your domiciles and remain there for the course of the night so that calm may be restored to Flood City."

"A curfew? You have got to be out of your tiny blue mind. There's still wounded people lying in the street! Who's going to—" Cortinas stopped talking. He knew the stubborn look on the captain's face.

The captain sensed victory and tacked toward graciousness. "Please have your friends evacuate the premises immediately." A big grin stretched across his face. Then, to Captain Gorus's great displeasure, Cortinas grinned too.

"No."

"I beg your pardon?"

"No," Cortinas said, still smiling. "No, I won't tell my friends to evacuate and no, you don't have my pardon. As a matter of fact"—he yanked a small walkie-talkie out of his vest—"come in, Tecla."

"Go for Tecla," a little voice scratched back.

"Under no circumstances are our people to leave this site until all casualties have been attended to and all booty looted from the wreck. Copy?"

"Copy."

Cortinas pocketed the walkie-talkie and grinned at the captain.

"This is open dissent, Mr. Cortinas. Rebellion!"

"So it would seem." Cortinas hovered in the air a few feet from the angry blue captain's face. Down below, a hush had fallen over the crowd. All eyes turned expectantly to the Star Guard captain.

"You will be punished!"

"Only," Cortinas said, powering up his jetboots, "if you can catch me." And with a burst of light, he was gone.

Max found Yala sifting through the carnage scattered around one of the ruined buildings. He yelled her name, breaking into a run, and felt all his anger and bitterness become relief. Yala turned, saw her brother, smiled wide, and opened her arms to him. They hugged, long and hard, and Max realized he was crying. He tried to wipe his eyes on her shirt, hoping that Djinna wouldn't notice from where she was standing.

"Hey," Yala cooed. "Stop that. I told you I was going to be alright."

"You said that about earlier. Then you were alright. Then everything went crazy again."

"I know. I know. But I'm still alright. And so are you."

Max nodded. He sniffled once, scrunched his face up and then released his sister. "You're really leaving tomorrow, huh?"

"At sunrise."

Djinna walked up behind Max and put a hand on his shoulder. Max felt little jolts of electricity shoot from her hand all the way across his body.

"Keep an eye on my little brother for me, okay, Djinna?"

Max cringed and rolled his eyes. Djinna laughed. "Will do, Yala. And you be careful." She seemed to want to say something else, maybe mention Krestlefax's one-word prophecy, but instead she just hugged Yala.

"C'mon, enough of all this lovey-dovey stuff," Yala said. "We got a lot to do."

They worked all night, lifting rocks, tending to survivors, finding shelter for the newly homeless. It seemed like almost all of Flood City was out that night, laughing in spite of the tragedy, finding ways to cheer one another on. Mr. Sanpedro showed up around four with a freshly baked batch of dougies. Every few hours, one of the Star Guard would trundle through and try to send everyone home, and then Old Man Cortinas would pop out of nowhere, do something wickedly mischievous, and disappear into the city again, forcing the blue giants to chase him.

As first light began to dawn over Flood City, the fires had all been put out and most of the debris dealt with. Fifteen people had died, counting the six found inside the cloud cruiser. The rest of the Chemical Baron crew had vanished without a trace.

Max finished cleaning up a pile of debris, wiped his brow, and looked over at his sister. "It's time," he said.

She nodded, frowning. "Yep."

"You ready?" Dr. Sarita said, walking over from the triage area, where she'd been treating cuts and bruises.

"Yeah. A little nervous, but I'll be okay."

Max had never heard his sister admit to being nervous before. She seemed to flow through any challenge with determined grace. "Okay," he said, trying not to sound doubtful.

They powered up their jetboots and flew the short distance to the launchpad. The city was coming alive around them, that laid-back dawn light pushing off all the turmoil of the night before.

The Star Guard ship was a huge transport freighter. It looked like an ancient skyscraper knocked on its side—big, boring, and gray. Max and Dr. Sarita watched Yala walk up the gangway along with Splink and about a dozen other recruits. Max couldn't help but feel like this giant flying monster was devouring his sister.

The ship grumbled, roared, and then sent blazes of fire exploding from its boosters. The crowd of family members and well-wishers took a few steps back so they wouldn't be incinerated. For a second it seemed like the massive thing wouldn't take off; it looked too big to fly. Max felt a guilt-ridden tinge of hope—maybe they'd just stay—but then it groaned and heaved itself up into the sky, only barely managing not to take out several buildings on the way, and shot off across the ocean.

PART TWO

Max jetted through the early morning streets of Flood City. The day after the pageant was always a quiet one, people sleeping off the night's revelry, but this morning the place looked downright deserted. Dr. Sarita and the other medical teams had headed back to the hospital, hopefully to get some sleep between treating patients. And everyone else must've finally trudged off to bed, exhausted from all the fiery explosions and sorting through rubble.

Max usually treasured a perfectly quiet moment in Flood City—they seemed to be more and more rare with each passing year as the population grew and the city itself didn't—but on this hazy morning he just felt lost. He could hear the waves crashing against the shoreline buildings, which usually brought him comfort but now just reminded him that his sister was gone, gone, gone to some unknown training camp across the water. Worst of all, Deezer's lifeless, dusty face kept burning through his mind like a migraine. Surely Deezer's parents had heard the news already.

They'd be bawling perhaps, or maybe just sitting quietly in a state of total shock. It would be a burial at sea like all Flood City funerals, and along with it all the dreary chores death required of the living.

Max shook his head, trying to clear the heaviness. He'd been half hoping Mr. Sanpedro's would be open and he could get a dougie, but now, crossing the deserted plaza, he saw all the shops were locked up. He grumbled to himself, accelerating up the face of the cliff. It was going to be a long couple of months.

He powered down his boots at the edge of the tunnel and heaved himself in. This was where Yala always came to think. She would sneak off late at night, probably thinking Max didn't notice, and spend hours on end in here by herself. Max never really understood it, but now he stood there panting and staring into the inky blackness and he felt some kind of peace come over him. It was an emptiness even more profound than the deserted city, and for no reason Max could explain, it was comforting. He walked forward, the clang-clang of his jetboots echoing up and down the tunnel around him. He'd have to ask Yala about this place, if he ever had a chance to talk to her again. Max smiled crookedly to himself and then tripped over a dead body and fell flat on his face.

For a full minute, Max lay perfectly still in the darkness. He wanted to move. He wanted to jet out of there as quickly as possible, in fact, but between the terror and the ickiness of it all, his body simply would not respond to even the most frantic attempts to rouse it. So instead he just lay there wondering what ridiculousness had caused him to *walk* through the tunnel instead of jet and why this had been the most endless day of his life and who might've met their lonely, dark end in the tunnel, of all places. He sincerely hoped it was no one he knew. He'd had just about enough of death for the moment.

His body still wouldn't let him move, but his breathing was finally slowing down. He wondered how the person had died. Maybe they were murdered. And maybe the killer was still around, lurking in the darkness. That thought had Max squirming to get himself up and running, but then the dead body rolled over and growled. Max yelled, scrambled to his feet, and ran.

He didn't stop till he was out of breath and could see the faint light from the other end of the tunnel. Then he threw himself against the wall and tried to listen over his own heavy panting for the sound of the zombie creature chasing him. He didn't hear anything but the echo of his breaths and the memory of the growl. It was more of a moan really. In fact, now that Max thought about it, it almost sounded like a word. And zombies didn't speak words, from what he knew about them; they just made horrible guttural noises while they gnashed their dead teeth on people's brains. Anyway, the noise the dead body made might've been a moan, and it might've been a word. And if it had been a word, it would've been something like *erp* or *emp* or . . . Max gazed back into the darkness.

Or *help.*

THE FLOOD CITY GAZETTE

ATTACK ON FLOOD CITY!!

CRAVEN BARONS STRIKE AT THE HEART OF FLOOD CITY FESTIVITIES, BUT THE STAR GUARD STRIKES BACK!

In the midst of Flood City celebrations last night, a Chemical Baron cloud cruiser launched a vicious attack on our beloved population. While initial damage reports are still coming in, at least nine Flood City Citizens were killed and over two dozen injured. The Star Guard, with some assistance from locals, fought off the attack and downed the cloud cruiser. The Flood City Star Guard Council and the Founders' Committee have been called into emergency session. **Please note: A mandatory curfew is in effect from nightfall to daybreak until further notice.** It is believed that several Baron-associated entities escaped into Flood City and are currently at large. STAY ALERT, CITIZENS! This is the greatest test we have faced since the Battle of Flood City.

RATIONS REPORT

Rations are back to their regular levels, as Flood City Day is now over. Please eat accordingly.

THE DAILY TIDE

Low tide today will be at **0436.**

High tide will be at **2317.**

Flood warning *is in effect for first six levels of domicile structures. Please be prepared to take emergency precautions (aka moving in temporarily with your upstairs neighbors) should conditions worsen. The Gazette will keep you updated!*

IGUANAGULL AHOY!

A massive incursion of iguanagulls visited the Flood City festivities just before the Baron attack. Accordingly, sightings have been up throughout the night. Stay safe and keep your eyes in the sky!

THE BOOO'CAST

Reported spectral/electromagnetic activity levels have been extra high by the Electric Ghost Yard. Please keep your distance from this area at all times!

THE VAPORS & ABANDONED OCEAN LINER REPORT

Still nothing to report. Those guys are weird.

CHEMICAL BARONS

An unknown number of Chemical Barons have infiltrated the city after the downing of their cloud cruiser (by the Star Guard). They are believed to be well armed and extremely dangerous. They are capable of masquerading as regular Flood City citizens, so please be extra vigilant as you go about your day. Report any unusual activity to the nearest Star Guard peacekeeper. Do not, under any circumstances, engage with the enemy.

Okay. Max's breathing was getting fast, which he took to mean that his body had realized that his mind was about to send it back into the place of utter terror once again. And it didn't want to go. But if it had been a word that the now maybe-not-dead body had spoken, and that word had been *help*, well . . . he couldn't just leave. He would never be able to get rid of the thought of some dying person wasting away in the tunnel, and that moaning plea would haunt him for the rest of his life.

Which would suck.

He scrunched up his face, told his breathing to *Cool it please*, and took a step back into the darkness. The clang of his jetboot sent fading echoes bouncing away from him. He took another step. Nothing ate him. No dead teeth sank into his brains. He started walking. *This is what Mom would do*, he told himself. *This is what Yala would do. But they would have a plan too. And something to fight with in case they were wrong.* Max had no plan and nothing to fight with. He didn't want to jet because he was afraid he'd either miss the body or singe it with the flame from his boots. That was about as much strategy as he had to work with so far; that and *Don't run away screaming.*

He was just thinking maybe the body had gotten up and walked away when he stepped on it again.

"Oof," said the body.

Max froze, his heart beating away like it thought it could break out of his chest if it went fast enough. "Hello?" he said. That seemed like a pretty useless conversation starter given the circumstances, but it would have to do. He reached down, felt fabric, flesh, hair.

"Help . . ." the body said, scaring Max half to death. But still . . . it was definitely a word this time. He had been right. He breathed a tiny sigh of relief and crouched down, trying to figure out what he was dealing with.

"Okay," Max said. It seemed to be a boy about his age maybe. Skinnier than Max, but then most boys his age were. Also, the boy seemed to have all his extremities intact, no blood-squirting stumps or gaping holes. That was a good thing. "Where does it hurt?"

"Everywhere" came the moaned response.

"Uh . . . where does it hurt the most?"

"Head."

Max touched what felt like dried blood on the boy's scalp. At least it was dry. "Okay," he said again. *Amazing conversationalist,* he thought. *Just amazing.* "I'm going to try to lift you. Somehow."

The boy just groaned.

Max slid his arms underneath him and tried to lift. The boy howled in pain, and Max put him back down. "Sorry." This would be harder than he'd thought. He walked around to the other side of him and crouched. Grabbed the boy under his left arm and by the pants leg and heaved him. The boy screamed again, but Max managed to get him awkwardly slung over his shoulder. He apologized again, felt silly for apologizing to someone whose life he was saving, felt even sillier for thinking so hard about it, and then started walking, trying to ignore the boy's moans of pain.

Sweat poured down Max's body by the time he reached the edge of the tunnel. The boy had gone unnervingly quiet during the last couple of minutes, and Max didn't want to put him down for fear he wouldn't be able to get him up again. An early morning downpour was covering Flood City in sheets of rain, and gusts of wind swooshed between the buildings like angry spirits. Max stared across the chasm to his family's twentieth-floor apart-ment. It was the same chasm he'd almost tumbled to his death into twenty-four hours earlier, and here he was about to maybe tumble to his death again. And this time he would be bringing someone with him.

Surely the boots will hold both of us, he thought. *Surely.* But he recognized the voice of trying-to-convince-himself. It was the same voice he used when he told himself that Djinna might be into him. Usually, after that voice came another one that always said the same thing: *Yeah right.* Still . . . Djinna had seemed kind of happy to see him, and if anything, the craziness of the night before had brought them closer together. *ENOUGH!* yelled the voice of reason. *You've got a half-dead kid on your shoulder and a plunge of death between you and safety. Stop thinking about the girl.*

Right. That voice always had a point. Max felt like he was in one of those annoying riddles that Mr. Essner would give them in school—the ones that always involved a catastrophic situation, a few disagreeable people, and not quite enough resources to deal with it. *Now solve it*, Mr. Essner would say, and the answer would always make people groan and slap their foreheads with its obviousness. Max never got the right answer.

In this situation, there were no resources except his jetboots, and Max was too exhausted to think of any clever way to get across. Plus he wasn't sure how much longer the kid would last, if he wasn't dead already. So Max powered up his jetboots as high as he could and launched out into the emptiness.

———————————

At first Max really thought he was going to make it. The jetboots carried him two-thirds of the way across the chasm before they faltered. *Two people is too much weight*, Max thought as the ignition jets sputtered and he started slowly descending. He pushed hard with his heels, sparking a little climb, but nowhere near enough to get him to the twentieth floor. Then his fall gathered speed as the boots began to fail entirely. Soon he would be in a full-on plummet.

"Uhhgg," moaned the boy, perhaps sensing his imminent shattering on the craggy rocks below. At least he wasn't dead yet. Max was close enough to his building that he could see into the apartments. They were falling faster now, but Max thought maybe, just maybe, he could grab one of the balcony banisters. He reached out, trying to edge himself closer, but couldn't quite make purchase.

"Oy," he said, shaking the boy on his shoulder. "I know you're in a bad way, but, um . . . I might need a hand here."

The boy stirred. "Urg," he mumbled, seeming, at least, to grasp what was being asked of him.

"I know everything hurts," Max said. There were precious few floors left before they began a free fall into the chasm depths. "But if I turn and you crawl forward, you might be able to tip us toward the building and grab a rail."

The boy didn't say anything for a second and Max almost lost his cool completely. Then the boy stirred. "Okay," he said.

Max threw his empty shoulder forward, setting them into a slow spin. There were only three balconies left. The boy shifted his weight, which seemed to send them spiraling down faster, and then howled with pain. *This is not good*, Max thought. But the boy was still moving, and then, Max realized, he was edging his body out across the emptiness. Max held tight.

Two more floors. They weren't going to make it. The rain smacked against Max's face as he looked up into the sky, maybe for the last time. Then he felt a sudden jerk and almost let go of the boy from shock. "You did it!" Max yelled. "You did it!"

"Yes," the boy said. "Now could you please climb up before you pull us both to our deaths?" He was grasping the railing of the last floor with one hand, barely hanging on. Max clambered past him, heaved himself onto the balcony, and then pulled the boy up. They lay there panting for a few minutes on the balcony, staring up at the falling rain, making sure they really were alive. Then Max looked over at the boy whose life he'd just saved.

"Oh," he said. "You're a Chemical Baron."

They both burst out laughing.

CHAPTER

30

What, Dr. Sarita wondered as she raced down a corridor between two brick apartment buildings, could Max possibly have done now? She sped across the plaza, noticing the first few Flood City folks beginning their days. It was raining again. Yala was gone. The jet fuel and smoke stench of the previous night's carnage still lingered in the air like a bad dream that wouldn't go away. Dr. Sarita sighed. And now Max wanted her to come home immediately and not ask any questions, just come home. Now.

"But you're okay?" Dr. Sarita had asked her son.

His face got all exasperated on the holodeck. "Mom! I said I'm fine. I'll explain when you get here." And with a blip he was gone.

Fine. Dr. Sarita was exhausted and worried, hadn't had time to process that her daughter was gone for who knew how long, and now Max wanted to act out. Fine. She sped up the cliff wall, through the tunnel, and up into their apartment.

Max stood up when his mom flew in from the balcony.

"Now, what," Dr. Sarita demanded, taking off her jetboots and rain jacket, "is oh-so-important that you—"

There was a boy lying on the couch. His hair was caked with blood and he was paler than most people on Flood City. And he was wearing Max's clothes, which were much too big for him. "Max?"

"Mom!" Max said in his don't-freak-out voice. "Lemme explain."

"Please do."

"He was injured in the crash last night. I found him unconscious in the tunnel." That all sounded true so far. "I don't know who he is." Less true. "He must not have a home. Or maybe he caught amnesia." And that was blatantly false and misleading; Dr. Sarita knew her son.

But he clearly knew her too, and now she was too busy being a doctor to pry more. Max had definitely counted on this. "That's odd," she said, kneeling beside the boy and inspecting his wounds. "Has he woken at all?"

"Just a little. He was pretty out of it though."

"Max, you carried him here? On your jetboots? That must've been . . . difficult."

Max nodded. "You have no idea, Mom."

"We need to get him to the hospital now."

"No!" He said it so suddenly that Dr. Sarita looked up at him in surprise.

She narrowed her eyes at him. "Why not?"

"Because he said he hates hospitals."

Dr. Sarita stood. "Max. Talk to me. C'mon."

Max looked like he was trying to come up with a hundred different explanations and all of them were just as terrible as the ones he'd already used. "Shoot," he finally said, collapsing in a heap on the old easy chair and covering his face with his hands.

"Max?"

"Okay, Mom, okay!"

"Why is he wearing your clothes?"

"Because . . . when I found him he was wearing these." Max reached under the chair and pulled out Ato's Baron uniform.

Dr. Sarita gasped. "He's . . ."

"A Chemical Baron, yes. But he's cool. I mean, he seems cool, and he's really hurt and I just couldn't leave him there, dying in the tunnel. It didn't seem right, so I just put him over my shoulder, even though it was dark and I couldn't see who he was, you know, and took him with me and we almost died getting here 'cause the weight was too much for my jetboots, but he grabbed the railing right before we slid down into the chasm, so technically he saved my life too, if you know what I mean."

Dr. Sarita stared at her son. Her eyes had gone from wide to narrow to wide again and finally settled on weary acceptance. It was an incredible story, but she was very familiar with Max's ramblings and kind heart and knew a true Max adventure when she heard one. "I do," she finally said. "I know what you mean."

"You do?"

"You did well, Max."

"I did?"

"Yes. You saved someone's life. You're right, he probably would've died if you'd left him there. Especially considering he's"—she had to pause to let the reality of it set in—"a Baron."

"Because most people woulda locked him up before they took care of him?"

"Well, I don't know about most people, but . . . yes, a lot of us have good cause to be angry with the Barons, especially after last night."

"He said he didn't know how bad it was gonna be last night," Max said. "He said—"

"Mmmmggghhh," Ato moaned.

Max shut up and looked at him. Dr. Sarita crouched back down and ran her hand along his head. It came back bloody. She looked at Max. "His wound opened up again. We need to do something *now*."

"Wha-what do we do?" stammered Max. "If we take him to the . . ."

"I know, I know," Dr. Sarita growled. She was pressing a towel against Ato's head to stop the bleeding. "Go in my bedroom and get my medical kit. Quickly."

Max ran into his mom's room and hurried back with the white box she kept under her bed.

"Get out the suture kit."

Max's hands were shaking. "You're going to stitch him up? Right here?"

"Max, now!"

Beneath a collection of shears and scalpels was a small plastic kit with thread and a needle in it. Max passed it to his mom, trying to steady his hand so she wouldn't notice the tremble.

"And one of those saline bottles. And some disinfectant. No, the other kind. Right."

Max peered over at his mom's perfectly steady hands as she poured saline over Ato's scalp. The gash spread in a red smile along the back of his head. Dr. Sarita dabbed it with orange disinfectant gel and then picked up a needle.

"Ugh," Max said before he could stop himself.

"Hush your mouth and glove up."

"What?"

"Put some gloves on. I need a hand."

Max did as he was told, trying to suppress the urge to run out of the room.

"Hold the wound the way I am and don't let go."

Max put his gloved fingers on either side of the gash along Ato's head. A trickle of blood slid out and Max closed his eyes. "He's not gonna wake up?"

"Not for a while, no. I gave him some sleeper meds."

A few moments later, it was all over. Dr. Sarita had slid the needle in and out easily, like she was jotting down a note. The bleeding had stopped and Ato had an ugly black caterpillar of knots running along the back of his head.

Max went into the bathroom and puked his guts out.

CHAPTER

Piece by foggy piece, the world slid back into focus. The shapes that had been dancing in front of Ato's face resolved themselves into objects. Objects with names and uses. Meaning. Yes. Then the past twenty-four hours trickled back into his mind.

He was in Flood City.

On Earth.

The cloud cruiser had crashed. Mephim. The nuke. The iguana-gull. So much had happened! He sat up, felt dizzy, and slid back down.

Where was he? Someone's bedroom. Max. Yes. The boy who had dragged him out of that tunnel and almost fallen into a chasm with him. He was in Max's bedroom. The rain pitter-pattered against the window. The sky was gray and dim in a way that could mean early morning or maybe nightfall. Ato had grown up on a spacecraft and wasn't familiar enough with planet living to know the difference.

A middle-aged woman with brown skin walked into the room. "Ah, you're up!" She had a thick halo of black hair and a sad smile. She sat beside the bed and put a warm hand over his. "I'm Sarita, Max's mom. I'm a doctor. How are you feeling?"

Did she know who he was? Surely she wouldn't be so kind. But then again, Max had known and still given him shelter. Perhaps it was all a trap. Ato's head began spinning again. "I'm okay," he said.

Sarita looked at him doubtfully. "Hmm, we'll see about that. I'm going to bring you some ration soup. It tastes like liquid towel, but you probably shouldn't be eating anything too exciting right now anyway. Give everything a chance to settle. Later, if you're up to it, Max'll run out and get you something from the bakery, okay?"

Ato nodded. Sarita smiled at him and he realized she did indeed know who he was and didn't care, or didn't care enough to judge him for it. Ato breathed a sigh of relief and passed back out.

———————

A plastic bowl full of thick greenish-brown goo was sitting on the bedside table when he woke up. It was lukewarm and Dr. Sarita had been pretty spot-on about the taste, but Ato scarfed it down and immediately wanted more when he was done.

He swung his legs over the side of the bed and carefully lifted himself into a sitting position. The room stayed pretty much still. His head throbbed but not unbearably. Alright. What else? His legs seemed undamaged. A few cuts and bruises decorated his pale skin, a little paler now than usual but nothing to be too concerned about. Everything seemed to be in pretty good working order.

He stood and made his way across the room, holding the wall for support.

"Hey there!" Dr. Sarita looked up from a textbook she was reading on the easy chair. "How was the soup?"

"Good."

Dr. Sarita raised an eyebrow and frowned at him.

"Towelly," Ato admitted. "But I was hungry."

"Max should be back any . . ."

A clanging and the roar of jetboots announced Max's return from the bakery. He walked in, jetboots in hand, and smiled. "He's alive!"

"Thanks to you guys," Ato said, rubbing the stitches on the back of his head.

"Don't touch 'em," Dr. Sarita said. "They need to heal."

"I got dougies," Max said. Ato had no idea what dougies were, but they turned out to be delicious. Some kind of buttery, doughy amazing thing that seemed to turn to syrup in your mouth and left you with a perfect aftertaste that made you want more and more. So far, Flood City was nothing at all like Ato had expected.

And he loved it.

Dear Max,

It feels so strange to be writing a letter the old old-fashioned way, but I think it's safer than any kind of transmission. The holowaves are being monitored, from what I hear, and they're keeping very close track of everything we do. I've seen the holographer's bird, Krestlefax, flapping around the training island the past couple of days, so I wrote this hoping he might get it to you.

The Star Guard transport dropped us off here three days ago. It's a huge concrete slab floating out in the middle of the ocean. It's probably only a little smaller than Flood City, but it's totally flat except for a few bunks and office buildings at the far reaches and some artificial mounds in the training arena.

There's three different species here at the academy besides us Earthlings. The giant blue guys we see all the time are here of course, the snells. They're almost completely brain-dead and utterly atrocious with their rudeness and body odor, but otherwise mostly harmless. And stinking Commander Uk—some kind of snell higher-up. He's one of the little ones though, and he's absolutely the most inconsiderate, hateful, foulmouthed, temperamental psychopath I have ever met. But we knew that. Fortunately, Uk just stops by to do inspections from time to time, and the main academy commander is another small snell in a hovercraft named Joola who actually seems pretty cool, surprise surprise.

annoying pout →

← hover thingy

Commander Uk

Then there's the triphenglotts. They're
basically just giant larvae with
billions of legs and pincer
mouths. They rear up on their
hindquarters when they're
angry and their whole front
is covered in some kinda
ick that I don't even wanna
think about. Probably battery
acid. Blegh. They have their
own quarters—some kind of cave
that leads to an underchamber behind
all the other buildings. They do the training exercises with
us—some of them even run exercises, yuck—but other than
that you don't see 'em much and there's rumors
going around they have some kinda special role in the Star
Guard hierarchy that no one knows about.

Questionable
stench

spikes?
baby legs?

ick

Triphenglott

Finally, there's the tarashids. Not sure what to make
of these guys. They have a hard armored shell like
a tortoise and large beaked heads with buggy eyes on
either side. Six great big elephant-size legs extend out
to surprisingly agile seven-fingered hands. Or are they

protective shell

safety goggles!

good with
tech

Tarashid

seven-toed feet? I don't know. They seem to be useful for whatever the tarashid needs it to be. Then they have an apparently endless supply of other little clawed arms that show up from within that shell from time to time. They're quiet creatures, and there's not very many of them. One appears to be their leader, his name's Osen and he seems somehow . . . I don't know how to explain this . . . trustworthy. We've barely spoken but it's just something in his eyes, like he's watching everything going on and taking it all in but always with a little skepticism.

Anyway, I think there's some issue between the lumbering tarashids and the icky triphenglotts, because there's always an uneasy kinda feeling in the air when they're around each other.

Every day an angry clique of Star Guard captains wakes us up at sunrise. Usually it's one of the blue giants but sometimes it's a tarashid, which is disorientating cuz they look so weird, or occasionally a triphenglott, which is terrifying because, ew—and they just end up snaking up and down the dorm aisles on all those hideous legs leaving a trail of nasty behind them and bellowing in some clacky bug talk that no one can understand.

Needless to say, it's no way to greet the day. (See how I make rhymes for you, bro?)

We do exercises all morning. Not just jump squats like in Mr. Arroyo's class either. These are the kinda calisthenics that make you feel muscles you never knew you had, make your whole body burn and feel broken by the end of the day. They give us some nasty grub for breakfast. (You don't wanna know. Neither do I, in fact.) Then we have weapons and pilot training all day, which would be pretty cool if it wasn't for this triphenglott called Ridge Commander Briggus. He's the chief weapons instructor and I swear it's like he's trying to kill us. I shot a slicer yesterday until my fingers were calloused and my arms could barely lift the thing, all because I'd missed the motorized target dummy a few times while it swung back and forth toward me. I know they want us to learn and be proficient little killers, but sheesh! Can a girl catch a break?

This place is weird, Max. It's so sterile—there's no smell at all except disinfectant and no colors except gray and I never thought I'd say this, but I actually miss your stinky socks, because at least it's something real, human—home. I guess I must be homesick if I miss your funk already, ugh!

And I get the feeling us Flood City folks are the most unwanted of the pack, even though we're the most normal looking! (Okay, okay, I know they all think they're the most normal looking, but still . . . I think even if I were a triphenglott I'd be repulsed by myself.) Anyway, they all frown at us and are extra hard on us in training. Well . . . not the tarashids, now that I think about it. They don't really give us a signal one way or the other. But the blue giants and the triphenglotts are downright rude and sketchy potatoes all day long! (Hahaha you remember how Jasmine used to say "sketchy potatoes" all the time?! Cracking up just thinking 'bout it . . . but it makes me sad too . . .)

And . . . the hardest thing was having to shave my locs. My locs, Max!!! You know how many years I been growing them! That was, like, a piece of my soul and with a quick buzz and unfriendly blue hands holding my head still, they're gone. I wanted to cry so bad, felt it rising up inside me, but I pushed it away because no way I'm gonna cry in front of everyone on day one of Star Guard Academy, you know?

Still . . . I feel so strange being bald-headed, like a part of me's missing.

I can't really describe how hard it was to leave you guys that morning, especially given everything that had gone down the night before. I feel like someone carved a hole out of my heart and it'll never be filled till I'm back in Flood City. Somehow though, through all this, I know I'm doing the right thing.

Love you always.

Give Momz a big hug for me and don't worry about me! I'm fine! Write whenever you can.

Y

PS: And thanks to Delta for the drawings cuz you know I can't draw!

CHAPTER

Effie Delano was ten years old when the scary men came to her house. It was already a terrible night: the rush of people escaping from the Music Hall, the flashes of light in the sky, and then that explosion that seemed to shake the whole planet. But they'd made it home safely—Effie; her older brother, Dante; little Arthur; and Mom and Dad—and then they'd lit candles and huddled in that flickering pool of light in the kitchen, talking in hushed tones about what had happened. Grandma Betty, who was too old to go out anymore, had listened attentively from her hoverchair in the corner. Then came the tapping at the window, which gave Effie a horrible knot in her tummy because she somehow knew exactly what was about to happen and wanted more than anything not to let Dad get up and see what the noise was. But she didn't; she kept her mouth shut, and Dad got up and then everything happened so fast.

Really, it wouldn't have made any difference, Effie told herself. She'd told herself the exact same thing each of the seven days that had gone by since that horrible night, and she still didn't believe it. Now she said it again, to see if maybe it would sound true the second time in a row, but it never did. She was standing in the bakery line. Her hands were shaking, but she couldn't tell if it was because she was afraid someone would realize what was going on or she was afraid they wouldn't.

"Ahem." The older man behind her cleared his throat, and Effie realized the people ahead of her had moved up in line. She skittered forward.

It was just her and Dante left. They'd kept her alive 'cause she was just a pathetic little girl and couldn't hurt anybody, and Dante had been blind ever since a jetboot racing accident when he was a kid, so the bad men must've figured they didn't have much to worry about from him. In fact, they didn't seem worried about anything at all. But they needed someone alive to run their errands and another someone alive to keep the first from running off. It was a clever plan, because there was absolutely no way Effie would ever escape without Dante, and he wouldn't get far wandering the narrow alleyways of Flood City by himself.

"Ahem!" The old man coughed again, and Effie stepped into the open space between her and the next person in line. The smell of freshly baked goods was intoxicating, a painful reminder of freedom.

If you run away, we will kill him, the tall one in robes had said. *If you do anything silly or stupid or clever or try any slick moves at all, we will kill him.* Effie had nodded, her eyes huge with ter-ror. *If I start to feel sick or find any weapons you've been hiding or wake up in a bad mood . . .* The man didn't finish the sentence, he just sliced his finger across his throat and arched his eyebrows. *Understood?*

Effie had nodded again, wishing the whole thing were just a horrible dream.

Now go get us some more dougies. Those things are delicious.

"How many'll it be, Effie?" Mr. Sanpedro said.

Effie mumbled something.

"What's that, dear?"

"Two dozen."

"Oh my, you guys must have a full house, huh?"

Effie shrugged, unable to look the baker in his eyes. He disap-peared into the busted old train car and returned carrying two big paper bags. Their bottom halves were already dark from the heat and grease of the dougies.

"You tell your mom and dad I send my regards, okay, Effie?"

She nodded, taking the bags, looking away.

"Effie?"

She looked up at Mr. Sanpedro, a million different thoughts, prayers, bargains, wishes, fears burning through her eyes.

"Everything alright?"

She nodded. "Everything's fine, Mr. Sanpedro." She even smiled at him.

He grinned back at her. "Alright, little one. See you tomorrow."

Efiie walked away, cringing inside herself.

"What we need," Get said, slamming his hand on the kitchen table, "is a plan."

"I've got a plan," growled Sak. "We get out of here now and never come back."

Tog shook his head. "How do you plan on doing that when the cruiser's down for the count *and* under armed surveillance by the Star Guard?"

"We can handle the Star Guard," Mephim said. Everyone shut up and turned to look at the shadowy corner he'd been lurking in. It was the first time the ArchBaron had spoken all day. "The cruiser is not salvageable, but the escape pods may afford us an opportunity to retreat for the time being. Baron Apix?"

"Hm?" Tog perked up, startled at being addressed with his formal title.

"Can you fix up whatever damage there is to the pods if we get you to them?"

"I don't see why not. I mean, there'll be damage, for sure." The strain was evident in Tog's voice, but he wasn't the type to make up a brighter scenario. "But I believe it's fixable with some tinkering. Thing is, it'll take some time."

"How much time?"

"Well, it depends how bad the damage is. Could be a couple of hours."

The ArchBaron stepped out of the shadows and turned his icy gaze on Sak. "Can we hold off the Star Guard and whatever nuisance the Flood City rebels bring for four hours, Chief Gunner Sak?"

"Well, I—" Sak started, but Get cut him off: "Of course we could! There's, what? Six of us. We have weapons, some at least, and we could cause plenty of trouble and keep the blue giants running in circles for . . ."

"I didn't ask you," Mephim seethed. The boy sat back down, his face reddening.

"I believe we could do it for four hours, sir," Sak said. "But it won't be easy. And we'll lose men and empty our resources."

"Which is to say?"

"We don't even know how badly the pods are damaged, and until then it's no use going in only to find out there's no point anyway."

"A little reconnaissance, then?" The ArchBaron seemed pleased with this idea.

"Right. We distract the giants for an hour, that shouldn't be hard, and send the boy—er—young Baron to sneak in, see what the situation is with the pods, and *then*, if they seem worth the trouble, we go in blasters blazin' and see what kind of time we can buy for old Tog here to do what he can for the pods, eh?"

"I'll fix the pods," Tog snarled. "Don't you worry about that."

A tap-tap-tap came at the door and the men all went for their weapons. Sak peeked through the peephole and waved to everyone to relax. "It's the girl," he said, unchaining and opening the door. "She's got the dougies."

"Thank god!" Get exclaimed. "I love those things!"

CHAPTER

The first thing Ato noticed about Flood City was that everyone was a different shade of brown. They'd talked about it up on the Chemical Baron base fleet, but they'd simply said broad things like "the remaining inhabitants of Earth are mainly brown-skinned humans." Only *brown-skinned* didn't really seem to cover it. Instead, Ato found a whole rainbow of variations from light pink like himself (although there weren't many of those) to Max's reddish tan, to Dr. Sarita's slightly darker, umber hue, to Dr. Maceo, whose skin was a rich dark brown.

At first it was confusing: Up on the base fleet, almost everyone was pale like Ato, so it took him a few days to adjust to all the different colors. But now it'd been more than a week since the crash and Ato had started venturing out into Flood City. He was getting the sense that just seeing faces that looked like his would never feel the same again.

"Push down!" Max yelled. Ato was still getting the hang of his jetboots—a pair of Max's sister Yala's. He was descending rapidly into a twisted ravine between two apartment buildings and he'd been so lost in thought he hadn't even noticed. "You got to pay attention on jetboots, man!" Max warned as Ato accelerated into a sharp upswing. A passing swarm of little kids chuckled wildly at Ato. "It's not like walking, 'cause everything's happening much faster. Things'll sneak up on you in seconds flat and you'll be toast."

Ato nodded. "It's kinda like information overload. All I've ever known my whole life has been on the base fleet and then only recently occasional missions to other spots. I never even put my feet on real terrain, I mean something that wasn't a spacecraft of some kind, until I was eleven."

Max looked at his new friend. "Wow. I can't even imagine. I mean, we don't put our feet down that much, and I suppose we're a ways over the actual surface of the earth, but still . . ."

"It's there."

"Right. You can sense it. Then again, I've never been to space, so, I guess we're kinda even."

Ato shrugged. "Space isn't really all that big a deal. You look out the window and it's just empty, empty, empty as far as you can see. Maybe there's a bunch of stars. Maybe a nebula or an asteroid belt somewhere way off, but even that barely breaks up the monotony of it. And the base fleet is huge, you know, but still you feel like it's this enclosed space that doesn't grow or change or have any life to it whatsoever."

They jetted along a larger throughway, ducking between passing families and various Flood City folks finishing their day's chores. Buildings leaned in odd angles on either side, looking more like spiky still life explosions than anything someone could live in. But laundry hung from metal escape ladders and faces gazed out windows. On one long balcony, folks were gathered around tables laughing and making fun of one another over some kind of game. It was a breezy, warm afternoon. The sky was just turning into that murky red that would soon slide into darkness.

"What you wanna do?" Max asked.

"Race."

"Oh, you got your skills together that quick, huh?"

"Maybe I do."

"It's gonna be dark soon."

"So?"

"I think the Star Guard put another curfew on tonight."

"So?"

Max grinned. "So we better hurry." And off they went.

———————

The city sped past Ato at a frenzied rush. Some of the buildings were ancient brick structures, half dilapidated and trashed, while others where majestic steel skyscrapers. They all became a blur as he amped up his speed and brushed past Max.

"Oh, think you're slick, huh?" Max called from behind him.

Ato laughed and leaned into the wind the way Max had taught him. For a perfect second, he rushed ahead. The air seemed to cleave to either side of him to make way. Then his tummy gave a lurch of warning, and he realized he was tipping too far forward. Panicked, Ato kicked his feet out, too hard, waaaay too hard, and sent himself into an airborne somersault. He bounced painfully off the side of a building and then spun back out into the sky upside down.

———————

Max hurtled forward with a burst of flame from his boots. He cringed, seeing Ato bounce off the building, and then aimed directly for the same spot so he could line up their trajectories. Shouldn't be too hard; he'd seen Yala do building bounces a hundred times but had never bothered to try it himself. She made it look easy, of course, because she was Yala, so anything having to do with agility was the most natural thing in the world to her. But Max knew the wall bounce took a careful balance of speed and precision. He burst toward the wall, his hand stretched in front of him. Perhaps a little too fast. Definitely way too fast, but it was too late. Max smashed hands, then face, then full body into the wall. A billion color splotches dotted across his vision for a second and then he could see again and he was springing backward right behind Ato. At least he got the angle right.

Max whirled himself around, reached out, and grabbed Ato's foot as it spun around again. "Gotchya!" He decelerated and brought them down carefully onto someone's balcony.

"You okay?" Max asked.

Ato looked stunned for a second and then smiled. "That was amazing!"

Max burst out laughing. He pulled a shaky hand across his face and it came back bloody. "Shoot."

"Oh, you're hurt?"

"Nah," Max said, ruffling through his pockets for some tissue. "Think I took the wall a little hard is all." He realized he was still laughing. "It happens."

"You wanna head home?" Ato said.

"Not really," Max said. "Mom's working the overnight and being home just makes me mad that Yala's gone."

Ato nodded. "The curfew?"

"I don't even care."

"What do they do if they catch you out after dark?"

Max shrugged. "Send you to the academy. Chop off your head. I dunno."

"What would they do to me?"

Ato had no ID of course. He was a stranger, and worse than that, he was a Chemical Baron. They had barely spoken of it since that first rainy day, and Max had simply let the fact that they were sworn enemies slip out of his mind. He'd introduced Ato as his new friend, and people generally just assumed he was from a different neighborhood of Flood City. But the Star Guard peacekeepers were something else entirely, always sticking their giant blue noses as far into people's business as possible. "I don't know," Max admitted. "Maybe we should go back."

The last traces of daylight were disappearing from the sky around them. A few gas lamps flickered on along the walls of some nearby buildings. A holocam drifted past, making little futzy noises as it went.

"No," Ato said. "I grew up following rules, being careful, minding my manners. The Chemical Barons live a military existence, glued to all kinds of archaic codes that most people don't even understand anymore. And I've left all that behind. I'm done following rules that don't make any sense."

"So you wanna stay out all night?" Max did too, but he didn't want his friend to get in trouble.

"What's the worst that could happen?" Ato said, jumping into the air and igniting his boots.

Max followed a few seconds later. "That's the kind of thing people say right before they get . . ."

They rounded the corner and Max shut his mouth. Three towering blue Star Guards frowned down at them.

". . . caught."

THE FLOOD CITY GAZETTE

SPECIAL MEMORIAL EDITION!!

Today we honor the nine honorable heroes lost during
the Chemical Barons' vicious sneak attack on Flood City.

BRANTLY BORAST	SARAPAT SINTO	BAILEY TIDEWIDTH
KIM SUKAYAMA	DEEZER MOZZAT	FELA BATU
MAREEN DANILO	ALESSANDRA TUMBAO	SARA SARA FLEX

RATIONS REPORT

Rations are at regular levels today.

THE DAILY TIDE

Low tide today will be at **0613**.

High tide will be at **2104**.

Please *avoid the city edges
during high tide, as conditions
can worsen suddenly.*

IGUANAGULL AHOY!

Star Guard peacekeepers near the holographer's tower report low
levels of iguanagull sightings. Stay safe and keep your eyes in the sky!

THE BOOO'CAST

Reported spectral/electromagnetic
activity levels are low by the Electric Ghost Yard. Please keep your
distance from this area at all times!

THE VAPORS & ABANDONED OCEAN LINER REPORT

We have nothing to report.

CHEMICAL BARONS

The Chemical Baron elements remain at large within the confines of Flood
City. Remain alert at all times. They are armed and extremely dangerous.
Stay vigilant!

CHAPTER

"Three o'clock," Effie said. Dante hucked his balled-up sock, heard it bounce off the wall and land softly on the wood floor. Effie went to get it. "Close but not quite. That was more like three thirty."

Dante sighed. He could've sworn he had it right. He'd had the layout of the bedroom memorized for two years now, and it was driving him up the wall that he couldn't seem to picture it correctly when it mattered most.

"You wanna take a break?"

Effie was always sensitive to Dante's smallest aggravations. He shook his head, and she put the balled-up sock in his hand again. "You ready?"

Dante projected the floating clock numbers into the air around him, trying to imagine exactly how far away the walls were. He nodded.

"Two-thirty," Effie said.

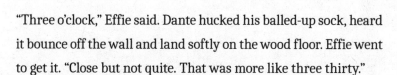

Two-thirty, Dante thought. *Almost three but back a half tick.* He focused on the hovering number three directly to his right and then tossed the sock a little before it.

"Perfect!" Effie yelled a little too loudly. "You nailed it, D!"

Dante put a finger up to his lips and heard Effie gasp as she realized her mistake. Footsteps were already clomping down the hallway toward them. Dante threw himself into the bed and pulled the sheets up to his neck.

The knob turned, the door swung open, and one of the bad men came in.

"What's going on in here?" the man said. It was a boy's voice, someone around Dante's age or a little younger. He sounded terrified, like he was doing his best to act brave and failing miserably. He had light brown hair and big blue eyes, and he looked like he was a little scared but doing his best to cover it up and act tough.

"Nothing," Effie squeaked.

"We said no talking, no?"

"Yes," Effie and Dante both said.

"So . . . what is so important that you are yelling, missy?"

"Nothing."

"Alright, pick up all those socks. Just 'cause your parents aren't here doesn't mean you get to be messy." And he was gone.

Effie let out a long breath of air as Dante tried to get his heart to stop roaring away in his ears.

"Identification cards, please," one of the Star Guards said in a gruff voice.

"Um . . . what?" Max said.

Another Star Guard stepped forward. Max recognized his wide forehead and furrowed brow—it was Captain Gorus, the same one who'd bothered him on the day of the attack. "We have word that several of the Chemical Barons escaped from the cloud cruiser last week and infiltrated the civilian population. They may be holed up in an old hideaway or seeking refuge with Baron supporters within the city."

Max scoffed. "There's no Chemical Baron supporters in Flood City," and then he swallowed hard, realizing that in a way, he qualified as exactly that. "Well, if there are," he added hastily, "we haven't seen 'em."

"Show us your identifications, please, and you can be on your way." Captain Gorus made it sound so simple.

Max closed his eyes. There was no easy way out of this. Ato was already trying to stutter out an answer, but he wasn't making much sense.

"He left his at home," Max said. "We'll go get it and bring it to you."

"No can do," Gorus said. "It is a crime in the confines of Flood City to leave your house without your identification card. Also, it's after dark, which means the curfew has begun, which means you're both in violation of it. So why don't you two young fellows come with us?"

Max had had his heels pressing lightly against the accelerators the whole time, ready to bust out at a second's notice. He pushed down as hard as he could and yelled, "Get out of here!" as he burst toward the shocked Star Guards. One of their huge hands was already reaching out for Ato. Max adjusted slightly and thrust himself at it, pushing it out of the way just in time.

"Hey!" the Star Guard yelled.

Ato powered up his boots and sped off, not caring where, just trying to put as much distance between himself and those blue giants as he could. He felt terrible leaving Max behind, but he knew it didn't make any sense to stay—Max had ID and knew how to get away from them anyway. If Ato was caught, it meant imprisonment for sure and who knew what else?

He rushed down the smallest, windiest alleys he could find, sped past curtained windows and abandoned buildings and floors that were wide open, revealing a whole family panorama for all the city to see. A few times he adjusted wrong—flying was particularly hard in the growing darkness—and scratched against walls or dipped too close to the jagged ground.

Finally, when he was sure the rumbling footsteps of the Star Guards were long gone, he stopped and threw himself breathlessly against a wall. He powered his boots down to a low levitate and looked around. Dim gas lamps hung in their flickering halos, but otherwise the city was almost as dark as the night sky above him. He had no idea where he was and even if he did, he wouldn't know how to get back to Max's house. The one thing he did know was that he was a million miles from home in enemy territory and that he could never go back. Never. The word felt like a brick in his chest. He'd been so caught up in the excitement of the crash and hanging out with Max and learning about this new place, he hadn't stopped to think about never going home again.

His mom and dad were probably freaking out and checking for updates constantly with the various War and Intelligence Barons. He thought about better times with Get—how they would gorge on syntenelle snacks after every mission, no matter how messed up it had been, and watch the holocasts and know better than to ask each other about any of it, even though the screams and laser fire rebounded endlessly through their thoughts. And the one time Get did start talking about being scared before a raid, his face wide open, that brave veneer suddenly gone. Ato had admitted his own fears too and how the roar of it all used to linger, long after the mission was over, and how maybe it becoming normal was even worse, now that the roar was starting to die out. They'd both cried, and it had been like releasing a huge, heavy balloon that had been lodged in him, shoving all his insides into the wrong places.

Maybe, somehow, they could piece this all back together. Maybe he could go home again and convince the Barons that the Flood City folks weren't so bad after all.

Mephim's snarl flashed inside Ato's eyes. He shook his head. There was no turning back. Not now. He could never go home again.

A few tears started to threaten the edges of Ato's eyes, but he didn't have time for all that. He was lost and the Star Guard was after him and it was well after curfew. He blinked the tears angrily away. No. Not right now. There'd be time to grieve and be homesick later. Hopefully.

Ato took a deep breath and tried to clear his aching mind. The thought of Mephim lurking somewhere in the city was almost too much to bear. Anyway, he had more important things to worry about, like how to get back to Max's.

He picked a random direction and jetted quietly off.

———

Max wound semi-aimlessly through some back alleys near Flood City Plaza. Surely Ato hadn't gotten far. Plus, thanks to the curfew, the city was virtually empty, and the only sounds were crashing waves and occasional iguanagull cries from above.

The Star Guard ruined everything, Max thought. They literally stuck their big ridiculous blue hands into every situation and caused endless amounts of trouble. It almost made it worse that half the trouble they caused was from sheer oblivious-ness. They just bumbled through their ludicrous protocols and bylaws and got in the way. Sure, they handed out food, but it was barely enough for everyone to survive, and they could make things difficult for the black market whenever they felt like it. And maybe they had played a crucial role in saving Flood City from the Chemical Barons all those years ago, but they obviously weren't doing a very good job right now. Cloud cruisers were fall-ing out of the sky. Barons had infiltrated the city. Everything was a great big—

A shrill whisper sounded from the shadows of a nearby alley-way. "Pssst!"

Max froze.

"Psst!"

"Who is it?"

"Come here."

There was too much intrigue in the air for that kind of non-sense. Max stood his ground, plotting the quickest escape route in his head.

"Come here!" the voice repeated.

Max shook his head. "Nope. You wanna talk to me, you come and do it. I'm not disappearing into some shadow never to be heard from again."

"Good lad," Old Man Cortinas said, buzzing out of the alleyway. "This isn't the time to be trusting strangers."

"Cortinas!" Max gasped. "What are you . . . What's up?"

The old rebel shrugged and swiped at the air. "Eh, you know—been lying low ever since the crash. Heard the Star Guard had a little bounty on my head."

"I saw you what you did that night," Max said. "I didn't know . . . you . . . knew how to do that."

"From the old days, is all. A few tricks I picked up back during the original Flood City rebellion." The original Flood City rebellion. Old Man Cortinas had been a fierce leader back in the day, people said. Max was suddenly full of questions, but Cortinas stopped him with a single look. "Max, I need you to do something for me while I'm in hiding."

Max tried to imagine what that entailed, being in hiding. It sounded terrifically exciting but was probably pretty drab after a couple of days. "Anything, Mr. C. Whatever I can do to help." Images of dashing into secret hideaways to deliver encrypted messages raced through Max's mind.

"Cause trouble."

"Um . . . what?"

"I . . . we really, the rebels, need you to cause as much trouble as possible."

"What kind of trouble?"

"That's up to you. Search within your wicked little heart and find that place of love for your city and wrath toward the big blue boneheads. But mostly, we want to make them feel like there's lots and lots and lots of us. Cause a little confusion, you know? Wreak some havoc of the highest order."

"I guess I understand."

"You'll figure it out. If nothing else, just get some paint and write *Property of Flood City Guerrilla Squad* on something the Star Guard feels like is theirs. That really makes them mad."

"Okay, Mr. C."

"And bring your friend with you, he looks like he could use some mischief making in his life."

"Who?"

"The little pale fellow you've been running around with. Apo . . . Aro . . ."

"Ato?"

"That's the one."

"How do you know about . . ."

"Thank you, Max," Cortinas said as he jetted straight up into the sky. "You have no idea what a help you are."

"Mr. C!" Max called, but the old warrior was already gone.

———————

Max zipped out into the plaza outside the Music Hall without even realizing it. He immediately eased off his accelerator. There would be Star Guards all over this place, presumably, to keep vigil on the downed cruiser. But there was the cruiser, lying like a dead animal in a heap of ruins, and no one else seemed to be around. Odd.

Max landed as quietly as possible and slow-walked toward the wreckage. Something wasn't right. He could feel it in the air all around him. The one time the Star Guard was actually supposed to be somewhere and they were nowhere to be found. Figured.

A hatch opened with a clang and Max froze. A hand came out, then a face. It was Ato.

"Ato!" Max said, sighing with relief and running toward the cruiser. "What are you . . . ?"

Ato lifted a blaster cannon and pointed it directly at Max.

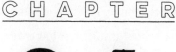

"Um . . . what are you doing?"

"Shut up!" Ato's face was contorted with fear and rage.

"What's going on?"

"Shut up, I said!"

Max refused to believe that his friend had been playing him this whole time. The pieces just didn't fit together right in his head. There was a scrabble of motion from the other side of the square and Ato looked toward it.

Max turned and felt all the air leave his lungs at once. There was Ato, jetting toward the cruiser at breakneck speed. And there, on the cruiser, was Ato, his face stricken. The Ato on the cruiser swung his blaster around just a second too late and his one shot flashed harmlessly into the night sky as jetboot Ato ran full force into him and they both toppled over the side.

Utterly perplexed, Max ran over to see what was happening.

There were two Atos. He hadn't been hallucinating. One was dressed in the slightly too large clothes Max had lent him and the other had on a school uniform a few sizes too small. Other than that they looked exactly the same. Twins. By the time Max reached them, the surly school uniform Ato had untangled himself and taken off down an alley with the telltale unsteadiness of a new jetbooter. Max's Ato was nursing a fat lip.

"There's two of you!" Max said.

Ato nodded. "I'm afraid so."

"Your brother seems like a real jerk."

Ato nodded again. "Pretty much. We better get out of here. He'll probably be back with more friends and bigger guns."

Max agreed and they jetted down an alley. "I wonder what he was doing in there, your brother?"

Ato shook his head. "Probably looking for the nuke."

Max burst out laughing. "Whoa! Ato . . . okay . . . nuke? As in nuclear warhead? That's hysterical! That's . . ." He looked at Ato. Ato wasn't laughing. "Wait. You're serious?"

Ato nodded.

"But . . . no one has nuclear weapons! That's absurd! The last ones were destroyed eons ago! Way before the Floods. They've been teaching us about it in . . ."

Ato shook his head. "I saw it, Max. It's real. We studied this stuff too, believe me, because it's, like, a crazy obsession with the Chemical Barons. I know all about nuclear weapons, and the thing that was stashed in the engine room of that cloud cruiser was without a doubt a nuke. I . . . I should've told you before, I just—I knew the Star Guard was there so the Barons wouldn't be able to get to it and . . ." His voice trailed off.

"Even if they were there," Max said, "you can't trust those guys. You know that."

They buzzed along in silence, looped around a corner, and came out of the alley right at the edge of the ocean. In the distance, Max could hear the crackling ghosts in their yard. A little farther along were the Tumbled Together Towers. All around them, the gray sea thrashed like an angry god. "I'm sorry," Ato said. "I should've told you."

Max made a face. "Yeah. I don't know what good it would've done. But yeah. It was in the engine room?"

"They've probably been trying to get it since the crash. I'm sure that's what my brother was after just now."

"But they couldn't because the Star Guard was watching it." Max frowned. "And for some reason they weren't tonight. I don't like this at all. We should tell someone."

"Who? Who do we really trust? And even if someone knew, they'd have to get past the Star Guard to get to it."

Max nodded. "That's probably true."

"And if you did tell them, how would you explain how you found out about it?"

There was no way around it. They couldn't alert anyone to the nuke without giving up Ato. And as long as the Star Guard were around, no one would be getting to the thing anyway. Still, something seemed very wrong about the whole situation. Max growled by way of a reply, and the two friends sputtered off toward home.

Dear Max,

I wish I could write you and say everything is fine, I'm doing great, training camp is a blast, blah blah blah, but I can't.

Everything is not fine.

Training camp is a mess. I'm scared, Max. And you know I don't even really get scared, and when I do, I don't tell anybody. And the last thing I want is to worry you, believe me, but I need to tell someone and I don't know who to trust anymore.

Commander Uk. Yeah, he definitely hates Flood City with a passion. Like we collectively flushed his life down the toilet somehow. I dunno. There's a rumor that it all has something to do with the original invasion/defeat of the Chemical Barons—Uk was an attack fleet commander back then and I think our guys mighta stolen some of his glory in the fallout.

Either way, now he's taking it out on us, and it's gone way past your average everyday power-hungry jerk with a grudge stuff. First it was just extra workouts for all of us humans, and you know, we all kinda laughed about it and put up with it, especially because none of us want to let it show that he's getting to us, you know? All except Splink, that is. He's the only Flood City kid that Uk has taken a liking to, so he gets away with anything and never ends up with the same punishments as us. I wish you could see how hard I'm rolling my eyes at this kid right now. And to think he tried to holler at me last year. Ugh.

Eventually though, our people started getting exhausted. It's just been too much, Max. I'm alright cuz you know I worked out all the time back home anyway, so it hasn't been too too bad, but Telly and Etienne are both sick, dehydrated I think, and can barely get out of bed. Delta was doing fine but then a few days ago she fell from one of the high-rise climbing traps and fractured her shoulder, but of course they won't treat her cuz they say that's part of training—recovering from injuries and survival. Ugh, I could scream...

The night she got hurt one of the tarashids showed up in our barracks. It was Osen—remember, the one I told you about that seemed like their leader and seemed somehow trustworthy? Well, he didn't say anything, just lumbered across the floor toward her. At first we all kinda freaked out, like, what this big-shelled space creature bouta do to Delta, right? Osen musta realized what it looked like cuz he stopped just beside her and looked around.

He raised two of those great big arm things. They say tarashids have telepathic powers and I always woulda scoffed at them but Max, if you coulda felt/heard what I felt/heard that night. It was like the most soothing voice in the world. There were no words, but somehow it was still saying, "I mean you no harm, I come to heal the girl." I swear to you, it was the most amazing thing. At first I thought I was making it up, but then I looked around and I could tell all the others had heard it too.

It was a good thing he said it too, cuz what happened next looked like anything but healing. Osen leaned over Delta and gathered her up in those big arms. She was knocked out from some medications we'd smuggled out of the first aid office, so she just hung their limply while all those tiny alien legs started swarming over her injured shoulder. I don't think any of us breathed the whole time it was happening. I don't even know how much time passed. Eventually he put her down and trudged off and the next day she was completely recovered. Not even sore or anything.

The Flood City Rebel Guerrilla Squad is on everyone's minds. The Star Guard guys keep whispering about it to each other, and then the other day Uk actually brought it up in a class; and the way they talk about it, Old Man Cortinas and them are like a hundred times worse than the Chemical Barons. At this point though, it's hard to imagine anything worse than Uk and his stinking calisthenics.

Commander Joola is still the saving grace of this place (there go another rhyme for ya). You can tell she's not impressed with Uk's grandstanding and actually wants us to be better soldiers—even us Floodites, as they been calling us. She monitored a flight simulator exercise I did and it was the first time I'd been alone with her.

Maybe I was bristling, I dunno. You know I never been able to hide my feelings. Commander Joola goes, "You don't like the Star Guard much, do you, Cadet Salazar?"

And I'm like: "Not really, no."

And her: "Can I ask you why not?"

And I mean, I dunno, I just launch into it, the whole thing, why we hate the Star Guard, and she's just nodding, her face deadpan. When I was done it dawned on me how much I'd just let out and I'm sure my eyes went wide but whatever, what's said can't be unsaid, right?

Commander Joola takes a long breath and then says: "Then why are you here?"

And I tell her because I want to help fight the Barons and learn skills and this the best way I know how.

Then she smiles very slightly and says: "Me too."

And I gape and go, "Really?"

Turns out Commander Joola is no big fan of the Star Guard either, even though she's a ranking commander and all that, but she says at their heart they're a good organization, just complicated and sometimes corrupt like any group of beings. They really just want to bring order to the universe, and that's cool I guess. The problem is, they're always understaffed and getting into messy intergalactic conflicts, and the Barons, while they don't have that many fighters on their side (and everyone kinda hates them for jacking up Earth), they have all the coolest weapons and technology and they're hiring mercenaries and sending drone ships against anyone that opposes them. So the Star Guard see a place like Flood City, where we ain't got much going for us and need help, honestly, and they think hey, we help you, you help us. Kick out the Barons and do some recruiting, everyone's happy.

In theory. Of course: no, no no and no, but I get the idea. And at least there are some good ones (or apparently good ones, because you can't really trust anyone) like

Joola out there to counterbalance hovering trash bags like Uk.

Alright bro, I love you, take care of yaself, don't do nothing too reckless and give Mom a kiss and a hug...

Y

CHAPTER

The men chatted incessantly into the night and Dante waited. He'd gotten very good at waiting in the past week. Every day the terror would rise up inside of him, almost choke him from within, and then he'd breathe as deeply as he could and remember little Effie. She was still alive. Her tiny rasping snores came to him from across the room (six o'clock, to be exact—that one he had memorized perfectly in case he ever had to get to her quickly). Eventually the frantic beating of his heart would slow, his breath would stop coming in short, choppy gasps, and his mind would stop playing out all the horrible things that might happen.

When the terror simmered down to a low boil, his senses would come back and the world became crisp around him again. There were the familiar smells of his family, lingering like ghosts even though their bodies had been dragged away days ago. There was the friendly buzzing of jetboots past the window, the murmur of conversation out on the street, and somewhere, way past all that, the sound of crashing waves. All sounds that used to bring him a certain joy when he'd pause from his exercises or studies and consider the world around him.

Now they only made him sad.

The men in the kitchen broke into another loud chorus of laughter and one-upmanship. Soon they would try to make it back to their spacecraft and Dante and Effie would become useless to them. Most of the men had settled in, drowning their fears of being trapped in their ruckus games and shouting matches, but one—the Quiet One, Dante called him—was biding his time, plotting when to leave. And he was getting restless. Dante could tell by the incessant shuffle-shuffle of his feet and the tiny flicking of his fingers against one another. On the rare occasions he did speak, there was a growing rage evident in his raspy voice.

Effie stirred in her sleep. *Hush,* Dante whispered inside himself. *Be peaceful in your sleep, little one. Soon our time will come . . .*

———————

This would never do.

Mephim watched as Get slapped down his cards on the kitchen table and then reached across and smashed his fist into Tog's face. The men let out a chorus of exaggerated *Ohhhh*s designed to egg on the violence.

"That's the best you got?" Tog growled.

More laughter. Blood trickled from his left nostril and wound its way around his mouth and down his stubbly chin.

Mephim cringed inwardly. Why couldn't he have been marooned with disciplined men? True warriors who could stay quiet and maneuver tactically, ruthlessly. Survivors. Just about anyone would've been better than this reckless group of hooligans.

"Hit him again!" Sak yelled.

Get wound up for another punch.

"Enough." Mephim said it quietly, but it immediately silenced the room. Get glanced at him. Mephim narrowed his eyes at the boy.

"But, Baron . . ." Sak said.

"Enough of these games. This stupidity. We must be preparing our escape, not getting comfortable and drunk on our own idiocy." The five men looked back at him with empty stares. Tog wiped blood off his face. Mephim crossed his arms. "We leave in three days. Make yourselves ready."

"How?" Get asked, that childish whine still edging his voice. "The Star Guard is—"

Mephim silenced him with a glare. "You really want to know," he said, "do you?"

Get nodded with a gulp.

"Very well, young Baron. Come with me."

———————

Get had never been on the roof before. Mephim led him up a dark stairwell and then out a metal door. Gray clouds drifted like fat ghosts in the dark sky around them. Flood City spread to either side, twinkling streetlights and illuminated windows. Families would be settling in for the night. Get felt a twinge of guilt. Families like the one Mephim had slain in their own home. Much as he tried, Get couldn't get the image of those crumpled, bleeding bodies out of his head. Seeing death and destruction in battle was one thing, but that single, sudden massacre had been something else entirely.

Mephim held a tiny holowand up and opened its beam into the sky once, twice, a third time.

"What're you doing?" Get asked, shaking off the memories of death.

Mephim didn't answer, flashed the holobeam again, then twice more.

"Is that code? Are you signaling the ba—?"

"Silence," Mephim said.

Get shut up.

A few moments of quiet passed. Get heard the shush of the ocean, the buzz of some jetboots. Somewhere, way, way above them, the Barons' base fleet waited. Home. Funny how Get was standing on the very ground every Baron worshipped and dreamed of and called *home*, and he'd never felt so lonely, so alien, so lost. Home was his small barracks on Starcharger 79X, with his mom and dad right down the hall and Ato in the bottom bunk.

Ato.

He'd tried to banish his twin brother entirely from his thoughts since they'd crashed. Mephim said he'd betrayed them all, caused the crash, and was a traitor to Barons everywhere.

"Good evening, ArchBaron," a low voice boomed, startling Get from his memories. A giant blue head peered over the rooftop at them. The snell's face almost looked human, except those huge eyes were so far apart and his nose was just a slight bulge between them.

"Not so loud, you fool!" Mephim snarled. "Do you want the whole of Flood City to— Never mind. This is my mentee, the young Baron Get. We seek audience with your supervisor immediately, Captain Gorus. There is no more time to wait."

The captain nodded at Get. "Hey there, young Baron."

Get nodded back, unsure what to say.

"I'm afraid that can't be arranged at the moment," the captain said. "He's indisposed and has to—"

Mephim pulled a small hand cannon out of his robes and pointed it right between Captain Gorus's eyes. "Allow me to repeat myself," Mephim said. "Perhaps you didn't hear me correctly the first time. We seek audience with your supervisor. Immediately."

Gorus started to say something, then thought better of it.

"No more runaround," Mephim said. "No more delays."

Gorus raised a giant blue hand to his face and pushed a button on the blinking band wrapped around his wrist. "Gorus to base, Gorus to base."

A pause, and then the wristcom responded in a crackling voice: "Proceed, Captain."

"Have the regional commander holomessage me immediately."

Mephim smiled.

CHAPTER

38

Finally alone in his room, Max took a deep breath and collapsed on the bed. He missed Yala, who always knew what to do and how to do it; at least she knew how to act like she did so everyone around her felt safe. Even when Max was doing something right, he cringed with the feeling that it could all collapse at any second.

He eyed his horn.

Except music.

That was the only exception to the "Max messes up" rule. Those notes turned to gold when they came out of his horn, and best of all it was effortless, like the music was playing itself and Max just had to exhale all the emotion he felt into it.

Max picked up his horn. It felt good in his hands, an old friend. Outside the window, the sprinkled lights of Flood City rose and fell beneath the crescent moon. The ocean was all around; Max could hear it raging through the night. He put his lips on the mouthpiece, closed his eyes, and blew.

A single note slid into another. Max walked up and down the scale one time and then burst into a sullen free form, allowing each phrase to lead him to the next, circling melodies around one another, echoing himself, teasing forward and dancing back. It felt so good. He was pretty sure it sounded great too. He brought the spontaneous song to a close and opened his eyes.

An iguanagull sat perched on the window, not ten inches from Max, staring at him. It was close enough that Max could make out each glittering scale on its face, the shiny reflections in its black, black eyes, those razor-sharp, spaceship-eating claws.

"Um," Max said. It took all his self-control not to get up and run out of the room. Any sudden movement would spook the thing, and if there was one thing worse than an iguanagull on your windowsill, it was a freaked-out iguanagull trying to eat through your skull. Which it could easily do if the notion occurred to it.

Max tried to smile but was pretty sure it came out more like a grimace. The bird-reptile thing shifted its weight from one foot to the other and flapped its great, feathered wings a few times.

"Ato," Max hissed. "Ato!"

The iguanagull turned its head from side to side, regarding Max suspiciously with one eye and then the other.

"Ato!"

"What?" Ato poked his head into Max's room and rubbed his eyes. "I was watching the holodeck and it's bad enough that you wanna practice at all hours of the night but now— Oh!" He gaped at the visitor. "How the . . . Where did . . . Wow." Ato took a slow, cautious step toward the window. "Where'd it come from?" he said quietly.

"I don't know. I was practicing, had my eyes closed, and when I opened them, there it was."

"Play," Ato said.

"What?"

"Keep playing your horn, Max."

"Ato—"

"Just try it."

Max sighed and picked up his horn. He started back in on the melody he'd been tooling around with, this time keeping one eye open and glued to the creature. The iguanagull closed its eyes.

"Ato!" Max whispered. "It closed its eyes!"

"I know," Ato said, still slo-mo walking toward the window. "Keep playing!"

Max took his melody off into some uncharted territory, bending notes and accenting each line with graceful pauses. The iguanagull swayed gently back and forth on the windowsill.

"It's listening," Ato whispered. "It's really listening."

Max finished. The iguanagull opened its eyes, favored Max with a piercing stare, and then flapped its wings twice and took off into the night.

CHAPTER

Max poked his head into the big, empty Music Hall. Some of the chairs still lay scattered and tipped over from the mad escape the week before. The gaping hole in the ceiling showed a tattered square of gray sky and sent a shimmering corridor of daylight down to the much larger hole in the auditorium floor. No one was around, not even the iguanagulls. Max walked up to the edge of the Hole and took in that deep darkness. Somewhere down there, life had once been normal on the surface of this planet. People went about their days and started families and fell in love. They played music and got into fights and worked things out. And now they were all gone. It was impossible to comprehend, that much life, that much death.

They'd sent explorers down there once, with cables attached to their belts, but their jetboots had run out of power and then they'd run out of rope and there was no sign of the darkness ending. The team had even thrown objects down to see if they could time out how far it took to hit the bottom, but the darkness seemed to just silently eat whatever they threw into it; no sounds ever came back up.

Max was wondering what it would feel like to be that far down in the Hole when he heard footsteps approaching from the dressing room.

Djinna stepped out onto the stage. "Max!" She smiled and Max felt all gooey inside.

"Djinna." He nodded at her, trying really hard not to look like he was trying really hard.

"We have rehearsal today?"

"I dunno. I figured I'd show up and see who else came."

"Me too."

They looked at each other for a few seconds, all their useless little words having been used up. Max felt perfectly content and terrified at the same time. It was awesome.

"That . . . song . . ." Djinna said the words carefully, like she wasn't sure if she should even broach the topic at all. "What you . . . we . . . played . . . last week."

"Yes."

"It was . . . I kinda felt like it was the music that I've always wanted to play but never been able to." She moved her mouth all the way to one side of her face, as if she wanted to swallow up the words she'd just said. "If that makes any sense," she added quickly.

"It does, it does. I feel the same way."

"LOOK AT THAT HUGE HOLE!" Fast Eddie yelled, bursting

through the double doors and charging down the center aisle. "It's huge!"

Max grudgingly peeled his eyes away from Djinna's face and glared at Fast Eddie. "You didn't see it during the attack?"

"Nah, I was out quick and didn't look back," Fast Eddie said. "Is it true about Deezer?"

Max frowned. He'd been trying to block out the image of Deezer's pale, broken body all week. "Yeah. I . . . we saw him."

Djinna nodded.

"Wow," Fast Eddie said. "That's really messed up." It looked like Deezer's death was dawning on him for the first time. Max really hoped Eddie wasn't about to cry.

"Alright, people." The voice made Max cringe like he'd done something wrong. It was Trellis, the conductor. He clapped twice and strolled to the center of the stage. "Let's come together, hm?"

The rest of the orchestra bustled in after him and formed a semicircle. "I have two sad announcements to make, my friends. Our beloved Deezer was killed during the attack." Word had already gotten out about Deezer, so most people just nodded sadly. "And of course, Mr. Cortinas seems to have disappeared."

"Hardly," someone muttered.

Trellis raised an eyebrow. "Apparently he felt the need to, uh, make himself scarce after all the, um, chaos last week."

General mutters of confusion rose up.

"As the most senior remaining member of the Flood City Orchestra . . ." Trellis began.

"You mean oldest." Fast Eddie snickered.

Trellis frowned but ignored him. "I will be taking over as director."

Max's heart slid into his knees. Trellis running the orchestra? No way. He could practically hear the music curling up and dying at the thought of it. They were just breaking into something new and exciting, and Trellis would never let them experiment. He was strictly by the book.

As if to confirm Max's worst fears, Trellis crossed his arms over his chest and announced: "And let me say right from the get-go, there will be none of that new whatever-it's-called that certain members were participating in during the Flood City performance. None. I won't tolerate it."

"What?" Max blurted out before he could stop himself. "Why not?"

The whole orchestra turned its glare toward Trellis.

"Well, it's very simple," Trellis said, crossing his legs and then uncrossing them again. "The Star Guard is here to protect us from the Chemical Barons, just like they have for the past twenty years. They say the pageant stays the way it's always been, so that's what we do. The pageant is wonderful, people, there's no need to . . . Max! Where are you going?"

Max was already halfway to the door. For the first time in a long time, maybe ever, he felt completely clear about what he was doing. He simply would not tolerate being in an orchestra that wouldn't let him play his music the way he heard it. It had been instantaneous and beautiful and everyone knew it, and if Trellis wanted to kowtow to the Star Guard, he could do it without Max leading the horn section.

There was a shuffling from behind him, but Max didn't bother looking back, he just kept striding down the aisle and then burst through the front doors and out into the bright day. He was startled a few seconds later when the rest of the Flood City Orchestra stomped out too.

"Oh," Max said, looking around at his fellow musicians.

"That's garbage," Djinna said. "If we can't play what we want, what's the point?"

"Yeah," chimed in Fast Eddie. "No one wants to hear that same old boring music anymore anyway."

People began to mill off toward their respective houses. Trellis came out a few minutes later, looked around miserably, and then jetted off to mope somewhere. Max stood staring at the Music Hall, thinking about the big hole inside it and all the dead people at the bottom of the ocean and all the music that wanted to come out of his heart.

"Wanna walk around inside for a bit?" Djinna said. She was standing right behind Max, her face sad and serious.

"Yeah," Max said. He hadn't realized she was looking at him, and he suddenly had no idea what to do with his body. "That'd be great."

"That was kinda awesome, Max," Djinna said as they strolled up and down the rows of seats. She flashed that smile for just a second and then it disappeared again.

Max grinned and then tried to focus on what had just happened instead of how flattered he was and how unwieldy everything felt. "It just makes me so mad. I don't know what they expect, but I'm done with the old stuff."

"Yeah."

Max glanced at her. Djinna looked she was waiting to say something. "What?"

"Your buddy—Ato?" she said. Max and Ato had seen Djinna a few days before and Max had given his usual not-that-convincing explanation about him.

"What about him?

"He just materialized out of thin air?"

"Well, you know, like I said, his mom—"

"Right. When'd you meet him?"

"Oh, you know . . ." Max shrugged. He hated lying because he knew he was terrible at it. None of the words wanted to come out in the right order, so he ended up mumbling a few strings of nonsense.

"Wanna try that again?"

"About a week ago, I guess."

"So right around the time of the crash."

Max nodded. Djinna seemed to be staring right through his skin and directly into his brain. It was charming and annoying at the same time. "Have you heard from Splink?"

Djinna's face softened and Max wished he'd thought of changing the subject earlier. He'd have to remember that strategy for the next time he was in a bind.

"No. Well . . . yeah, kinda."

"How have you kinda heard from him?"

They walked down the center aisle of the Music Hall toward the double doors that led out to the plaza.

"He sent, like, a general hologram to all his friends and family about everything. You know, they don't have much time to send stuff with all the training and everything, so . . . yeah."

"General, huh?"

Djinna tensed her face up and for a second Max thought she was about to shout at him. Then she just frowned and looked away. "Yeah," she whispered. "Sounds like he's having fun."

"Oh yeah? Yala sounds miserable."

Djinna stared at Max. "You heard from her?"

"Um . . . she wrote me, yeah."

"As in a letter?"

"Uh-huh. A couple." Max was trying as best he could to not sound like he was bragging, but Djinna looked even more hurt than before.

"How'd she send them to you?"

"The bird, Krestlefax, brings 'em."

"The one that perches in the tower I live in."

Of course that bird, Max wanted to say, there's only one bird left in the world. But Djinna hadn't meant it as a question.

At that moment, they walked under the gaping hole that the Baron cloud cruiser had torn out of the Music Hall ceiling. An orange-tinged blast of afternoon sunlight streamed through it and lit up Djinna's brown face as she looked directly at Max. "Okay," she said, the single word soaked in disappointment. "I see."

"Sorry," Max said. It seemed useless, but it was better than nothing.

"For what?" Djinna said, suddenly defiant. They walked out of the sunlight and through the double doors. "I don't care. It is what it is." She shrugged.

In the plaza they studied each other for a few seconds. "I'll see you at practice next week?" Max said.

"Yeah. Listen, Max, I don't have a problem with your friend or anything, I'm just saying: Be careful. Things are getting real weird around here and it's hard to know who to trust, is all."

Max nodded at her. "I will. Thanks."

They both leapt into the air and jetted off in opposite directions.

DID YOU KNOW?!

Earth's population when the Chemical Barons caused the Floods was approximately 10 billion. That means that with survival estimates at less than 1 percent, approximately 10 billion people died as a result of the Floods. And if not for Star Guard intervention, that number would be far higher.

SYTHILIUM

The chemical compound the Barons mass-produced that caused the Floods. They originally tested an ether form of this on various drug addicts they pulled off the streets, but the experiments went wrong and turned the unwilling participants into a whole new species, our weird and enigmatic friends, the vapors!

THE *GALLANT* TO THE RESCUE

The *Gallant* was an intergalactic academic frigate that was taking off for a field trip to Tarashidex Prime on the day of the Floods. On board was an entire school, plus several dozen teachers, staff, and crew members. The surviving members of this voyage became known as the Founders. Because the Chemical Barons had already escaped into orbit and formed a military blockade around Earth, there was no way for the *Gallant* to make it to deeper space. The crew elected instead to hover over the surface of the waters, which they did until they came upon the mashed-together buildings that we now know as Flood City!

STAR GUARD ACADEMY

Where the next generation of elite Star Guard peacekeeper troops go from regular citizens to first-rate fighting machines. And keepers of the intergalactic peace!

Ato looked up from one of Yala's old history textbooks as Max came zooming into a landing on the balcony. "Um."

"Um what?" Max said, panting a little as he pulled off his jet-boots and flopped into a reclining chair.

"The Star Guard think the Barons caused the Floods?"

Max squinted at Ato. "Y'all did."

Ato blinked. "That's not what . . . I mean . . ." He held up the book. "You believe this stuff? It's so obviously propaganda to make the Star Guard look good."

"Of course it is, and they bend the facts on some stuff, but that doesn't mean other stuff isn't true. The Barons causing the Floods is a known fact. Why do you think you guys all made it out and basically nobody else did? The Barons left before the Floods. Didn't bother telling anyone, just caused 'em and booked."

"Well . . ." Ato started. "I mean . . ."

"Do you honestly think the Barons would be admitting it openly in their textbooks if they had, Ato?"

Ato shook his head, tears welling up in his eyes. "I didn't think . . ." It couldn't be. The Baron Academy holodocs were equally slanted, the other way of course, but Ato had always figured there was some truth to them anyway, just like Max said about his. The Floods being a natural occurrence, as the Barons claimed, wasn't an entirely impossible theory. Floods . . . happened. But still . . . "If you believe that," Ato said, "how can you . . . ? Don't you . . . hate me?"

Max looked him up and down carefully, eyes narrowed. "You aight," he conceded with a shrug.

Ato's eyes were wide.

Max punched him on the shoulder. "I'm kidding! You're, like, my best friend! Of course I don't hate you. Your folks are bad people though. I definitely hate them. They can rot. So I guess that's kinda messed up, now that I think about it. And if you ever go all Baron on me and decide you wanna blow us up or whatever too, I mean, then we'd have a problem. But somehow I feel like if things came down to it, you'd have my back, Flood City's back, in a fight."

Ato nodded. He'd only been here a little over a week, but he knew it was true. He'd never felt so accepted, never felt like he could fully be who he really was, not some twisted version of himself, until he'd gotten to Flood City. And without having to think about it, he knew what Max said was true.

"Even against the Barons."

"Yes," Ato said.

"Bet." Max pulled out a bag of dougies and held one out to Ato. "Why you crying, man?"

"I'm not!" Ato said, wiping his eyes. "I just . . . it's a lot. I don't know." He shoved a dougie in his mouth, let the sweet juiciness of it fill him.

"You're overthinking, my dude, and anyway, we got more important things to talk about than world destruction and your responsibility in such acts."

Ato almost spat out the dougie. "Oh my god!" He wiped the last few tears away and then wiggled his eyebrows. "How'd it go with the holographer's daughter?"

"Fine." Max shrugged. "I guess."

"Man, you have got to learn how to lie better. You're squirming!"

"I am not! I mean, I always squirm after I jetboot around."

"Lies."

"I just feel . . ." He looked around the room, then just walked out to the balcony without saying a word.

Ato followed him. For a few moments they both just stared at the gaping tunnel across the chasm, the spot where they'd first met. A soft drizzle fell from the gray skies.

"I don't know what to do with myself around her," Max said. "You know?"

"No, actually," Ato said. "I've never had a crush on anyone."

"Never? Whoa."

"What's it like?"

"It's like the best thing and the worst thing ever all at the same time. But I dunno, now that we're becoming friends, it feels like everything has calmed down a little."

"Even while the rest of the world has ratcheted all the chaos up to ten."

"Ha . . . I guess so, yeah." He cracked a sudden smile. "Anyway, let's get out of here."

"Where you want to go?"

"I dunno. Cause some trouble."

It felt good to be out and about. Max had too many different thought lines rushing through his mind to just sit at home. At least out here, zipping easily down alleyways and swooping up above the city, he could feel fresh and free and not tied down by everything going on. It was amazing how well Ato seemed to be adjusting to this whole new life. He'd probably left behind one that was unlike it in every way, not to mention all his people.

"Awkward question coming," Max said as they sloped into a downward trajectory toward an open area between two brick buildings.

"Impossible!" Ato snorted.

"Do you, like . . . miss your parents?"

"Oh."

Max cringed as Ato slowed his jetboots to a hover. Why did he always put words to thoughts? "I'm sorry! I shouldn't have asked. I just—"

Ato waved him off. "It's fine! I'm okay. I just slowed because . . . I had to think about it. Which I guess is your answer, huh? I mean, I do, but I also don't?"

They fell back into a slow glide, skirted around the edge of Barge Annex toward the Music Hall. "My parents . . . my whole family—they're not the warmest people, really. Like you know how when you come home, your mom kisses you on the cheek and asks about your day? Yeah, that's . . . that's not a thing for us. They're not mean! They're just not . . . they don't show a lot of love. Outwardly."

"That sounds kinda rough," Max said.

"What about you?"

"Huh?"

"Your . . . dad?"

"Oh, ha!" Max didn't know why the mention of his dad made him laugh—there was nothing funny about the situation at all. Maybe it was the absurdity of not even realizing what Ato had been asking about at first. Ato looked a little horrified. It was hard, Max realized for the three hundredth time since he'd started hanging out with his new friend, to explain a place like Flood City.

"We've lost a lot of people here. People get lost at sea, they disappear without a trace sometimes. They go on expeditions and never come back. It's part of life here. My dad joined an exploratory mission to try to find land before I was born and never came back."

"Oh man. I'm sorry," Ato said. "Maybe he's—"

Max shook his head. He'd never liked the idea that his dad was out there somewhere, living some other life faraway. Sure, it was possible, but only barely. And what if he was? Max had never known him, so it hardly mattered. "No, man. He's dead. Or presumed so anyway. We say his name at the Hole every year along with all our other dead—well, almost every year. And I'm sad for my mom, but it's not something I sit around and think about."

"Wow," Ato said.

They loop-de-looped through the mini-plaza, sped under a crumbly bridge, and then fell into a slow glide down one of the more impossible-to-navigate corridors.

"Anyway," Max went on, finally getting to what he'd only just realized he'd been trying to say all along, "the first group of kids here, our parents, had lost almost all their families in the Floods, so the adults kind of became everybody's parents, and that's just how this place is: We all look out for each other."

Ato opened his mouth, probably to say something deep, but stopped. "What are you doing?"

Max had pulled a can of spray paint out of his satchel and was shaking it up. "Shhhh!" he hissed. "Keep an eye out."

"But—"

"I said shhh!"

They were hovering in front of a Star Guard transporter. The crew had left it parked on top of someone's house, as they often did, and probably all gone to sleep inside. The ship itself seemed to be slumbering. A gentle hum emanated from it, but otherwise everything was still and quiet.

"You're not gonna . . ." Ato started to say, but then Max sprayed a line of paint across the wall of the transporter. "Max!"

"Look, Ato," Max said without taking his eyes off the wall. He started another line, this one curving around from the top of the first and connecting back to it halfway down. "You can either stay and shut up or go home and shut up. But either way, I need you to shut up."

Ato nodded and glanced up and down the alleyway.

"There," Max said a few minutes later. "All done." He jetted back a little and took in his work.

PROPERTY OF THE FLOOD CITY REBEL GUERRILLA SQUAD

"You've lost your mind," Ato said.

Max shrugged. "Maybe I have. But I'm sick of the Star Guard ruining everything. I've had it. They took away my sister and now they've ruined my music. Hey, what is a guerrilla squad anyway?"

"You say it guerrilla," Ato said, pronouncing the *el* sound at the end instead of the *y* sound Max had used.

"Oh. In Flood City two *l*'s together sound like *ya*."

"Well, not in space. Anyway, it's a kind of warfare where a smaller army fights off a larger invading one by hiding out in the jungle or buildings or something. Back before the Floods there was an animal called a gorilla that was like a big muscley human covered in black fur that lived in trees."

"What does one have to do with the other?" Max asked.

"Nothing actually," Ato admitted. "I just love animals."

"Awesome. Anyway, Old Man Cortinas asked me to cause trouble the other night."

"Cortinas the rebel leader? You saw him?"

"Yeah," Max said. "The night we saw your twin. He asked me to help him cause some trouble for the Star Guard. Said I should bring you too, actually."

"He knows about me?"

"I don't know if he knows who you are, but he's got spies everywhere, and I'm sure they've seen us hanging out."

Ato had nothing to say to that, so they jetted quickly away from the crime scene.

———————————

"It feels good," Max was saying as they rounded another corner. He'd tagged up three more Star Guard ships and it was getting toward dawn. "Like, I've never done anything really bad my whole life, because it never made sense to. But now . . ."

Ato put up his hand very suddenly. They both let their jetboots simmer to almost nothing and slowly sank toward the wall. "You heard something?" Max whispered.

Ato nodded. "Look!" Across from them, DOWN WITH THE STAR GUARD!!! was splattered in big angry letters across a wall.

"Did you write that?"

Max shook his head. "Did you see me write it?"

"No, but . . ."

"Shh!"

Someone was coming. If it was a Star Guard patrol, they were done for. Even though they hadn't done the tagging, they were standing right in front of it with a backpack full of spray cans. And whoever had done the tagging was probably long gone by now. Max tried to prepare himself for the worst. It had been fun, being completely reckless, but now that it was over he really, really didn't want to get caught.

Bartrum Uk rounded the corner in his little hovercraft. His eyes stared blankly ahead, but there was no way he could miss Max and Ato hovering right in front of him. Max felt his belly churn. It really was over.

"Get back to your patrol, you mangy grunts," Uk barked. His voice sounded squeakier in person, like he was fighting a cold.

"Um . . . what?"

"Get back to your patrol, you mangy grunts."

"Should we play along?" Ato whispered.

Max shook his head, speechless.

"Get back to your patrol," Uk said again. "You mangy grunts."

"Something's not right about this," Max said, squinting at the Star Guard commander. He zipped cautiously forward. Uk didn't move.

"Get back to your patrol, you mangy grunts."

Max reached his hand out toward Commander Uk and watched in amazement as it passed right through him. "It's a . . ."

"Hologram," Djinna said, jetting out from the shadows and pulling off the balaclava she'd wrapped around her face. "Not one of my best, but still, it usually scares off the Star Guard right quick."

"Djinna!" Max yelled, hoping he sounded just happy enough to see her that it didn't seem desperate. "You made a life-size hologram of the Star Guard regional commander?" The idea was so audacious and brilliant, Max couldn't help but smile even through his surprise.

"Sure." Djinna shrugged. "I just used an image of him off the regular holonet and blew it up. Enlarging a 'gram is like the easiest thing on the planet, so you know, no biggie. Then I cut together clips of his voice to get him to say something that'd scare off the troops, and voilà! Oh, I see you brought your suspicious friend!"

Ato waved awkwardly at her.

"And you did this too?" Max said, pointing at the wall behind Djinna.

She looked around and then nodded enthusiastically. "And by the paint all over your hands I'd say I wasn't the only one out here causing trouble in the name of Flood City."

Max grinned.

"Well, then," Djinna said. "What are we waiting for? Now we're a team!"

The walls all around Mephim were peopled with smiling, jet-booted superheroes and shooting stars.

It was hideous.

Even the bedsheets on all three beds had happy little cartoons on them. It was no wonder these petty holdouts had been so easy to infiltrate. If it hadn't been for that asinine young Baron interfering, they could've dropped the nuke and obliterated the place and gone ahead with figuring out how to make Earth reinhabitable. If it hadn't been for that . . . child . . . the Barons would probably already be sending exploratory missions by this time.

Mephim took a deep breath, trying to push out all those negative thoughts as he exhaled. A big plastic star dangled from a cord in the ceiling and sent tiny light shards spinning around the room. The curtains dulled the streetlamps outside and so the room was mostly dark. Even better: It was blessedly quiet compared to the kitchen, where Clowns Number One through Five continued to bask in their own stupidity.

In with the good, Mephim told himself glumly as he sat cross-legged directly beneath the rotating star. Out with the bad. That buffoon of a boy. In with the good, out with the bad. He'd come so close. Soooo close. The sounds of another useless argument came from the kitchen and Mephim winced, trying to block out the distraction and resist the urge to go tear someone's head off.

In with the good. Earth. He was on Earth. *Home.* Even if it wasn't in the ideal circumstances—it was something. He'd made it home, after so many years in exile. After the shame of defeat. Somewhere, amidst all this water, there was solid ground. And somewhere beneath it all was the place he'd been born. The cradle of the Baron Empire. And he'd survived this long, which was no small feat considering the cards he'd been handed. Considering the ignorant, ridiculous, unstrategic, useless . . . Out with the bad.

The argument in the other room dissolved into raucous laughter.

Mephim fumbled with his robes and retrieved the iguanagull head, now dried out and crusty. He held it up so his eyes met with those empty sockets. Just that simple touch and already Mephim could feel the power surge through him.

"Soon, my pretty little friend," he whispered. It felt like electrical jolts were blitzing through his veins. His whole body convulsed one time, and then he put the shriveled talisman away with trembling hands. "Our time will soon come."

THE FLOOD CITY GAZETTE

The Intergalactic Star Guard Conglomerate would like to officially remind the citizens of Flood City that they are a member-municipality of the Intergalactic Star Guard and that membership comes with both rights and responsibilities. Further shenanigans directed toward the property and personnel of the ISGC will *not* be tolerated under any circumstances. This warning has already been issued a number of times. Consequences for these acts of public nuisance will be in effect shortly if the culprits are not apprehended. It is up to the citizenry of each ISGC municipality to hold one another responsible. Punishments levied on rebel perpetrators can include up to seven weeks in the off-world Star Guard brigship, mandatory service in the Star Guard, cutting of rations, loss of citizen rights, and public execution.

Please note: The mandatory curfew is still in effect from nightfall to daybreak until further notice.

RATIONS REPORT

Unfortunately, rations are at half level today. Maybe when the shenanigans let up there will be more food available.

THE DAILY TIDE

Low tide today will be at **0456**.

High tide will be at **2214**.

Please *avoid the city edges during high tide, as conditions can worsen suddenly.*

IGUANAGULL AHOY!

Star Guard peacekeepers near Barge Annex report moderate levels of iguanagull sightings. Stay safe and keep your eyes in the sky!

THE BOOO'CAST

Reported spectral/electromagnetic activity levels are unusually high by the Electric Ghost Yard. Please keep your distance from this area at all times!

THE VAPORS & ABANDONED OCEAN LINER REPORT

We have nothing to report.

CHEMICAL BARONS

The Chemical Baron elements remain at large within the confines of Flood City. Remain alert at all times. They are armed and extremely dangerous. Stay vigilant!

Djinna had her back pressed against a crumbly stucco wall when Max and Ato rounded the corner. "We gonna do things a little differently this time," she said.

"What do you mean?" Ato asked.

"The lookout can stay right here while we tag up the transporter."

"But the transporter's way up ahead on the other side of the square," Max pointed out. "How's Ato gonna let us know if someone's coming?"

"He's gonna use one of these!" Djinna pulled two little black boxes strapped to wristbands out of her knapsack.

Both Ato and Max's eyes got big real quick. "Holowatches!" they yelled at the same time. "Coool!"

Djinna beamed. "See, there's a little holocam on this end and the top is a deck. It's pretty low-tech really, but you know there's some advantages to being—"

Max snatched one of the holowatches out of her hands and brought it up close to his face. "Amazing!"

"—a holographer's daughter." Djinna rolled her eyes. "Sure, you can look at it. No problem."

"Oh, sorry, Djinna," Max said without looking up. "I've just never seen one of these before."

"Well, there it is. Can you give it to Ato now?"

Max looked up. "Oh. Right. Here, Ato." He handed over the holowatch, keeping his eyes on it as Ato strapped it around his wrist and fiddled with the controls.

"Your dad really is pretty much one of the coolest people in the world," Max said.

Djinna shrugged. "He's alright. Now . . . let's move." She nodded at Ato and headed across the open square. Max sped after her. For that wild couple of seconds they were in the open, all by themselves. It was after midnight, well past curfew, and if anyone had seen them, they'd have been in huge trouble, probably thrown into prison or who knew what else. The Star Guard had been upping their patrols, threatening worse and worse punishments for anyone caught damaging their property or engaging in "rebel activity." And Max was terrified, it was true. But somewhere beneath all that terror there was something else, a rising tidal wave of excitement that got bigger and bigger every time the stakes got higher. He couldn't help it; as much as he knew it was ridiculous to risk everything just to draw some words on the side of a spaceship, it felt right to finally have a mission. And every time the Star Guard issued new angry proclamations about the rebels and their scoundrel pranks, he felt a little thrill of pride that he'd actually gotten to them some.

"You comin'?" Djinna hissed.

Max snapped out of it and swooped against the side of the transporter. He nodded. "Let's do this."

"Wait," Djinna said. She raised the holowatch (Max still peering at it in total amazement) and a shimmering blue Ato appeared in front of them. "All clear?"

Ato looked confused for a second, squinting at them and scratching his head. Then he glanced around a few times and nodded. "Clear!"

"Okay, now let's do this!"

They turned and pulled out their spray cans in one fluid motion. Max had to marvel at how easily things seemed to flow with Djinna. They'd only been going out on runs for a few nights and already they'd fallen into a smoothness that barely required speaking. And now they had holowatches? It was almost too much.

Max did a quick outline of the letters in an obnoxious metallic green, and Djinna started filling them in using dark blue for shading and a thick goopy orange for highlights. They were finishing the first word when a soft whizzing noise rang out and Max felt himself stuck fast to the wall he had just been painting.

"What happened?" he yelled, squirming against what felt like a hundred thick ropes wrapped around his whole body.

"I don't know!" Djinna said.

Max could tell from the strain in her voice that she'd been tied down too. He shook his head back and forth a few times and managed to get it free enough so he could turn and look at her. "You okay?"

"Yeah, I think so. Can't move though."

"Me either."

"The holowatch?"

"Can't reach the button."

This was it, then. Well, not *it* necessarily, but close enough. Max tried to take a deep breath, but the net wrapped around him made it hard to do anything. He felt oddly calm for about ten seconds, as if his mind hadn't quite caught up to the sudden turn of events. He took another breath and then panic set in. Whatever was about to happen, it was going to be awful. That much was certain.

The wall rumbled painfully against his face and he realized one of the giant Star Guards must be approaching. Or maybe a few. Hopefully Ato was smart enough to get out of there before they showed up. He only hoped Djinna would be okay. Djinna. Her face took over his thoughts like a perfume cloud, blotted out all his terror and uncertainty. She looked so peaceful over there, even in the midst of all this mess.

"Pssst!"

Max wrestled his head back to the other side, his heart pounding away in his chest with sudden hope.

"Max!" It was Ato, hovering in the air a few feet from him. "What are we gonna do?"

"You have to go, Ato!" Max hissed. "They're gonna be here any second!"

"I'm not leaving without you guys! What kind of a friend would I be? Besides, your mom would *kill* me!"

"He has a point," Djinna said.

Max sighed. "But what are we gonna do? No one has a knife. The Star Guard's on their way." The ship gave another rumble as if to confirm this. "And you're . . . you know."

"What?" Djinna asked.

"Nothing," Max said. "I'll tell you later."

Ato leaned backward, pointing his feet at the edge of the net. "I'm gonna try using my jetboots to singe it off."

Max winced; the burst of flame was so strong he could feel it cover his body like an instant sunburn, but when Ato zipped back over, the net was still intact. The rumbling got louder.

"They're here!" Djinna whispered. "Hide!"

But it was too late: Two ugly blue heads appeared over the top of the transporter ship like a pair of big annoying moons. Max groaned. Ato just hovered there looking up at them, his mouth opening and closing uselessly. Neither of the Star Guards moved, and for a few seconds, Max thought maybe nothing at all would happen—they'd all just stand there gaping at one another until the sun came up.

Then one of the giants said: "Hello, sir."

Realm: Milky Way
Sector: 12A-14079
Planet: Earth
Region: Flood City

From: Regional Commander
Bartrum Uk, Earth Forces
To: Star Guard Command

Esteemed Co-Commanders:

It pains me to report, but the ungrateful citizens of the noble municipality Flood City have been howling louder and louder for our evacuation of the premises. How quickly they forget! How easily history slips away from them beneath the rising tide (no pun intended, of course!) of daily drudgery and the merest taste of independence.

What will they do, I wonder, if they get their wish and we remove ourselves entirely from the situation? What will they eat, even? How will they fend off the next Chemical Baron attack?

It seems the Chemical Barons are more open to negotiations than we'd previously realized. More to come.

And perhaps we will find out these answers sooner rather than later. We'll meet via holosphere presently, but this memo is to note in advance of that session that I'll be recommending a full pullout from Flood City, including all civilian and military services.

Magnanimously,
RC Uk

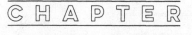

Max sputtered. Who was the giant talking to? He couldn't tilt his head enough to tell where they were looking.

"Hello?" Ato said doubtfully.

"What are you doing out and about so late?" the other giant asked.

"Um . . ." Ato said.

"Gathering more intelligence, eh?" the first Star Guard said. "Right. Is that other fellow around? The skinny robed fellow?"

Realization dawned on Max with such a confusing mix of emotions he didn't know what to do at first. "Oh, he's asleep right now," Ato was saying, somewhat unconvincingly. At least he seemed to have caught on. And not a moment too soon.

"And who might these two be? Some Flood City rebels you've caught, eh?"

"No!" Ato yelped. Then he got himself together. "Um, no. They're actually my men. Um, my troops. Barons, that is. Disguised as rebels! To, you know . . . infiltrate. The rebels."

Good thing the giants aren't too bright, Max thought. Both the Star Guards were nodding and shrugging. "Oh, but they're all caught up in our booby trap," one of them pointed out.

"Yes," Ato said. "Would you mind just, um, er, letting them out? Now?"

"You're sure they're Barons?"

"Absolutely!" Ato sputtered. "And without a question."

With a blip and whir, all the horrible pressure on Max's back suddenly released and he almost hurtled down into the building ravine before igniting his jetboots and stopping himself. He exchanged a very confused glance with Djinna, who must've been completely lost, and then smiled up at the Star Guards. "Thank you, good gentlemen!"

"Give our regards to the robed fellow," one of the Guards said with a little salute. "Hope the negotiations work out for you folks."

Max had to fight the urge to hurl his spray can at them. *Negotiations?*

A quiet whir sounded, not too far away, like the sound of an approaching hunterfly except . . . shriller. Max, Ato, Djinn, and the two Star Guards looked around just as a magnificent bolt of lightning tore through the night and slammed into the side of the ship, vaporizing a huge chunk of it.

"Yeegads!" one of the Star Guard yelled.

The ship caught fire.

"Rebels!" shouted the other.

Max, Djinna, and Ato dove out of the way as another bolt sizzled past.

"Greetings, huge blue clowns!" It was Tecla, zooming through the night with a long metal cylinder perched on her shoulder. "Your ship looked a little musty, so I decided to help you clean it with my trusty sharazar!" She let out another bolt, demolishing the cockpit. "Ayo."

The Star Guards' big blue heads poked up behind the flames. "Call for reinforcements," one said. "And load up another netblaster."

"Oh, hey, kids," Tecla said, gazing down. "You guys might wanna scatter right about now. Things about to get—"

The thunder of approaching Star Guard troopers filled the air. It sounded like a whole lot of them.

"Messy."

A sharp, wet sound rang out, like a fresh bag of dougies smacking into a wall at light speed, and long, sticky tendrils filled the air above them—it was the same material that had pinned them down a few moments ago.

"Go!" Tecla yelled, spinning into a midair cartwheel as she released an extended blast from her sharazar. It shredded flaming gashes through the netting, which then floated in cinders out of the sky. Max, Djinna, and Ato blasted down the nearest alley as the shouts of Star Guard peacekeepers grew louder.

————————

The sproinging slap of those netcasters kept bursting out around them. Every time Max looked up, another tendril was stretching across the sky. Plus, the whole world kept shaking beneath the boots of those huge snells. A few jetbooted rebels whizzed past overhead, and then the sound of more sharazars blasting away echoed through the night.

"This way!" Djinna ducked down a narrow alley. Max and Ato zoomed after her. The whole place was all shadows and the trickle of running water somewhere nearby.

"Do you think they're following us?" Ato asked.

"No idea," Djinna said. "They probably have their hands full now."

"Those rebels . . . are . . . so awesome," Max panted.

Djinna flashed a wily grin. "I legit wanna be Tecla when I grow up."

"Me too," Max said. "What happens now?"

The booming footsteps and sharazar blasts sounded like they were getting farther away.

No one said anything for a few minutes.

Then Ato spoke: "If the Star Guard thought—"

"Shh!" Djinna snapped. The whole place was shuddering again, ever so slightly. "They're coming back."

The rumbling got louder, then the Star Guard netcaster let out another wet slap in the air right above them and everyone flinched and crouched against the wall.

"See any?" a booming voice whispered.

The other just grunted in reply.

"Wait 'em out? They couldn'ta gone far."

Max held his breath. How long would they stay? What if—

"Nah," the other said. "We keep looking. C'mon."

The rumbling footsteps faded again.

Max exhaled. "We gotta get outta here."

All three exchanged glances; each nodded. They powered up their jetboots and took off into the night.

A few hours later, Ato and Djinna sat at the edge of the tunnel. The darkness stretched behind them. Up ahead, beyond Max's apartment building, was the endless ocean. Somewhere down below it all were the millions of dead souls that had been lost when the whole world flooded. When Ato's people had flooded the Earth, he reminded himself. The reality of that was starting to become more and more real with him. And he couldn't keep pretending it wasn't true just to make himself feel better. A few lights twinkled from buildings around them, but most of the tiny part of the planet that was still alive was fast asleep.

"You're a Baron, aren't you?" Djinna said.

Ato nodded. "You've known for a while, huh?"

"I had my suspicions."

"But I've sort of renounced the Baronhood. I mean, I'm not really a Baron anymore."

"You mean you're not sworn to destroy my home? So pleased to hear that." Djinna pulled her legs up to her chest and wrapped her arms around her knees. She didn't look at Ato, just stared out into the night.

"Well, not all the Barons want to destroy Flood City."

Djinna shrugged.

"But you're right," Ato said after a pause. "That night they attacked, the plan was to drop a nuke."

"What?"

"But it wasn't everyone. We didn't know, it was just this one . . ." Ato felt himself flailing for explanations, but none of them seemed to make any sense or even matter.

"So the rest of you guys just wanted to attack and shoot us up with regular lasers, but one guy wanted to nuke us, and *that's* supposed to make me feel better about your people?"

"No," Ato said. "Most of us thought it was just an exploratory mission. Or intelligence, really."

"So you were just spying on us, no big deal."

"I mean—"

"What if you all just left us alone? You already destroyed a whole planet. Wasn't that enough?"

Ato opened his mouth to say that *he* hadn't personally destroyed anything, but it just felt like dodging somehow. He hadn't—he hadn't been alive when it happened, but the only reason he was even alive was because his parents had known the Floods were coming and left Earth in time to survive. A decision he didn't make yet benefited from anyway. It was all so confusing.

He just knew that he wanted to do better. To be more intentional about what he did with his life. Even if it meant being awkward and not having answers.

"Anyway," Djinna said, "what happened to the nuke?"

"It's probably still on the downed cruiser, but no one can get to it because the Star Guard's there. Of course, after tonight, I'm not so sure the Star Guard and the Barons are even enemies anymore."

Djinna just shook her head and then buried her face in the curve of her elbow. They were silent for a little while as the ocean snarled and swirled.

"It's my brother," Ato said. "My twin. That they thought I was tonight."

"Figured something like that." Her eyes were red when she looked up. "You guys all look the same to me anyway."

That stung, but Ato was pretty sure that was the point. And anyway, him being defensive wouldn't do any good right then, and he knew it. He sighed. "The fact that they thought I was my brother though . . . that means—"

"The Star Guard and the Barons are negotiating. And Flood City loses again."

It was true. Whatever was going on, it could only mean trouble for Flood City. Probably total destruction.

"I'm going to do," Ato said slowly, "everything that I can"— Djinna finally turned to him, her eyebrows raised—"to stop whatever horrible thing might be about to happen to Flood City because of my messed-up people."

Djinna studied his face very carefully for a few seconds, then nodded ever so slightly and went back to staring out at the night.

Far above them, Max swooped through the air.

No matter what he tried, he couldn't clear his head. The Star Guard was negotiating with the Chemical Barons. And not even the ones up on the base fleet: Those big obnoxious giants were talking to the very same Barons who had terrorized the pageant and were hiding out somewhere in Flood City.

It was so infuriating!

Max looped up over a half-destroyed building and kept going up, up, up until he was surrounded by clouds and the moon looked closer than the city lights. Somewhere up there, the Chemical Baron base fleet was churning along, waiting for the moment to come destroy Flood City once and for all. Probably wouldn't be long now. And way out over the ocean, Yala was training to become one of the very things Max hated the most.

Max sped in wild circles, letting the night air rush over him as he dipped and glided. Then he remembered he'd brought his horn. Way up here, he could play as loud as he wanted and no one would tell him to shut up or not to make that new music. He smiled as he put his lips against the brass mouthpiece, the one moment of ease and joy he'd felt in all this turmoil. Gliding along through the sky, Max let out a long and beautiful song, gave voice to the very saddest parts of his soul.

He was somewhere over the Tumbled Together Towers when he realized he wasn't alone. Iguanagulls. Lots of them. He sputtered, almost choking on his own saliva, and then calmed himself. They weren't attacking. In fact, they were looking rather comely, soaring along on either side of him, their squinty little eyes peering in his direction. *They tear apart ships with those claws*, Max reminded himself. *Don't get too comfortable.*

Still, the great flying monsters just kept pace with him, flapping occasionally against the autumn wind. Max put the horn back up to his lips and returned to his song. Maybe he was crazy, but it seemed almost like the iguanagulls were responding to him. He upped the tempo a little, broke into a sweet little boogie. At first nothing changed. Then one of the iguanagulls surged ahead. Another followed. They looped around each other and dove off to either side. A few more rushed forward, and soon the whole flock of them was spinning and diving in frenzied circles.

Amazing, Max thought. He'd already figured they liked the music; why else would they keep showing up? But this—this was something else all together. Max slowed the song down again, and the flock triangulated around him. He took the horn away from his mouth just long enough to let out a great big belly laugh and then shot off through the night sky, surrounded by a growing flock of ferocious new friends.

PART THREE

INTERGALACTIC STAR GUARD CONGLOMERATE

Realm: Milky Way
Sector: 12A-14079
Planet: Earth
Region: Flood City

From: Regional Commander
Bartrum Uk, Earth Forces
To: Earth Forces/All

Esteemed Co-Commanders:

To my loyal Star Guardians! Peacekeepers, battalion heads, administrative cogs, and various bureaucrats and secretaries! The time has come. RC Command Order 47589-22 is in full effect as of today at sunrise, Flood City time. You may begin immediately.

Please do not hit reply all when replying to this message.

Magnanimously,
RC Uk

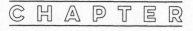

Ato was staring at the holodeck with his mouth hanging open. "Are they serious?"

"What?" Max called from the other room.

"The Star Guard. They're . . . they're . . ." Ato flailed his arms around for an explanation. "Get in here!"

Bartrum Uk hovered over the holodeck. The words *Regional Commander, Earth Forces, Interglalatic Star Guard Conglomerate* circled around him.

"That's the guy my sister was talking about at the training camp!" Max yelled, walking in. "The one Djinna made the holo of. He's a real iguanagull turd."

Ato swatted at him. "Shh! Listen."

". . . in regards to this unfortunate situation with the Flood City Rebel Guerrilla Squad," the commander croaked, "we are forced into a position that no one likes being in. Of course, we have limited resources, particularly in regard to our rescue mission on Flood City . . ."

"Drives me nuts that they're still calling it a rescue mission after all this time," Max growled.

". . . and a population that harbors resentments to the point of self-delusion toward the Guard . . ."

"Uh-oh," Ato muttered. "This is the way they talk on the base fleet when they're about to really drop a hammer on someone."

". . . which in consequence leaves us no other choice"—Bartrum Uk paused and then smiled sadly—"but to cease all food supplies to Flood City . . ."

"WHAT?" Max and Ato yelled.

". . . in order to divert resources to our hunt for the participants in this ragtag gang of terror plotters and saboteurs. Most notably, their leader, one Rodolfo Cortinas, is still at large and has been since the unfortunate incident at the Flood City Day pageant two weeks ago. Until the time that he and his inner circle can be brought to justice, food rations will cease entirely." Uk cast a sorrowful gaze downward and shook his head. "It is a terrible situation, I'm afraid. Just terrible."

"This is . . ."

"Perhaps a noble leader of the Flood City community will take a stand for his or her brethren and turn in these foul schemers. Otherwise, I fear the rations ban may go on"—he paused again—"indefinitely."

Max kicked the holodeck off and the staticky figure blipped out of existence. "This is ridiculous!"

Ato nodded.

"It's . . . tyranny! Injustice!" Max said, pulling his jetboots on. "Our stored food might last us, I dunno, a few weeks. Maybe a month or two. And as long as Tecla's water filtration machine holds out, we'll have that, but . . . they're leaving us to die."

"Man!" Ato followed suit. "Where we going?"

Max stopped and looked at his friend. "Well, we're gonna go do something about it, obviously!"

"What?"

"I have no idea." Max took a running jump off the balcony and jetted into the sky.

All over Flood City, people were pouring out onto the streets, shouting their complaints to one another or no one in particular. A spontaneous throng of protestors spilled into the plaza. People jetbooted in tight angry circles, passing along information and gripes, their eyes darting around for any sign of the Star Guard.

"Wow!" Ato said as they jetted into the center of the plaza. He felt like he was standing in the nucleus of a giant, furious atom and a thousand protons and electrons were swarming around him waiting to explode. "Seems like something's about to happen, doesn't it?"

Max just nodded. He hadn't had a clear thought in his head since Bartrum Uk had said they were cutting the food rations. All he could think about were people he knew and loved starving to death, one by one. When he closed his eyes, he saw his mom's face growing thin and empty with hunger. Without land there was no way to plant crops. The only animals worth bothering with were the iguanagulls, and there was nowhere near enough of them to feed all of Flood City. And of course, the Star Guard had already considered all these facts and were using them to their advantage.

Each angry beat of his heart thumped a mini-earthquake through his brain. He could barely see straight. The Star Guard ruined everything. And what they didn't ruin, the Chemical Barons did. And now they were doing it together. He realized he was clenching his fists and made a conscious effort to relax them, which lasted all of twenty seconds and then they were tightly balled again.

"Max?" It was Ato, trying to be the calm voice of reason.

"What?"

"You alright?"

Max shook his head. "No."

There was a commotion at the edge of the plaza. Max and Ato both whirled around to see a Star Guard convoy ship ignite its liftoff engines. "It's the last food supply ship!" someone yelled.

It probably wasn't true—the last supply ship had surely left hours ago—but no one seemed to care. The crowd surged toward the ship as one.

"Max," Ato whispered. "What're we doing?"

They were caught up in the momentum of the crowd, flushing forward almost against their will. Max shrugged. "We're being angry."

"But . . . but . . ."

An explosion erupted along the side of the convoy ship. The crowd stopped short. No one seemed to know where the blast had come from. A hatch opened and one of the Star Guards poked his head out. He had one of those headsets on that they used to broadcast announcements of the food delivery, so his voice boomed across the plaza: "Back off, Flood City rebels! We don't have your food! We're under orders to evacuate and evacuate we will, even if we have to shoot our way out!"

The laser cannons emerged all around the ship and whirled toward the crowd. People yelled in protest and took some anxious steps back.

"That will be difficult," boomed another voice. "Since I've disabled your laser cannons."

The snell glanced from side to side. "Who's that?" His voice crackled out. "Show yourself!"

"Happily" came the response, and Cortinas jetted out of the tunnel and directly toward the disabled ship. He wore a headset that he'd obviously ganked from a Star Guard trooper, and a very mischievous smile. "Now, if you don't mind lending me your ship, we can negotiate the terms of your surrender."

A wild cheer went up from the crowd.

THE FLOOD CITY GAZETTE

CITIZENS!! GATHER TODAY AT CENTRAL PLAZA! THE STAR GUARD IS ABANDONING FLOOD CITY! A NEW ERA IS UPON US! JOIN US TO FORGE THE FUTURE FROM THE ASHES OF THE PAST. IT'S A BRAND-NEW DAY!!

NOTE:
THIS MEDIUM HAS BEEN LIBERATED FROM THE STAR GUARD HAPPY JACKALS WHO SUBJECTED US TO THEIR BAD PUNS AND GOOFY BANTER FOR FAR TOO LONG. THE REGULAR *FLOOD CITY GAZETTE* WILL RESUME BUT BE LESS ANNOYING, WE PROMISE. ONCE WE FIGURE OUT HOW TO UNDO ALL THESE SETTINGS, ANYWAY.
AND TAKE OFF CAPS LOCK. AYO.

RATIONS REPORT

NO MORE RATIONS!!!!! UH . . . WE GOTTA FIGURE ALL THAT OUT TOO.

THE DAILY TIDE

NO DAILY TIDE TODAY.
FREEDOM!!! ALL DAY!!!!

Please *avoid the city edges during high tide, as conditions can worsen suddenly.*

IGUANAGULL AHOY!
IGUANAGULLS ARE HAPPY THE STAR GUARD IS GONE TOO!! AYYYYY!!!

THE BOOO'CAST

NO COMMENT.

THE VAPORS & ABANDONED OCEAN LINER REPORT

MAN, LISTEN.

CHEMICAL BARONS

THAT JACKED-UP CLOUD CRUISER STILL LYING IN THE RUBBLE, Y'ALL.

"What does this mean?" Ato asked.

Max could barely hear him over the cheering crowd. "It means we're fighting back."

"Against the Star Guard or the Chemical Barons?"

"Whichever comes for us, I guess." Max shrugged. "Maybe both! Let's see if we can talk to Old Man Cortinas." They elbowed their way up to the edge of the transporter. A group of Flood City rebels was escorting the giant away. Cortinas stood on top of the ship, consulting in hushed tones with a few of his lieutenants. Max and Ato waited until they'd all zipped off on their missions and then approached the old warrior.

"Ah, Max!" Cortinas grinned and put a firm hand on Max's shoulder. "How are you, son?"

"Mr. Cortinas, what's going on?"

"Our plan is working; the ration ban is only the beginning. Soon the Star Guard will evacuate completely."

Max was horrified. "That was the plan? But . . ."

Cortinas looked down at him solemnly. "Of course it was the plan, Max. What did you think? Aggravate the Star Guard until they get off our backs and pull out of Flood City once and for all."

"But what'll we do without the rations?"

"We'll find a way, Max. We always do. We're survivors. But one thing you can be sure of, we'll never figure out how to do it ourselves as long as those big blue clowns are hand-feeding us pasty basura day in and day out. Something had to give."

"What about the Ba—?"

"So many questions, Max." Cortinas waved his arm out over the thundering crowd. It seemed suddenly like all of Flood City had poured into the central plaza. Max saw Sebastian and Dr. Niska. There was Mr. Essner from school, and beside him stood Mr. Sanpedro. Most of the kids Max knew were swarming toward the center of the crowd. It was exhilarating and terrifying all at once. "Things unraveled more quickly than we thought," Cortinas said. "And I have to disappear again."

"But . . ."

"I'll be back though. We're gathering strength. Preparing for different disasters. Don't worry. Just keep at it."

"But, Mr. Cortinas, the Barons have—"

"I want to give you these," Cortinas said. He handed Max two thick cylinders with straps and handles.

Max's eyes got wide. "Shiolyders? But Mr. Cortinas, I'm only a kid."

"Yes, I know, son. But these are dangerous times. The population of Flood City must be ready to defend itself at a moment's notice! What if the Chemical Barons were to descend once again from the sky?"

"Yeah, about that . . ."

"We wouldn't have time to go house to house, arming the citizenry. No, we must be prepared. The shiolyder is a powerful weapon. It can shoot a pressure blast strong enough to crush every bone in the human body. Enough hits from it can take down even the largest Star Guard transporter ship, as long as you power it up all the way. Give one to your friend. The other to your mom if you want. But don't be caught out here without something to defend yourself."

"I don't even know how . . ."

"You'll figure it out, Max."

"Cortinas! Wait!"

But the old rebel had already jetbooted into the sky with a wild chuckle.

Max looked at the weapons. They were about the size of his forearm and made from some heavy-duty metal Max had never felt before. Surely from the steel mines of the Jupiter moons or something. Maybe they were even Star Guard weapons that the rebels had liberated for their own uses. And now they were Max's. The shiolyders seemed awkward in his hands, and the fact that they could inflict so much damage on a person, kill someone, made it even worse. He stuffed them in his satchel, wrapped a sweatshirt around the top ends, and then turned to Ato. "What's wrong?"

Ato was staring into the crowd with a look of absolute terror on his face. "Nothing. Let's get out of here."

"Right. Tell me another one." Max followed his friend's gaze to the face of a tall, middle-aged man who seemed to tower over the crowd. The man was glaring at Ato, his eyebrows arched. Then he smiled in a way that made Max shudder inside. It was a smile that said *I'm coming to get you.*

CHAPTER

47

Djinna found her father crouched over one of his computers, tapping away as if his life depended on it.

"Dad?"

"Just a sec, my dear," Dr. Maceo said. His eyes stayed fixed on the dancing numbers that blipped to life in the air just in front of him. "One . . . more . . . second." He tapped a few more keys and then sat back. The little glowing numbers congealed into a cylinder that spun several times around and then exploded back into a chaos of digits.

"Whatchyou doing, Dad?"

Dr. Maceo stood up and stretched his long arms over his head. "Trying to prepare for the collapse of the holonet."

"You think the whole net will collapse now that the Star Guard is pulling out?"

"Probably in the next few days. Either way, it's high time we have our own system. I've been preparing over the years just in case, and hopefully the ghost net I planted beneath the Star Guard one will be able to go live once they strike theirs. Hopefully."

Djinna looked at the numbers hovering over the holodeck. Each one had a little scratchy version of itself glimmering beside it like a tiny shadow. "That's your ghost network?"

"Indeed," Dr. Maceo said.

Djinna scooched past her dad and sat in his chair, still staring at the swirling numbers. "You reconfigured the net addresses to our server."

Dr. Maceo nodded, smiling.

"And you concealed the secondary network with a firewall so that if the Star Guard detected it they would just think it was a stray fragment of their own."

"Mm-hmm."

"Have you tested it?"

Dr. Maceo turned his daughter's chair so it faced the glowing holomap of Flood City. It was slightly dimmer than usual and flickered occasionally with little jolts of static. "That's from the ghost network?" Djinna jumped out of her chair and hurried over to it. "Daddy, it's nearly perfect!"

Dr. Maceo beamed. "Well . . ."

"So Flood City now has it's own fully functional holonet."

"Well, for the most part . . . We'll have to see how it holds up when—"

"Daddy, you're brilliant!"

Djinna wrapped her arms around her dad and squeezed him as hard as she could. "It's amazing!"

A blip-blip noise from the holodeck announced an incoming call, and Dr. Maceo untangled himself from his daughter's embrace to see who it was.

"Djinna?" Max's 3-D form blipped into the air. "You there? Oh! Hey, Dr. Maceo."

"Hello, Max. You staying safe and inside in the midst of all that chaos out there?"

"Mostly, sir. Is, uh, Djinna around?"

"Hey, Max!" Djinna stood in front of the holocam and smiled.

"Hey, Djinna." Max looked like he wasn't sure what to do with his body. "We, um . . . me and Ato . . . need your help with something."

"What?"

"It's about what we talked about . . ."

Dr. Maceo poked his head back in front of the holocam. "Max, I'm sure you don't think Djinna will be leaving the house with all the danger going on in the street."

"Well, sir, the thing is . . ."

"You mean," Djinna said, "the thing we talked about in rehearsal? The *thing* thing?"

"Uh-huh."

Dr. Maceo looked at his daughter. "Djinna, please don't tell me that . . ."

"I'll meet you at your house in twenty minutes," Djinna said. She hit the hang-up button just as Dr. Maceo was opening his mouth to object. "Dad," Djinna said, "I can't explain this, but I have to go. It's really important." She started toward the door.

"Djinna," Dr. Maceo said. She stopped. "The Star Guard is up to no good. There's who-knows-what kind of chaos breaking out in the streets. I can show you the footage if you want; it's not pretty. Things are being destroyed. Star Guard ships burnt up. It is chaos, my girl. There's no telling what could happen. On top of that, if the Star Guard do eventually pull out, the Barons could launch a full-on attack at any second!"

"I know," Djinna said quietly. "I'm scared too. And that's why I have to go. I don't want to grow up being scared. I want to do something about it. Even if it . . ." Her voice trailed off, and they looked at each other for a moment. "You taught me that, Daddy. To fight for a better world."

"I do worry about you," Dr. Maceo said. "But I am also proud of you."

They hugged, and then Djinna headed for the door.

"Make sure you let me know if you need any help from your old man," Dr. Maceo called after her. "I still have a few tricks up these old sleeves, you know."

"So who was that dude?" Max asked. They were jetting along a windy passageway toward the docks.

"No one," Ato said. He kept looking behind him.

Max stopped, set his boots to hover, and waited for Ato to turn around.

"What?" Ato said.

"Tell me what's going on, Ato. I know you don't like talking about the Barons—you never even told me you had a twin brother till he showed up and tried to zap me—but there's obviously something that's got you terrified. What's the deal?"

Ato sighed. "I'd been hoping he was dead."

"Who?"

"Mephim."

"The tall creepy guy that just gave you the murder face stink eye of death?"

Ato nodded. "But of course he's not dead. That would be too easy."

"Who is he?"

They fell back into a slow glide toward the ocean. "He's the Chemical ArchBaron that was in charge of the secret mission to attack Flood City. He's very powerful in the whole political food chain up on the base fleet. Taught me and my brother almost everything we know about fighting and flying and all that. He was the one trying to nuke everybody the night of the attack!"

"Great."

"And . . ."

"What?"

"I don't know how to explain it. He has some kinda magic thing going on."

"Magic?"

Ato looked agitated. "He's . . . I think he's a sorcerer of some kind. There's rumors; it's not spoken of much, but there's whispers that once upon a time, generations ago, the Chemical Barons were sorcerers. They dealt in magic—could transform themselves and go invisible and all kinds of other things."

"Whoa."

"Uh-huh. And Mephim, well . . . I don't know really. It's just, the day of the attack, he got his hands on this iguanagull that had infiltrated our ship, right, and he . . . well, he tore its head off with one quick rip, and I think he . . . kept it."

"He kept an iguanagull head? Ugh!"

They swooped out of the alleyway a little closer to the Electric Ghost Yard than Max had planned and both stopped short. The crackling blue lights erupted all across the mesh of burnt-out wiring and charred spaceship hulls. Max shuddered. All the excitement of the day evaporated between Ato's creepy sorcerer stories and the memory of those flashing phantoms. "Let's go another way."

Ato agreed and they doubled back into the alley. "I think," Ato said, "he wanted to perform some kind of magic with it, but I never found out cuz then came the attack and then we crashed and that was that."

"What kind of magic?"

"I have no idea, Max."

"Well," Max started to say, but then he stopped because something slammed against his back and he found himself hurtling toward a wall at Mach 10. "Baaaaaaaaah!"

He jerked to a sudden stop, his face inches from the rough concrete, and heard a familiar voice giggling in his ear. "Djinna!" Max yelled, shrugging her off his back and spinning around. "What the—?"

Djinna tried to contain her laughter. "You gotta stay on guard, man! These are troubled times."

"You're awfully chipper considering we're all about to starve to death."

Djinna shrugged. "I know. I don't know what's come over me, I just . . . We've always been so afraid of what would happen if the Star Guard stopped supporting us. And now they're gonna be gone and it's terrible, I know, but I'm thrilled too. I mean, yes, we might not find a way to get food. And of course there's that little issue of the rogue Chemical Barons and their nuke to deal with, but hey! We're alive! And pretty soon, we're gonna be free!"

"If we're not annihilated in a nuclear meltdown."

"Right! But still . . . exciting times!"

Ato zipped over to them. "What are you so happy about?"

"She's in blissful denial," Max said, shrugging, "and has managed to forget that we live on a concrete slab surrounded by poisoned water with no possible means to grow our own food whatsoever."

"Oh!" Ato slapped his forehead. "I completely forgot!"

Djinna and Max raised their eyebrows at him.

"The iguanagull!"

Max rolled his eyes and made a get-on-with-it gesture.

"The one Mephim beheaded."

"What about it?" Max demanded.

"Wait," Djinna said, holding up her hands. "Who's Mephim and why is he beheading iguanagulls?" She didn't look nearly so excited anymore.

"Some wild magic ArchBaron that ran the attack mission Ato came in on and for some reason has a thing for tearing animals to pieces," Max explained. "Okay, what about the iguanagull, man?"

"I retrieved the headless corpse out of the ship's refuse chute just before it was ejected, you know, so I could do an autopsy."

Djinna shook her head. "Your friend is weird, Max."

"I know. You get used to it."

Ato ignored them. "And those razor-sharp claws? They scoop

like little scythes and have a kind of hollow area in the middle, like a mini-canyon."

"And?" Max and Djinna said together.

"There was soil in there."

"You mean like dirt or engine crud?" Djinna suggested.

"No, I mean soil."

"Soil soil?" Max said.

Ato sighed. "The kind of soil that things grow in."

"But that's impossible!" Max blurted out. "There's no soil any-where! Where would there be soil? It's not . . . it's . . ." He followed Djinna and Ato's gaze out to the faraway line where the ocean met the sky. "Oh. But how . . . ?"

"I don't know," Ato said.

"We could be self-sustaining," Djinna whispered.

Max nodded. The ocean seemed to go on forever and ever, but maybe not. "We wouldn't need the Star Guard to survive."

"I'm sorry to break up the fantasy," Ato said. "But there's still the small matter of the Star Guard probably being about to aban-don a nuclear warhead in the middle of Flood City where the Barons can snatch it."

"I know," Max said. He kept his gaze set on the endless ocean. "I just wish Yala was here to help us out. She always knows how to do stuff like this."

"Right, stuff like this." Djinna rolled her eyes. "Cuz stuff like this happens all the time."

"What about the bird?" Ato said.

Max raised an eyebrow at him. "Huh?"

"Krestlefax?" Djinna said. "That's actually not a bad idea, Ato. You could send Yala a message. It's worth a try, anyway."

Long shot though it was, the thought of seeing Yala gave Max a momentary rush of joyfulness. "Is he at your tower?"

"He comes and goes, but maybe. Let's see if he's in the cupola."

The neighborhoods of Flood City rose and fell like still waves around the holographer's tower. Up above, the sky painted itself in brilliant swaths of orange and purple. The sun had already dipped into a cloud bank just above the far horizon.

Djinna hoisted herself up onto the slanted roof and made her way toward the one open window with alarming speed.

"How does she do that?" Ato gaped. "She's not even wearing jetboots."

Max shrugged. "She grew up in this tower. Been climbing it all her life."

"He's here!" Djinna yelled. "Come up!"

"Ugh," Max muttered. "I knew she was gonna do that. Can't the dang thing fly down here?"

"Stop complaining." Ato laughed. "We don't have much time."

The uppermost section of the tower was a drafty stone room. Djinna stood in the middle, staring up into the shadows of the cupola.

"Max," she whispered. "Scribble a note or something about what we're doing!"

"Is he sleeping?"

"What? No."

"Then why are we whispering?"

"Because . . . Just do it, please."

Max took a music notebook from his courier bag and tore out a scrap of paper.

Yala,

We're in trouble. The Star Guard's pulling out of Flood City, taking our food rations with them. People are going wild in the street and an ArchBaron from the crashed cloud cruiser named Mephim is trying to nuke the whole planet!! If you can get out of that horrible training camp, come back. We need your help.

—Max

He nodded at Djinna, who craned her neck and whispered: "Krestlefax!"

Something shifted in the darkness above them and then the ancient bird spread its wings and alighted in a flurry of feathers. It cocked its head to one side, regarding the three friends with an intelligent eye, and then lifted up one foot and put it back down.

"We need your help. We need you to take a message to Max's sister, Yala."

Krestlefax tipped his head to the other side, which could easily have meant yes, no, or nothing at all.

"Would you bring her this letter?" Djinna said. She stepped forward and held Max's note out to the magnificent bird. Krestlefax regarded her for a few seconds without moving. Max wondered if he was somehow weighing the honesty of her soul or something. Then the bird reached his beak out, plucked the note gingerly from Djinna's hand, and placed it in his own claw. He flapped those huge wings a few times and made some short jumps and then leapt into the air and swooped out through the window.

"Well," Djinna said once they'd climbed back down. "All we can do is hope she gets it in time."

It was coming. Any second now. ArchBaron Mephim stood at the window, his tall form just a shadowy silhouette from the outside. The streets were dark and mostly deserted, but something out there was brewing and gathering like a hurricane. Mephim could feel the excitement move through him like all the platelets in his blood were jittering and frothing. Soon, the call would come in. Then, as long as things continued to move along the vast network of outcomes he saw when he closed his eyes, it would be time to strike. A vibrating buzz erupted from the bedside table where Mephim had placed the portable holodeck. He smiled as the blue alert light flashed across the dark room.

Mephim walked slowly over to the holodeck and flipped it open.

"Good evening, ArchBaron," said the flickering image of Regional Commander Bartrum Uk. "Everything is in place. You may proceed."

Tonight was the night. Effie could tell by the sudden silence that had fallen over the men in her house. They were only this quiet when they were planning something. From the other room, she heard the clicks and hums of weapons being cleaned and prepared for battle. Soon they would come in and send her and Dante to wherever it was that they'd sent the rest of her family. She wondered if it would hurt, if it would last long or just be sudden nothingness in a flash of light. She tried to calm herself, for Dante's sake if not her own, but each breath came faster than the one before it and her tummy was tangling itself into a fist of knots.

"Shhh," Dante said. Effie hadn't realized she was whimpering. "Stay as quiet as you can and come close to me."

She made a conscious effort to stop trembling and crossed the room to her older brother. Dante sat in his favorite stool and held so perfectly still, with his eyes closed, that if he hadn't just spoken she would've assumed he was asleep. She had a million questions to ask him and mostly she wanted to burst into tears and sob on his shoulder, but he'd asked her to be quiet and she was resolved to do everything she could to concede. Dante had never asked her to do anything before.

Any second now. They would send one. The door would open. The coward would keep his distance best he could. He would want to get it over with. Dante could hear the determined frenzy in all their movements. They were getting ready for something big and they didn't have much time to do it in. Surely they wouldn't send the Quiet One. He would be too busy taking care of last-minute preparations to bother with such a menial execution. They would send one of the henchmen, someone low in the hierarchy. After all, who wanted to murder a little girl and a blind kid? That was the point of moving up in the world, so you didn't have to do messy things like that. Leave it to some sloppy fool, right?

Dante hoped he was right.

THE FLOOD CITY GAZETTE

CITIZENS!! WE BEGIN A NEW ERA OF FLOOD CITY HISTORY. ONE OF FREEDOM. ONE OF LIBERTY. ONE OF INDEPENDENCE FROM THE CORRUPT AND POWER-HUNGRY STAR GUARD!

SPEAKING OF HUNGER . . .

IT'S ESTIMATED THAT THE RATION PACKS WE LIBERATED FROM THE DEPARTING ISGC VESSELS WILL KEEP US SUPPLIED FOR APPROXIMATELY THREE MORE MONTHS, EVEN WITH A CAREFUL RATIONING SYSTEM IN PLACE. AS A CITY WE MUST STEP UP AND DEVISE NEW AND INGENIOUS SURVIVAL TACTICS, INCLUDING HOW TO MASS-PRODUCE NUTRIENT-RICH CONSUMABLES, AKA FOOD. AS SUCH, THE FLOOD CITY REBEL GUERRILLA SQUAD AND THE FOUNDERS' COMMITTEE ARE HOSTING A FOOD CREATION CONTEST. ALL CITIZENS ARE ENCOURAGED TO SUBMIT THEIR IDEAS! THE WINNER WILL RECEIVE A LIFETIME OF FREE FOOD!! HA, JK . . . KINDA. A SUITABLE PRIZE WILL BE ANNOUNCED IN THE COMING DAYS!

RATIONS REPORT

SEE ABOVE.

THE DAILY TIDE

NO DAILY TIDE TODAY.

FREEDOM!!!

Please *avoid the city edges during high tide, as conditions can worsen suddenly.*

IGUANAGULL AHOY!

IGUANAGULLS BEEN OUT AND ABOUT THESE DAYS, FOLKS REPORTING. KEEP AN EYE OUT FOR 'EM.

THE BOOO'CAST

NO COMMENT.

THE VAPORS & ABANDONED OCEAN LINER REPORT

THEY STILL WEIRD.

CHEMICAL BARONS

NO NEW ACTIVITY REPORTED FROM THE BARONS, BUT WE BELIEVE THEY ARE STILL HOLED UP IN THE CITY SOMEWHERE. YOU SEE ONE, JACK HIM UP FIRST, ASK QUESTIONS LATER.

"Okay," Djinna said. "So the Barons have a nuke and they want to use it on Flood City. Why?"

Ato grumbled inside himself. It wasn't his favorite topic to cover, especially when Djinna was involved. But he also knew that discomfort was exactly what he had to face most of all, what had kept him quiet this long. And that keeping quiet was the one thing he couldn't do anymore. It had almost gotten them all killed already and might still, depending on how things played out. "Because all the Barons want to do is get back to Earth."

Djinna opened a bag of dougies and started eating one. They were in the kitchen of the holographer's tower. Djinna had scooted up onto the counter, and Max and Ato were at the table. "Mmkay, but Earth is covered in water," Djinna said. "That's why they left us all here to die in the first place, from what I hear."

Ato decided to ignore her sarcasm. "Right, and the Barons think that somehow the key to getting rid of the water is on Flood City."

"So they're gonna decimate it? That makes sense."

"No, it doesn't, Djinna, I'm just saying that's what they think. The Barons are sick and tired of space—"

"How terrible for them."

"And they'll do anything to find a way back to Earth. Somehow, the higher-up Barons got it in their heads that Flood City holds the secret to their return. That's why we were doing the exploratory mission."

"Nice exploring method."

Ato rubbed his eyes. "Well, we—I didn't know it was gonna go like that! Otherwise I wouldn't've gone! And it's not like I had much of a choice anyway!"

"Alright, guys," Max said. "We need to be figuring out what to do, not arguing about what happened."

Djinna took another bite of dougie and gazed out the window. "And what I'm saying is, in order to figure out what to do, we also gotta understand what happened. Even if it makes certain people uncomfortable."

Ato looked like he was trying to swallow a brick for a few seconds and then calmed down. "Djinna's right. I'm . . . sorry. What I was trying to say was . . . they want to be able to explore Flood City without having to deal with the actual people who live here. Thus, the bomb. I think Mephim and the others will be plotting a way to get far enough away from Flood City to nuke it without getting nuked themselves."

"Great," Max said. "All they need is to mug someone and gank their jetboots and we're toast."

"I don't think that'd do it," Djinna said. "Jetboots'll get you high enough, but then what? It'll take a while for the dust and fallout to settle before the place is inhabitable again, and there's no way they could wait it out on jetboots."

"She's right," said Ato. "That's probably the only reason they haven't done it yet. My bet is they're banking on the cruiser."

Djinna made a face. "The one that nose-dived into an apartment building? Good luck with that. Yala and the rebels put a hole in the hull. That thing won't fly again."

"No," Ato said, blinking as the realization dawned. "The cruiser won't, but the escape pods might."

"There's escape pods?" Max gaped. "Crud!"

"And if they can get to them, they take off in a group of let's say three. They shoot straight up into the air, one has the nuke and the other two run interference, and the second they make it high enough . . ."

"Pow," Djinna said. "Flood City becomes a nuclear wasteland. How high are we talking?"

"About a mile, give or take."

"So, wait," Djinna said, her arms crossed over her chest. "What's the plan?"

"Well," Ato said, "since we're still here, I guess it's safe to assume that the Star Guard hasn't already given them access through whatever creepy contact they have. So, we stake out the cloud cruiser, right? Take shifts or something, maybe set up a holocam?"

Djinna made a noncommittal growl.

"And then when the Star Guard leaves," Max said, "we get there before the Barons do, confiscate the nuke, and disable the escape pods, and then be out!"

"And if they get there *while* we're there?"

This was the part Max didn't like thinking about. "We fight 'em."

"With what?"

"With these," he said, pulling the shiolyders out of his knapsack.

"Shiolyders!" Djinna said in a half whisper, half yell.

"Cortinas gave them to me earlier. Said we had to be prepared, arm the population and whatnot."

"Do you know how to use 'em?"

Max shrugged. "Point and shoot, I guess."

Djinna rolled her eyes. "This is quite a plan."

"You got a better one?"

"A better plan to stop a bunch of trained soldiers and an evil wizard from breaking onto the crashed cloud cruiser and stealing back their nuclear weapon?" She thought for a moment. "Nope. But what if they get away, or get there before we do? We need a backup plan."

"Or ten," Ato added.

Max made a kind of gurgling sound and they both turned to look at him. "Um . . . Max?" Djinna said. "You alright?" He just stared off into nothingness. "Look, I know you're worried about the city and everything, but you gotta get with it. We need you—"

"Remember the other day?" Max snapped his head toward her, his eyes suddenly sharp and focused. "When you told me that enlarging a hologram was like the easiest thing in the world?"

"Well, I think I said it a little differently, but yeah. Why? What's going on?"

"I think," Max said calmly, "I sort of more or less have a backup plan that might stop Mephim from nuking Flood City."

Djinna and Ato stared at Max for a few seconds.

"Great," Djinna said. "Let's hear it."

CHAPTER

51

Dante could smell the fresh evening air, feel the sunset breeze coming through his bedroom window. Something was going on in the streets of Flood City—it wasn't the usual tranquil sounds of people chatting on their way home from work. Jetboots dashed past the window, voices cried out in anger and fear. Somewhere not too far away, a Star Guard transporter was taking off in a hurry. Whatever it was probably had to do with the intruders' hasty departure. They were almost done preparing now, which meant it wouldn't be long.

Dante reached out his hand till it touched Effie's little shoulder. He could feel her trembling, the poor thing, and knew she was doing everything in her power to keep from bursting into tears. The door handle turned and Dante heard someone take a deep breath. It wasn't the Quiet One. He never would've hesitated like that. The killer closed the door behind him, took one step into the room and then another.

Fear made everything seem very crisp and sharp suddenly. Dante felt like he could smell each flower growing in the little soil pot outside the window. He was aware of murmurs in the bowels of the building that he'd never noticed before, ambient groans that shifted every few seconds in tone like some endless whale call. The killer's sweat, his however-many-days-without-bathing funk, came rushing to Dante like a messenger warning of the attack.

Get stared across the room at the girl and her brother. He hadn't given them much thought up till this point. He'd felt bad for them at first. He'd been grateful that Mephim and Sak had taken care of the rest of the family. Just thinking about it still made him nauseous. He'd seen death before but always in the thick of battle: glorious deaths, sudden, horrific yes, but at least they had context and made some . . . sense. If death can ever make sense. But that family . . . Get shuddered. They'd all known before it happened, and that look of utter helplessness and desperation would haunt Get forever.

Anyway, he had to focus on the task at hand. These two had gone from objects of pity to vague nuisances as time had worn on. More mouths to feed, prisoners to be checked on. And now they were useless. Now everything pointed to a quick, clean escape, and these two being alive made that impossible. *Two quick slices*, Mephim had said, handing him the knife. *That's it.*

Get had nodded, meeting the ArchBaron's eyes with confidence. But now, staring down these two living, breathing beings, he felt all weak and pathetic. The whole thing seemed wrong. He took a step toward them. Tried to ignore the girl's whimpering and how much she reminded him of his little cousin GeeGee up on the base fleet. Then he thought about what he'd do if anyone ever hurt GeeGee. A flash of rage reared up inside him. These Flood City scumbags wanted to take over everything. To stand against the Chemical Barons. He directed his rage at the boy across the room, who couldn't be much older than he was, and took another step forward, this one with more confidence.

"Hey there," the killer said, his voice wavering just slightly. "Brought you some lunch." He was just a boy. Dante's own age, maybe younger. And he was afraid.

Dante stayed perfectly still. Effie had stopped trembling. Her breath came in quick little gasps. The killer would probably go for Dante first to get him out of the way. A few more uneven steps and he was right in front of them, panting for breath. Dante figured he was within arm's reach, but it was too risky to strike out and miss, so instead he picked up the chair he was sitting on and swung it as hard as he could. It wasn't a direct hit, no satisfying crunch that Dante had been hoping for, but he definitely caught the killer off guard and smacked his knife hand. Something heavy and metallic clanked to the ground and that was all Dante needed to hear: the killer was unarmed, at least for the moment. Dante hurled himself forward, catching a fist directly in the jaw as he threw both arms out and tackled the boy in front of him.

For a few terrible seconds, everything was a scattered chaos of scuffling and painful jabs. "Effie," Dante hissed. "The knife!" He felt the killer scramble beneath him. There were a few more moments of terror and confusion as Dante fought to control all the flailing arms and legs. Then, very suddenly, the boy on the floor stopped moving. Dante caught his breath. He was still alive. He wasn't bleeding. "Effie?"

"Yes."

"You have the knife?"

"Yes."

"Where is it?"

"Pointing into the man's neck."

The boy was still breathing. There hadn't been any horrible cutting sounds. "You didn't stab him, right?"

"Not yet."

"Okay, that's good." Dante felt his heart pounding in his head. "I'm gonna find something to tie him with. If he says anything, stab him."

"That's my plan." Effie's voice wasn't shaking anymore.

"Why, in the hologrammiest of hologram kingdoms, is this holodeck so difficult to work?" Max said.

Djinna shoved him out of the way. "Because it's a special one and does special things." She pouted her lips and started tapping away on the keypad.

"Is one of those special things making a very basic holocall from one deck to another, or is that beneath the might—"

"Yes!" Djinna said. "That is one of the many things it does, but you have to know how to work it."

"You have to be special," Ato offered.

Djinna glared at him and then went back to the keypad. "There. It's all set up for you non-special people to use. Here, gimme the number."

Max passed her the crumpled piece of paper that Biaque had handed him what seemed like forever ago. She furrowed her brow, tapped a few keys, and then stepped out of the way. Max walked up to the holodeck. "It's gonna be weird seeing a vapor on a holodeck," he announced to no one in particular, "cuz they're already kinda—" A perfectly crisp image of a vapor blipped into existence in front him. "Oh!" Max gaped. "It looks so real! This *is* a special holodeck, Djinna." Max could make out the vast hull of the ocean liner stretching out into the darkness behind the vapor.

The vapor looked nonplussed. "Os Olendak."

"What?"

"Os Olendak."

"I, uh . . . don't speak . . . vapor."

"It is my name," the image croaked, looking expectantly at Max.

"Oh! Uh . . . Maximiliano Salazar," Max said. "Nice to meet you." That part wasn't necessarily true, but it was the best he could come up with. The vapor just looked at him. "I'm, uh, looking for someone named Biaque?"

Os Olendak raised a suspicious eyebrow and squinted at Max. "Reeeeeally?"

"Uh-huh. Is he . . . home?"

Without a word, Os floated off and Max was left staring at the ruined labyrinth that was once a luxury ocean vessel.

"Max!" Biaque popped up out of nowhere. His smile seemed to go on forever. "Was wondering about you the other day."

"Hey, Biaque!"

"How's your sister, Max?"

"She's good. Well, no . . . she's not that good actually."

Biaque frowned. "Well, the Star Guard boot camp is definitely—"

"Biaque, we need your help."

Biaque's eyes narrowed and his long mouth moved all the way to one side of his face. "You're in the holographer's tower, yes?"

"Yes."

"I'll be there in six and a half minutes."

"Great. And, Biaque?"

"Yes, Max?"

"Bring your friends. All of them."

———————

Six minutes and forty-one seconds later, Max, Ato, and Djinna stood at the foot of the holographer's tower facing a floating semi-circle of vapors. There must've been hundreds of them. Max had no idea that so many even existed. Ten minutes and seventeen seconds after that, Max had explained the ins and outs of his plan. There was an odd silence as the crescent of vapors hemmed and hawed and swayed gently in the breeze. They seemed to be consulting somehow, although none of them spoke a word or even exchanged a glance.

Biaque floated out of the crowd. "It will be tricky, but we'll do it."

"Great!" Max said. "Now . . ."

"Djinna!" Dr. Maceo's voice came from somewhere overhead. "Djin— Oh my! That's a lot of vapors!" Djinna rolled her eyes. Everyone looked up at Dr. Maceo's startled face peering out from one of the tower windows. "Hello, vapors!" he yelled with a friendly wave. The vapors didn't reply.

"What is it, Dad?"

"Max's mom is on the holodeck. She wants to talk to him."

Biaque put his hand on Max's shoulder. "Go. We know what to do."

Max smiled at him. "Thanks, Biaque."

"I don't know why my dad couldn't just tell you that," Djinna grumbled as they walked up the winding tower stairwell.

"What?"

"You were standing right there! And he's all"—Djinna affected a pretty convincing imitation of her dad's accent—"'Djinna, Max's mom is on the holodeck.' You know? What's the deal? Just tell the person you're talking to."

"I guess."

"I'm not the emissary."

"Max! You're okay!" If Dr. Sarita hadn't been standing on the holodeck, you'd swear she was really there.

"Of course I'm okay, Mom! Whatsup?"

"I was just worried. There's so much going on right now. The Star Guard pulled out their last ships."

"What?"

"Commander Uk came up on the holodecks all over Flood City and said that they'd had it with the rebels and we're on our own."

Max bristled. What epic timing they had. "And they're already gone? All of them?"

"Yes, Max, that's what I've been trying to tell you! It's not safe out there right now."

The crashed cruiser, the nuke—all unprotected.

"Mom, I gotta go."

"Max, wait! Max!"

Mephim snapped shut the mini-holodeck that Bartrum Uk had given him and grinned. It was one of those true from-the-soul grins that Mephim only very rarely made, and when he did it usually made people around him stop what they were doing and edge carefully away. Everything was going just right. Better than he'd hoped. Maybe it was the power of that iguanagull working inside him, bending the universe toward his will, but somehow, things seemed to be falling perfectly into place.

Bartrum Uk was a slippery, unreliable negotiator. He was not to be trusted, that was for sure, but he seemed at least to have delivered so far. It had taken several extremely tense and risky overtures to the blasted giants before Mephim could get an audience with the Star Guard commander, and even then the guy seemed ready to throw everything away and lock him up at any given moment. Get, who Mephim had dragged along to try to give him a much-needed lesson in diplomacy, had almost blown the whole thing to pieces with his loud mouth and relentless hard-headedness. He would have to be dealt with more severely in the future, when everything settled down again.

The growl of a Star Guard transporter taking off startled Mephim from his reverie. He pulled the curtain away from the window with a long finger and craned his neck just enough to see the spaceship blast into the sky over Flood City and then zoom away. Yells of confusion, anger, and celebration came from the streets. Mephim smiled again. The moment had arrived. He let the curtain fall closed, took a long, satisfied breath in the darkness of the bedroom, and then stormed out into the kitchen to prepare for the attack.

"Are we ready?" Mephim said, looking around the room. Tog and Sak had packed up all their supplies and were standing by the door. Tamin was almost done shoving canned food into a bag. Everything seemed to be in order. Everything except . . . "Wait, where's Get?"

"He went to deal with the you-know-whos a few minutes ago," Sak said with a nod toward the hallway.

"And he's not back yet? Someone go . . ."

The roar of jetboots revving up sounded from down the hall. "Uh-oh," Sak said.

"Go find out what happened," Mephim muttered. "Now."

Sak rushed out of the room and a second later ran back in. "Take cover!" Sak yelled, throwing himself on the ground as Dante exploded into the room with little Effie clinging on to his back. Mephim lunged out of the way just in time to avoid getting smashed. Dante and Effie careened directly into the far wall. The whole building shook and some plaster flaked down from the ceiling.

"Get them!" Mephim yelled.

Dante had already swung around and was wobbling back and forth, shaking plaster off his head. "Left!" Effie screamed in his ear. "No! A little more to the right!" He turned slightly, following her commands. "There! Now go!" Dante jumped up in the air and was about to blast off when a huge weight collided against him. He hit the floor hard. Tog was on top of him and Effie, thrashing his arms and legs madly.

Dante heaved himself to one side, throwing Tog off, and then pushed down on his jetboot accelerators as hard as could. He surged forward faster than he'd expected and threw his hands over his face just before crashing into the far wall. Effie wasn't with him, he realized in a panic. There were bad guys all around, four he figured. Effie must've been flung off when he rolled to shake the one who'd tackled them. Dante scrambled to his feet. His face was burning and his whole body ached, but there wasn't time to think about that now. The guy he'd knocked over at the door was still recovering over at nine o'clock, but someone else was rushing toward him from three. Dante grabbed the first thing his hands could find, which turned out to be a small table, and swung it like a baseball bat in front of him. The impact reverberated through his whole body and the attacker groaned and collapsed.

"Effie!" She should be somewhere around midnight. Yes! That was her whimpering at eleven thirty. Her little footsteps rattled toward Dante, but there was someone else nearby. Someone tall and silent: the Quiet One. Dante could almost feel the hatred radiating from him. He barely made any noise as he swept across the room from two o'clock, making a direct course to intercept Effie. Dante leapt, pushing down on his accelerators just hard enough to jolt him toward his little sister. Flying through the air at that speed was terrifying, but he had choice. He wrapped his arms around her, felt the wind knock out of her little body as he swooped her up in his grasp, and then pivoted hard to avoid crashing headfirst into another wall.

Effie swung herself around to Dante's back. The guy from the hallway was coming from one o'clock. The guy who'd taken the table stumbled around at eight thirty. The Quiet One was . . . nowhere. Dante gulped. They had to get out of there. "Effie, the window! Quick!"

"But it's closed!"

"Doesn't matter. What time?"

"Twelve thirty!"

A sharp pain erupted across Dante's face as he lunged forward. It was the Quiet One, lashing out from wherever he was hovering, but Dante couldn't be bothered with things like pain. He pushed as hard as he could on his accelerators, wrapping one arm around his face with the elbow pointed out, felt the rush of motion, and then the shattering glass around him as he and Effie burst through the window.

Behind him, he heard the frenzied shouts of the tall one. "Tamin, Sut, jetboot up! After them! I'm heading to the ship with Sak, Tog, and Get. Destroy those two children and meet us there, or you'll pay for it with slow, horrible deaths, believe me!"

There was a smashing sound and the roar of the jetboots.

"Swing right!" Effie yelled. "Two o'clock! And then it's a clear run straight ahead."

Dante swerved hard, praying he didn't hit anything, and blasted off through the streets.

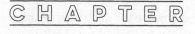

"You're all dead!" Ridge Commander Briggus hollered from his platform above the training grounds. "You hear me?" The triphenglott's hundred little appendages straightened and then erupted into a wave of squirming.

Yala rolled her eyes. It was about the eighty millionth time Brig had declared them dead, and she was beyond over it. Plus, she was lying face-first in a man-made mud puddle while stun lasers whizzed over her head. And she'd been up since daybreak and as usual had barely slept the night before.

"How can we be dead if we did everything right?" Delta whispered.

"Silence in the field!" Briggus yelled. "Dead children of Earth don't chitter-chatter."

"I wonder if dead triphenglotts do," Yala muttered.

Delta stifled laughter.

"What is this you say, Earth scum?"

Yala rolled over onto her front, careful not to get fried by a passing laser, and growled, "Shut off the stun cannons and I'll explain better."

"Ridge Commander Briggus has had just about enough of these Flood City arrogants!" Ridge Commander Briggus yelled into the sky. "We challenge!"

"I can never figure out who triphenglotts are talking about," Delta whispered.

Yala gritted her teeth. "I've had it with all of 'em."

Briggus clicked a button and the stun lasers stopped pulsing. "Let's see what this puny brown four-appendages creature has to offer in the realm of battle, yes?"

"Excuse me?" Yala said, springing to her feet. "You said what now?" She stepped through the mud toward the platform.

Delta stood up behind her. "Girl, I got your back."

"Ridge Commander Briggus said," he began, and then he screamed: "Braaagggghhh!!" A huge dark shape burst out of the sky, closed on the triphenglott in seconds, and, with a terrible caw, knocked him right off the platform.

"Krestlefax!" Yala yelled.

Briggus sprawled on the concrete, little appendages flicking frantically at the sky.

The huge bird swung in a sharp circle over the training grounds, swooped low past the mud ditch, and landed on Yala's outstretched arm. Yala still flinched a little—those claws never drew blood, but it was enough just to see the formidable creature flapping down toward her. Krestlefax had a rolled-up sheet of paper clenched in his beak. Yala took it, unrolled it, and stared blankly at it for a few seconds.

"What is it?" Delta called from the mud pit.

Everything suddenly seemed so clear. Biaque had said going to the academy was something she had to do for Flood City, not the Star Guard. That she'd be needed, and her position on the inside and training would be useful later. She just didn't think later would come so soon. Vapors really could see the future; all those whispers and myths were true. She could feel the moment arrive around her like a thunder crash. "I gotta . . . I gotta go."

It was dinnertime—Yala and Delta had been made to stay late at training—so the Star Guard Academy grounds were empty. The two girls sprinted across the open training zone and then crept along the wall of the barracks. Yala peered around the corner at the landing strip, where the Star Guard's massive transport unit stood. "It's clear," she whispered. They ran, the ocean breeze howling in their ears, reached the shadow of the transporter, and were about to lower the boarding ramp when someone yelled, "Hey!" from behind them.

Yala spun around. Commander Joola zipped toward them in her little hovercraft at the edge of the barracks. Osen lumbered along beside her, his long, thick legs sticking out at all kinds of awkward angles. Yala braced herself to fight. She didn't want to hurt Joola, but she wasn't going to be held back either.

"We just got word," Commander Joola panted. "Commander Uk has been negotiating with the Barons!"

Yala's eyes went wide. "He's what?"

Delta gasped. "I *knew* that guy was up to no good!"

"Apparently it was some top-secret back-channel thing with the survivors of the attack on the Music Hall. Even the some of higher-ups at the Star Guard Conglomerate didn't know, but others did—it's all very hazy. They're holding an emergency session to figure out what to do."

"Well, we can't wait for no emergency session," Delta blurted out. "The Barons have a nuke and they're about to use it on Flood City!"

"They what?" Joola yelled. Osen reared back, his big eyes squinting in shock.

"My brother just sent me a message," Yala said. "We can't . . . Commander, we can't sit back and let this happen."

Joola glanced up at the transporter and then back at Yala and Delta. "Ah . . ." she said as understanding took hold.

"Commander," Yala said. "I don't want to . . ."

"Cadets Salazar and Brown," Joola said, suddenly sharp and formal.

Yala cringed, her whole body tensed to fight. "Yes?" they said together.

"I cannot let you leave this base. There are proper channels to go through, and we must go through them." The snell's fingers hovered just above the stun-pistol holster on her waist, twitched once.

Yala took a step back toward the ship. "The proper channels mean my whole family and everyone I love getting killed."

"We'll put a rush on the orders to send an evacuation team."

NO. Everyone froze. The buzzing, nasally voice seemed to come from everywhere and nowhere at the same time. Slowly, all eyes landed on Osen. The tarashid leveled a withering stare at Commander Joola. *Not . . . good . . . enough.*

"I . . . You have no authority to debate me!"

Mm . . . we shall see, Osen said, and then he lumbered forward.

Joola pulled her stun-pistol. "Stop!"

Yala's eyes went wide. Now beneath the enormous hull of the ship, she took a step onto the gangplank. Delta stood beside her.

I am a medical officer, Osen muttered, clearly unimpressed with Joola's threats. *A nuclear attack on Star Guard territory means my services will be required.*

"But!" Joola yelled. "The Star Guard is evacuating Flood City!"

Even more reason, then. The tarashid stepped directly in front of Yala and Delta, blocking them from Joola. *Start the ship, cadets.*

Yala locked eyes with Joola. The snell growled, face twisted with anger. Then Yala turned and ran up the ramp to the cockpit.

The engines rumbled to life. Delta gave the all clear from the gunner port, and Yala hit the propulsars, launching them into the air. Below, Joola looked up at them, still holding the stun-pistol.

Let's move, Osen's voice warbled from somewhere nearby, and Yala blasted them out across the sky toward Flood City.

"Alright," Djinna said as she walked out of the holographer's tower and sighed. "Dad's cool with the whole thing, although he thinks it's completely ridiculous. I think he's impressed though; he got that glint in his eye and then got right down to it."

"Great," Max said. "I think."

"So we ready?" Ato asked.

They exchanged queasy glances. Tiny lights began popping on all around Flood City. The sky was dark blue with a splash of magenta at the far horizon. "You scared?" Djinna asked.

"Kinda," Max admitted.

"Yeah," Ato said.

Djinna nodded. "Me too. We probably should be—this is ridiculous."

"But I'd rather be doing *something*," Max said, "than just sitting around waiting for that Baron to obliterate us. Even if it's a ridiculous something."

"Same," Djinna and Ato said at the same time. Then they both glanced at each other in shock; it was the first time they'd ever agreed.

"Let's do it, then!" Max said, and they launched out down an alleyway. They stayed north of the Electric Ghost Yard, jetbooting along a winding succession of narrow passages. Around them, Flood City seemed to bristle with anticipation—something was about to happen and everyone could feel it. Folks skittered from doorway to doorway, watching the skies and cutting sharp glances around corners before scurrying into the shadows. A few times, Max, Djinna, and Ato stopped short as huge crowds swarmed past. Max scanned the faces for the long scowl of the Baron Ato called Mephim, but he was nowhere in sight.

"Uh-oh," Djinna said as they rounded a corner. The Music Hall loomed above them. Across from the entrance, the cloud cruiser still lay in a charred pile of rubble. It looked the same as it always had, except the top hatch hung wide open.

"Looks like we're too late," Ato whispered.

"How does it look?" Mephim snarled.

Tog Apix poked his grease-stained face out from the escape pod. "Like a mess."

Mephim opened his mouth to unravel some unutterable curse.

"However!" Tog said quickly. "I think I should be able to fix it up no problem."

"How quickly?"

"Shouldn't take long, probably just . . ." He stopped talking because Mephim's fingers were wrapped around his neck, crushing his windpipe.

"Say a number and then a say a unit of time." Something flashed in Mephim's eyes that Tog had never seen before. He wasn't sure what it was, but it definitely wasn't human. The ArchBaron was already renowned as a cold-blooded killer, but still—an even more sinister presence lurked in that furious squint now.

The pressure eased just enough for Tog to whisper, "Twenty . . ."

Mephim raised his eyebrows.

"Minutes . . ." The pressure returned.

"Don't say maybe, or probably, or hopefully. Just do it in twenty. Understood?"

Tog nodded. Mephim put him back in the pod and stormed off down the passageway to check on the others.

"Status?"

"Pretty much all set," Get said. "We just need the other two Barons to show."

"Don't worry about them. Prepare for liftoff in fifteen minutes." Mephim turned, his cape flowing around him like some nefarious cloud.

"Um, Baron?"

"Yes, Get."

"What's the plan?"

"The plan is you do exactly what I tell you, when I tell you, in the way that I tell you, or I will kill you."

"Yes, sir." Get went back to preparing his supplies and tried to ignore the growing fear inside him.

———————————

"It's so quiet all of a sudden," Djinna said.

It was kind of eerie, the sudden silence after all that chaos and running around all day.

"But not the peaceful kinda quiet," Ato muttered.

"More like the way my mom gets quiet when she's really, really pissed off," Max said.

They peered out of the narrow alleyway. The open square in front of the Music Hall was empty, not a soul about. "You really think they're already in there?" Max said.

Ato scowled. "Sure looks that way."

"Alright," Djinna said. "Here's what I think: We go in anyway. They're not expecting anyone to roll up on 'em. We enter quiet. Ato disables the escape pods while Max and I go get the nuke."

"Me?" Max said.

"Yes, you! Then if the Barons come we can give the heads up to Ato, or vice versa, then he comes up behind 'em while we're all fighting and pow! It's a trap!" Djinna had gotten pretty animated by this point and was boxing her fists against Max's shoulder.

"That's a wild plan," Max said, swatting her off. "But I'm in! You sure the holonet will work with the Star Guard evacuated and everything?"

Djinna grinned. "It just so happens that my daddy is a brilliant genius and prepared for the Star Guard evac in advance by creating a ghost holonet that is officially up and running as of earlier today."

"Nice," Ato said.

"I know. Now . . . let's move." They headed out across the open square. Scaffoldings wrapped around the front entrance of the auditorium like skeletal casts over its broken façade. The rubble had all been cleaned up and the area looked pristine in the early evening stillness.

Max watched Djinna sprint toward the cruiser. She moved like a ghost, so smooth and easy it seemed like she wasn't even touching the ground. Max sighed and hurried after her. Ato reached them a few seconds later.

"You coming?" Djinna whispered.

Max grabbed a rung and hoisted himself up. "Yep," he said, trying to keep the panting out of his voice. The top of the cruiser was dented and stained with smoke. Djinna poked her head out from one of the escape hatches and hissed at Max. Max crawled down the ladder and found himself in a cylinder-shaped tunnel. All kinds of pipes and wires snaked along the walls, forcing Max to stand a little closer to Djinna than he was quite ready for. "Which way?" he said, trying not to breathe all over her.

Djinna didn't seem to notice or mind. "Here comes Ato. Man, where the nuke at?"

"Nuke is that way," Ato said, climbing in and pointing down the corridor. "Escape pods the other way."

"Alright," Max said. "We're splitting up. You good, Ato?"

Ato nodded, but his face was creased with worry.

Djinna stepped between them. "Listen, both of you: We got this. You hear me?" She put her hand in the middle. Max put his over hers. Ato topped Max's hand. "We got this," Djinna said again.

Ato looked brighter when they let go; he even smiled a little. "The engine room is around that bend on the left. The nuke is behind a panel at the far end of the room. Access code 7785B."

"Got it," Max said, feeling a surge of wild confidence.

Ato ran off down the corridor.

Max looked at Djinna, took three clanky, echoing steps in the opposite direction, and then froze.

"What is it?" Djinna hissed.

"Someone's coming!"

"Left!" Effie yelled. "More left!"

Dante felt her little fingers dig into his shoulders. "You're gonna have to do better than that!"

"Uh . . . ten o'clock. No! Ten thirty! Ten thirty!"

The wind rushed against Dante's face. He'd managed to stop scrunching it up like he was about to crash into something and had even picked up a little speed. So far, little Effie hadn't gotten them caught or turned into paste against the side of some building.

"Good, keep going like that. But, uh"—Dante felt her little body squirm on his back as she glanced behind them—"faster!"

They'd gotten a good head start thanks to Dante's inadvertent rampage in the kitchen, but they'd also lost a fair amount of time trying to adjust. Now Effie watched in horror as two of the bad men jetted around the corner behind them. "Go!" she yelled. "Straight ahead."

They careened down a narrow throughway, one of the relatively straighter ones in Flood City. Somewhere up ahead things got a little more complicated, but at least they could make use of this clear shot while they had it. If they could get far enough ahead of the bad men then maybe, just maybe, they could duck down an unseen passage somehow and wait it out. "Just a little faster, Dante. Keep going. I know it's scary."

But Dante was somewhere else. The wind wailing in his ears, through his hair, that dizzy joy that only extreme speed could bring—it was just like he remembered it. And he thought he'd never feel it again. He could almost hear the crowd roar as he looped another time around Flood City, as he pulled into the lead, as he . . .

"WALL!" Effie yelled. "To the right, D, to the right!"

Dante adjusted a second too late; the concrete side of a building scraped along the side of his face and down his arm, sent him spinning off. Effie tightened her grip around his neck just to hold on as they whirled out of control and nearly crashed into another building. "Down, down! Up! To the . . . Yes!"

Dante shook his head against the stinging pain and found his center of gravity, easing into a low-burn hover. "I'm alright."

"You sure?"

Dante nodded. "Which way?"

"Turn. Turn. Turn. There. That way."

Dante pushed down hard on his accelerators just as the two men zoomed around the corner. "They're here, Dante!" Effie squealed. "Go! Go!"

They were closer this time. Effie could hear them panting and mumbling gruffly to each other just behind them. "A little to the left. Turn coming up ahead, right turn. One o'clock. One thirty. Two o'clock . . . turn!"

Dante veered hard to his right, nearly scraping another wall, and then evened out. "Nice!" Effie yelled. "Oh no!"

Dante flinched and slowed his burners but they didn't hit any walls. He felt Effie jerk violently. "They're alongside of us, D! They're grabbing me!" Dante veered hard to his right, directly into the attacker, and felt the bulky man swing off-balance. He grunted as several blows landed on his head and back but kept pushing to the side. Eventually there had to be a wall. He would just keep pushing till he . . . with a sudden impact, the man groaned and went limp against Dante.

"You got him," Effie said. Dante swerved back out into the center, listening to the man slide down the wall into the pit below.

"He dead?" Dante asked.

"Just hurt, I think."

"Okay."

"But the other one's close on us, D. We better go."

Dante nodded. He didn't know how much longer he could last without smashing into a wall. From the sound of those approaching jetboots, the Baron was only a few feet away and gaining fast. Plus he had the advantage of not having a little girl strapped to his back. Also, he could see.

"Right!" Effie screamed into his ear, and Dante rounded a corner, barely missing another wall. Suddenly a thick hand wrapped around his left ankle. He yelled and tried to kick at it with his right foot, but his weight was all messed up from the sudden shift in balance.

"Effie, can you pry his fingers loose?"

Effie glanced over her shoulder, saw the angry eyes glaring back at her, and then almost lost her grip when a flash of light burst out of nowhere and enveloped the man holding her brother's leg.

"What happened?" Dante asked, slowing down.

"The man," Effie said. "He blew up."

"Hello, young ones." An old man with a thick mustache and big wrinkly smile jetted out from a trash-strewn corner. He carried a long weapon of some kind over his shoulder. "Comandante Cortinas of the Flood City Rebel Guerrilla Squad at your service. You want to tell me why that angry man was chasing you?"

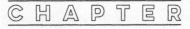

57

"What should we do?" Max whispered.

"We could go the other way," Djinna said, but she looked doubtful. "Do you think they already know we're here?"

"Probably, we were making enough noise."

"There's a turnoff up there, looks like it leads to another corridor. We could try and make it."

The steps suddenly broke into a run. Max saw a shadow stretching toward them along the dimly lit piping. A short, older man with thick sideburns appeared around the corner. He had been scowling, but when he saw Max and Djinna, his mouth dropped open and his eyes got wide. For a second, the three of them just stared at one another across the corridor. Then the man turned around and ran. "Intruders!" he yelled. "Launch the pods!" His words echoed up and down the hallway.

Max and Djinna looked at each other. They had come to the crashed cruiser to stop the Barons from nuking Flood City. The impending destruction of everything Max loved in the world was enough to wipe away almost all sense of caution from his mind. That, plus he was staring into Djinna's eyes and they seemed to be on fire with the thrill of adventure. Then she actually smiled, a wicked, confident grin—something akin to the one she'd given when Max had first broken out into the wild horn solo. Max turned down the hall, jumped up into the air, and launched after the man in a fiery burst of jetboot flame.

———————

Tog's voice was scratchy over the intercom. "ArchBaron Mephim!"

"What is it, Apix?"

"Someone's on the ship, Baron!" He had to pause to catch his breath. "Someone's—" There was an explosion of static. Tog could be heard yelling on the other end of the line and then it got very quiet.

Mephim turned to Get and Sak. "Get to your pods. We leave now." He didn't yell, but there was enough threat and authority in his voice for Get to jump into his pod without another word.

"Are you sure they're ready to . . . ?" Sak started to say. Mephim shot him a look and he shut up and disappeared into the hatch.

———————

"Now what do we do?" Djinna said.

They'd caught the guy off guard and it had been easier than either of them had expected to take him down. He'd fought back a little, but eventually Max had pinned each arm down, and after a little squirming the Baron had realized there was no escape.

"We gotta get to those escape pods," Max said.

"Obviously. But I mean, what are we gonna do with him?"

"Just get off me," Tog moaned. "I'll be good."

"You shut up," Djinna snapped. "How 'bout you stay here with this dude and I go see about the nuke?"

"Alone?"

"What—you don't think I can go at it alone cuz I'm a girl?"

Max stood up. "I didn't say that, Djinna!"

"You implied it."

"No, what I meant was—"

Tog stumbled to his feet and swung a haphazard fist toward Max. Djinna was there before Max could react. She intercepted Tog's punch with one hand and then spun her whole body around and dropped him with a swift kick to the head. Tog lay in a crumpled heap at her feet.

Max looked at Djinna with awe in his eyes. "Wow."

"We don't have time for all that, Max. C'mon."

A dim red light glowed in the engine room. Pipes and air ducts crisscrossed the walls around a massive control panel. About a billion little screens glared above it, most of them full of numbers and diagrams of the ship.

"There!" Djinna said, pointing to the far wall. "Oh no!"

The little cove in the wall was open. The nuke was gone.

The escape pod hangar was deserted. Tog Apix's tools lay scattered around the floor, along with some greasy rags and a can of engine fuel. He'd left in a hurry, probably to get some supplies. Which meant he'd be back any minute, along with whatever Barons were still alive. And Mephim . . .

Ato bolted out of the corridor, stepped around the tools, and jumped headfirst into one of the three escape pods. Inside, the cushiony seat took up most of the cramped space. Two control sticks poked up from the floor in front of it, and a screen displayed the horizon line within a series of circles. If he could destroy the control sticks, the pod would be . . . A door slid open somewhere nearby. Ato ducked into the tiny crawl space behind the seat and held his breath.

"Everyone out!" Mephim's voice yelled. "Someone's boarded the cruiser. Get in the pods and head out immediately!"

Footsteps stormed toward the pods. Ato cringed. Someone got

in, their weight pushing the seat back against Ato. The door slid shut with a whir and then the whole ship rumbled as the pod igniters burst to life. Ato peeked up at the figure in the seat and almost gasped. It was Get.

The pod shivered and then burst up into the sky.

———————————

Max and Djinna ran into the pod hangar to find three empty slots.

"We're too late," Max gasped.

"No we're not," Djinna said. She swung around and sprinted back down the corridor.

Max hurried after her. "What do you mean?"

"Those pods don't have much push." She was already halfway up the ladder. "They gotta get at least a mile over the city to nuke it without getting hit themselves." She crawled out through the hatch and reached down for Max as he scrambled after her. "And we have shiolyders. We can get within firing range and knock them off course before they reach a mile."

"And then slide on into Plan B," Max said. "Brilliant!"

Djinna had already leapt into the sky and ignited her jetboots.

———————————

The pods were fist-size bursts of flame against the darkening clouds. Max had never pushed his jetboots to their full acceleration, mostly because the Flood City streets were too windy and crowded for that kind of speed, but he'd always wondered just how fast they could go. The rush of air against his face felt incredible. He closed his eyes for a second, allowing the sudden jolt of speed to settle with his body, and when he opened them, the escape pods were much closer than they had been before.

"We're gaining!" he shouted.

"I know!" Djinna yelled. "You ready, Max?" Djinna zoomed up alongside him. She unholstered her shiolyder.

Max nodded and took his own out. It was heavy and he had to readjust his balance some. "You think Ato's in one of 'em?"

"Gotta be," Djinna said. "But he'll be alright. The blasts will just throw them off course and give us a chance to sabotage 'em."

The shiolyder had a wide mouth, which Max was grateful for because he didn't think precision would be his strong point while hurtling upward at about a bajillion miles an hour. He pointed it at the nearest escape pod and pulled the trigger. A beam of light burst out across the dark blue sky and Max hurtled off to the side.

When he recovered, he saw the pod had been tossed laterally and was wobbling in jerky circles. "It worked!" Max yelled.

"Nice one," Djinna said. "Just ease up on the accelerators next time so the pushback doesn't knock you so far off course."

"Gotchya!"

"We're not in the clear yet," Djinna said. She was racing after one of the other pods, shiolyder at the ready.

"What is it?" Max asked.

"That pod on the right, Max! It's . . . glowing!"

"What?" Two pods remained. The one on the right pulsed with a sickening green glow. "Maybe it's from the nuke somehow! And that other one is way ahead. I don't know if we're gonna catch them in time!" He blasted full power toward them.

"That's not all," Djinna said, slowing her jets. "There's a ship coming."

A massive Star Guard transporter had warped into the sky and was bearing down on them.

Ato had been holding his breath again. The front of the pod was a dome of glass, which meant the entire sky opened up around them as the clouds sped past on either side and Earth got farther and farther away. Get's brow furrowed as he pushed hard on the engine blasters and swung the control sticks back and forth, trying to stay level.

Ato would have to jump him. It shouldn't be hard—he had the element of surprise—but still: It was a tight space and there was no telling how things would go. He was about to stand when a tiny version of Max materialized in the air beside Get.

"Ato? Can you hear me? Listen, man," holo-Max yelled over the screaming wind.

"What the—?" Get grunted, spinning around in the seat. He saw Ato and scowled, swinging at him. Ato threw himself over his brother, crashing them both back into the chair.

"I dunno where you are," Max went on, oblivious. "But if you're anywhere near that pod on the right, we think it has Mephim and the nuke on board. You gotta smash it or something! We're too far back. Oh, and there's, uh, a Star Guard transporter bearing down on us too, so yeah . . . watch out for that. Wherever you are."

Get freed a hand and cracked Ato across the face. It wasn't a very hard hit—he had no room to wind up—but it caught Ato off guard and he reeled back, stunned. Get shoved him backward and pounced, pinning him to the rounded glass. The lights of Flood City seemed to spin circles around them, and then the open sky. In the corner of his eye, Ato glimpsed the pod Max had described, a speeding splotch that glowed green against the night.

"Ato, man, come to your senses," Get said, still holding him fast against the front of the pod. His eyes looked sad, scared, the way they had when he'd admitted how terrified he was going out on missions. Ato thought his brother might be about to cry. "I know the ArchBaron's messed up, Ato."

"You do?"

Get nodded. "We can stop him together. We can make things better on the base fleet. Together. The way we do everything."

The base fleet. Home. Ato had wiped the idea of going home out of his mind entirely—it was too painful and totally impossible. But with Get on his side, maybe . . .

"We just have to reason with him. With all of them."

"Reason?"

"They're old and out of touch, but they'll hear us out if we stay on 'em. I know they will. And if not, we can work the system and outmaneuver them politically. We're Barons too, after all. We'll be grown in a few years and—"

"*Years?*" Ato blurted out. "Get, there's an ArchBaron about to drop a nuke on Flood City *now*!"

"He wouldn't," Get said. "He's mean, but he's not *that*—"

"And you want to reason with him?"

"I mean . . ."

"And you think it's *just* him? They're all like that up there, Get. Mom and Dad would probably shake their heads and be kinda disappointed, but that's it. They don't care about Earth or any of the people down there. They just care about themselves. You can't reason with that."

Get's eyes narrowed. "Either way, I'm not gonna let you get us both killed by attacking an ArchBaron, Ato. No way."

Any second, Mephim would drop that nuke and annihilate Flood City. The two brothers locked eyes and Ato thought about the world below him, this strange, crooked place of survivors who had embraced him even though he was their sworn enemy. He thought about the way everyone up on the base fleet was pale like him and everyone down on Earth was brown, about the textbook saying the Barons had caused the Floods, killed billions of people, and Max's shrugged acceptance of it, and how Max somehow still had room in his heart for someone like Ato, even after all that death. Ato glared into his brother's eyes and headbutted him with all his might.

"Ah!" Get yelled, splaying backward with his hands over his shattered nose. Blood streamed down his face. He lurched at Ato, fist pulled back for another hit.

And stopped. His wide eyes looked past Ato's head to Mephim's pod. "It's . . ." His mouth dropped open.

Ato turned. Mephim's pod glowed with a sickly, menacing green. "Whoa . . ."

"He's mad," Get said. "He's really gone mad, hasn't he?"

Ato looked back at his brother, who was now cradling his nose again. "I think he always has been."

"But he's . . . he's Mephim. He's an Arch. How . . ."

"We have to do something," Ato said. "Or a lot of people are going to die."

Get's fist opened. He slumped backward into the chair. "He k-killed a whole family. Almost a whole family. And he wanted me to kill two of the kids but I couldn't . . . I mean, they jumped me before I could but I don't think I—"

"Get," Ato said. "Move over. We have to stop him. *Now.*"

Get looked up, his eyes flush with tears. "You're right!" He shoved the control stick all the way to one side and the pod swung hard. A horrible crack sounded and both Get and Ato were thrown to the side. Ato crawled into the pilot's seat. Mephim's pod still sailed along beside them, glowing bright green.

"Again!" Get yelled.

THE FLOOD CITY GAZETTE

SPECIAL ALERT EDITION

CITIZENS!! THE INFILTRATING BARONS APPEAR TO HAVE MADE THEIR MOVE. THERE'S JETBOOT ACTIVITY AND REPORTS OF FIGHTING IN THE SKIES ABOVE THE CENTRAL PLAZA. CITIZENS, IF YOU HAVE WEAPONS STASHED AWAY, RETRIEVE THEM AND PREPARE FOR AN ATTACK OF ANY KIND. REMEMBER, THE BARONS WILL BE DRESSED LIKE US. DO NOT BE SUCKERED IN. FIGHT FOR YOUR FREEDOM! FIGHT FOR FLOOD CITY!

CHAPTER

The escape pod was not built for tall, angley people like Mephim, and it was making him sweat. And now Get's pod was crashing against his. To top it off, he was starting to mutate. A thousand microscopic fireballs burst through his blood vessels. His fingers stretched longer, each nail extended and curled forward. His trembling arms began aching and his vision blurred.

This was good, this was part of the plan, but still . . . he'd never been through mutation before, and the pod kept shuddering with Get's attacks.

The control panel suddenly burst to life with flashing red lights and then smoke poured into the cabin as Get rammed him again.

The codex on this pod was a metal box above the pilot seat. Mephim reached for it with a trembling claw. Surely the most senior officer on that Star Guard carrier would have some inkling about the secret negotiations. Maybe that freakish floating frog Uk was on board. He fiddled with the buttons, leaving deep gashes in the control panel. "This is ArchBaron Mephim to Star Guard transporter, come in."

Static. Then a girl's voice, scratchy across the airwaves: "Star Guard transport rig H479-X to ArchBaron Mephim, proceed with your message."

"Put me in contact with your highest-ranking officer immediately." The boy who had knocked the first pod off course was gaining, raising that wide-nosed weapon of his, and the girl wasn't far behind him.

"That would be me, ArchBaron."

"What?" Mephim spat into his headset. He absolutely did not under any circumstances have time for games. A surge of wrath burst through him with such explosiveness it surprised even him. "But you're only a child, I can hear it from your voice. STOP THIS FOOLISHNESS!" His voice crescendoed into an inhuman snarl.

There was a pause, during which Mephim sweated profusely and watched with growing alarm as his chest heaved up and down, his whole body trembling through the transformation, and then the staticky voice returned. "This ship has been commandeered by the Flood City Rebel Guerrilla Squad, ArchBaron. I am Captain Yala Salazar and as such, the highest-ranking officer on board. How may I help you today, sir?"

Mephim tried to scream *No!* but all that came out was a raspy howl.

"Guys!" Ato yelled. "He's gonna make it! You need to go faster."

Max frowned. He was accelerating with all his strength and

had reached maximum speed. The Baron was still out of range, and now the Star Guard transporter was on the scene and probably about to blast him and Djinna out of the sky. "The vapors deployed?"

"Everything's set," Djinna said. "And my dad's got the holography covered."

A hidden portal slid open on the underside of the Star Guard ship and three laser cannons wheeled their heads out in a spinning fury. Max cringed, wondering whether he'd die in midair or make it all the way to the ground and then shatter into a million squishy pieces.

The cannons burst to life, bright red flashes exploding across the sky, but they weren't aimed at Max and Djinna.

"What on earth is going on?" Djinna gasped.

Max just shook his head, his mouth hanging wide open. They both slowed to a hover. Up ahead, Mephim's escape pod was taking a serious whupping from the laser cannons. Three direct hits had knocked it into a pathetic spin, and a fourth tore a chunk of metal from its side.

"Max!" A scratchy voice fizzled through Max's earpiece.

"Yala?"

"Max! It's me! It's me!" She was laughing hysterically. "We, uh . . . borrowed a ship!"

"Yala! You're . . . you're in the Star Guard ship?"

"In it? I'm piloting the thing! It's mine! Well . . . ours. I got Osen and Delta with me."

"Osen the weirdo alien creature thing with all the big weird elephant legs?"

There was an uncomfortable pause. "Uh, yeah. And you're on speakercom, Max."

"Oh. Hi, Osen. Um . . . so the guy in that escape pod has a nuke."

"I know," Yala said. "Krestlefax delivered your note and we busted outta the academy and came right away."

"Well, looks like you pretty much . . ."

"Incoming!" Djinna's voice crackled over the headsets.

Max spun around just in time to see a fireball crest across the sky toward Yala's transporter. "No!" Cortinas was flying up above the city. He lowered his slicer for a second, fiddling with it. Reloading. "It's not a Star Guard ship! It's Yala!" Max yelled, but the old rebel was too far away to hear him and didn't have a headset. Max dove toward Cortinas. Behind him, the blast exploded against the side of the transporter. A direct hit, of course. Max didn't even have to turn around to know. Cortinas was apparently an expert at the flying precision shot. One more and Yala would be fried.

"Cortinas!" Max yelled. It was no use. He watched in horror as Cortinas raised the cannon up to his shoulder for a final blast and peered through the viewer. Out of breath, Max could only let out a choked sob as he careened forward.

But the old rebel didn't shoot. Instead, Cortinas squinted up past Max as if he couldn't believe what he was looking at. Max slowed his jets and glanced behind him. Hunterflies, hundreds of them, were scattered out in the air directly in front of Yala's transporter. Max spotted Tinibu right in the middle of them all, twirling around and flapping his tiny wings. Cortinas lowered his weapon, still looking puzzled.

"It's one of our ships!" Max yelled, finally close enough to be heard. "Yala's on board! Don't shoot!"

"Your sister jacked a Star Guard transporter?" Cortinas gaped. "I'll be . . ."

It did seem even more amazing when he said it like that. But there wasn't time to be impressed. Mephim was still out there and still had the nuke. "Cortinas, the Barons are in those pods. We need to stop them!"

Cortinas nodded. "I'll blast them!"

"No!" Max yelled. "One of them has a nuclear weapon on board. If you blow the whole pod up, it'll kill us all. We're just trying to disable the thing so we can get to . . ."

"I'll round up the troops and we'll track down the other two pods!" Cortinas announced, and he zipped off. Below, a huge mass of clouds congealed where Flood City once was. Instead there was just a mountain of fluffy gray clouds.

"The vapors came through!" Djinna's voice crackled in Max's earpiece. "Nice!"

"Excellent!" Max gazed at the vast cloud wall of vapors stretching across Flood City. He wondered briefly which one was Biaque, or if it even worked like that—maybe they all just scattered their molecules and become a mass of nothingness all together. But there wasn't any time to sit there thinking about it. He'd have to remember to ask later.

"Um, Max," Djinna said. "You might want to see this." Max whirled around and watched in horror as a long, scaly arm reached out of Mephim's escape pod and dug its metal-shearing claws into the side.

"That hit demolished our shield!" Delta yelled from the control panel behind Yala.

Yala shook her head. "Yep, that's Cortinas. He doesn't miss. Looks like Max called him off though, thanks to those hunterflies."

We have another problem, Osen warbled in his strange telepathy. *Look.*

The escape pod they'd blasted still hung in the air, levitating in some eerie miasma of green light. Worse: a huge green arm with long claws and scattered feathers was reaching out of it.

"What is it?" Yala gasped.

Amalgamation, Osen muttered. His thick appendages circled the control board. *Abomination. Must increase shield capacity.*

"We're still depleted," Delta called. "I can't recharge them yet."

Yala squinted at the pod. "Is that a . . . giant iguanagull?"

Combined with the ArchBaron, yes. This one has employed a secret and terrible magic.

The arm was followed by a long green head with a man's face. Hideous fangs poked out of his scaly mouth, and his eyes were glowing red and full of hatred. He let out a shriek and then tore the tattered escape pod to shreds with a few quick swipes of his claws.

When the debris fell away the creature hung in the air, flapping those great wings and clutching a metal case in his long, horrible arms. The nuke.

"Oh no," Yala said. "Things just got worse."

Max was making gagging sounds into his mic. "It's a . . . and it's Mephim . . . and it's a . . . Yala, you there?"

She hit the codex button. "Here, Max."

"We need to get that thing away from Flood City, preferably to the east toward the holographer's tower."

"We'll do what we can, Max, just get ready to make a mad dash to catch that bomb in case he drops it." The creature screeched and flapped higher into the sky. He moved awkwardly, like one of those monsters from old holoflicks that wasn't animated quite right. Mephim must still be getting the hang of his new body, Yala realized. This was their only chance. "Delta, open up with those lasers, but careful not to hit the nuke."

"On it." The Star Guard cannons released a barrage of fire. Mephim spun and thrashed frantically, sending bloodied feathers whipping out around him, but still he climbed, and then he snarled suddenly and scurried out of view. She narrowed her eyes. "Prepare for maximum acceleration, Osen."

Osen nodded.

"On my command."

Any second now . . . there was a screech and Yala yelled, "NOW!" just as the long, gnarled creature burst into view. That fanged mouth opened wide as his lower claws reached up, poised to shred into the glass. Yala let a tiny smile curl up the side of her face. And then the transporter jolted forward. Yala was thrown back in her chair. For a few seconds, all they could see was Mephim, flattened against the blast window.

Then his green face contorted, and with a screech, he was gone.

———————

Max watched in horror as Mephim curved his huge green body away from the rumbling transporter and nose-dived toward the clouds above Flood City. "He's gonna suicide-bomb it!" Djinna yelled. "Max!"

"I know!"

The creature swept past Max and Djinna, his claws wrapped around the nuke, mouth curved into a triumphant smile. Max didn't know if Mephim was simply reckless enough to die for his cause or, worse, could somehow withstand a nuclear blast in his heightened mutant form. Either way, it wasn't part of the plan. In a daze, Max let his head fall forward so he was pointed directly down and accelerated as hard as he could.

"Max!" Djinna yelled. Seconds later she was beside him, the wind whipping her hair back. "What's the plan?"

Max pulled out his horn. He always kept it close, so stashing it in his satchel before they took off had barely been a second thought. Now it was his last hope. "We call for backup."

It took a few tries, what with the wind blowing against the mouth of the horn, but eventually Max found the right angle. He tilted his head just so and, still rocketing toward the cloud-covered Flood City, let out a long and sorrowful blast. He heard Djinna click in right on time with the metal rods she'd brought, dinging out that same slick syncopation she'd used at the pageant.

It felt absurd, of course, to be playing music at a time like this, but Mephim had simply exhausted all their plans one by one. Max thought of Flood City erupting into a mushroom cloud, of every single one of his friends and family members, the people who had raised him and made him who he was, all being disintegrated in a fiery hailstorm. He put all that sorrow into the notes he played, and then he saw the first iguanagull.

He wondered if it was the same one who'd perched on his window. Then he saw another. And then another. They were soaring all around him. They were zooming past him, their claws extended, mouths wide open. Max didn't know how, but he felt they understood what was going on. Maybe he'd said it with the music. Maybe they could just tell. Either way, he was suddenly in the center of a great airborne reptilian army.

Mephim hurtled toward the clouds, clutching the nuclear bomb. Just before disappearing into the nebula, he glanced back and then shrieked.

Iguanagulls.

Hundreds and hundreds of them, all racing toward him. And those two horrible kids were right in the middle of it all. The first iguanagull reached him before he could finish his shriek. Mephim swatted at it with all the strength in his arm and the thing went hurtling away, but two more were right behind it. They sliced at his wings with their talons and Mephim had only one free arm to fight back with. He dodged to one side and then flapped frantically away as the iguanagulls kept coming.

He had to drop the nuke, even if he was torn to pieces in the process. If he could just break away for a second or two and figure out where Flood City was in all these clouds. The boy swooped past him, blowing on that infernal horn, and the girl followed quickly after. They had some kind of plan, that much was clear. Mephim clobbered an attacking iguanagull and then felt sharp teeth close over his shoulder. He was so surprised he almost let the nuke slip out of his grasp, but he caught it at the last second and then flung the creature off him. Blood poured freely from the gash it had left behind. Feathers were everywhere.

Where was Flood City?

The beasts seemed to be pushing him somewhere. He sensed their drive as they swooped, snapped at him, and then retreated. The music those kids were playing must be having some kind of hypnotic effect on them. Mephim snarled. Where was the boy?

Suddenly, though, it didn't matter. The clouds cleared below and Mephim spotted the towers of Flood City, standing like ghosts in the night.

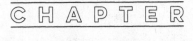

Mephim made a smile that showed all his teeth. Three iguana-gulls were swooping toward him, talons out, but he didn't care. He stopped flapping, felt gravity take him, and then squinted down at the city rising out of the cloud bank. He had wanted to hit it smack in the center, but really any old spot would do. A nuke was a nuke, after all. When it was over he'd lick his wounds and begin the exploration. But first: With a shriek of laughter, ArchBaron Mephim released the nuke.

The trio of iguanagulls had caught up to him. He hissed and scratched two of them with his back claws and then clobbered the third. Any second now. A fourth showed up, seemingly out of nowhere, and snapped a chunk of flesh off his leg. He batted it away. Too much time had passed. Mephim dove past the flock-ing iguanagulls. The whole world should be a fiery apocalypse by now, not a pleasant autumn evening. There should be mountains of toxic dust and flame exploding across the sky. There should be chaos!

Mephim flapped farther toward the city. Nothing. No explosion. Nothing. The clouds were clearing and so was Flood City, floating away in a flickering light like a . . . hologram.

Mephim howled. He raged back and forth in the sky, shrieking and thrashing his claws at whatever iguanagull dared come too close. Below him, the empty ocean stretched for miles and miles. Somewhere beneath the surface, a nuclear bomb was descending harmlessly into the depths.

The boy. It had all been a trick. Mephim craned his head up and saw the little scumbag hovering in midair, staring back at him. He gnashed his teeth and charged.

Max felt a strange calmness as Mephim came howling toward him. The creature wanted him to flee, he could see it in those flaming red eyes. A good chase, and then he'd tear Max to shreds and rain his entrails over Flood City. Max decided not to turn away. Instead, he powered up his jetboots and shot forward, directly into Mephim's charge.

Behind him, Djinna yelled, "Max! No!"

Max felt the wind go out of Mephim's lungs as soon as they crashed into each other. The creature had been taken completely off guard and was all flailing limbs and flapping wings for a few seconds. Max pushed forward, wrapping his arms around that scaly torso, and thrust his jetboots into their highest setting.

Before Mephim could regain his balance, they were over Flood

City, the real one this time. They hurdled between towers and over alleyways. Max felt claws slash across his back. He knew he was bleeding but there was nothing he could do about it. He reached around and found where the tattered wings connected to the creature's shoulders. The iguanagulls had already done a number on them—most of the feathers were gone, and one was hanging awkwardly to the side. Max grabbed the other, tried to figure out the least pleasant angle for it to be in, and then pulled with all his strength.

Mephim screamed and slashed at Max again, but his arms had been weakened by the iguanagulls' attacks. The wing was broken. Max was fading fast, but he knew exactly what he had to do. He only hoped he'd made it close enough for everything to work. He released his bear hug on Mephim, put his jetboots up against the creature's chest, and blasted off. Beneath him, the creature hovered there for a full three seconds, his broken wings flapping pathetically, and then a blast of freakish blue electricity sliced through the air and wrapped around his waist. Mephim's eyes, which just seconds earlier had been narrowed with murderous intent, suddenly opened wide. Another streak of electric ghost burst out into the sky and wrapped around his leg.

The air grew heavy with the static of the angry electrified dead. Max didn't know if he could keep climbing; everything was starting to get all foggy and weird looking. He was pretty sure he was about to pass out and probably vomit too. How terrible it would be to puke midair and then fall forward into it and then get eaten by electric ghosts and/or Mephim. Then he chuckled, in a ridiculous, morbid sort of way, because he was thinking about barf at a time like this, when his life and the very existence of Flood City was in the balance.

One of Mephim's gut-wrenching shrieks rang out. Max swiveled his body slightly and saw another blast of bright blue enveloping the horrible thing, pulling Mephim slowly into the static-filled wire graveyard.

Wonderful, Max thought as he tried to point his descent in a trajectory that wouldn't land him in the ocean or the ghostyard or impaled on some pointy steeple. *And I didn't even puke.*

Max exhaled for what felt like the first time in years and gradually decreased the power of his jetboots until he reached the ground, just in time to pass out.

THE FLOOD CITY GAZETTE

FREEDOM FREEDOM FREEDOM!!!!!

RATIONS REPORT

We finally figured out how to take off caps lock! Here's to small victories amidst large ones!! The Sustainable Food Creation Competition has already yielded some amazing results. We're so proud of all the brilliant minds here on Flood City. Such ingenuity! We'll have presentations from all the finalists at our community-wide meeting next Wednesday, and then everyone who submitted an entry will split into teams and get to work! It won't be easy, but we got this!

THE DAILY TIDE

Low tide today will be at **0515**.

High tide will be at **2121**.

Please *avoid the city edges during high tide, as conditions can worsen suddenly.*

IGUANAGULL AHOY!

Iguanagulls spotted by the Holographer's Tower and near the Music Hall. Don't mess with them, we're gonna get this food situation sorted out some other way.

THE BOOO'CAST

Lots of heightened electrospectral activity by the EGY, probably because they're still monching on that wicked wizard dude.

THE VAPORS & ABANDONED OCEAN LINER REPORT

The vapors have decided to openly join Flood City society now that they helped save all our lives! Catch them out and about in Barge Annex or take one of the tours of the Ocean Liner they're offering every weekday afternoon!

CHEMICAL BARONS

Gone for now, but they'll be back. Meanwhile, let's all make sure we're ready for 'em . . .

"Max?"

The dream was too pleasant to let go of. Hundreds of plants were rising from the ocean; vast crop fields and forests stretched out all across Earth, where waves had once been.

"Max!"

"What?"

It was Yala, and oddly enough, she was standing outside. Behind her, Max could see the ocean stretched out all around them. It was a beautiful day; the sun was streaming through a bank of blue and white clouds, shimmering across the water. "You're alive."

Max put a hand to his face. It was solid, so that was good. He nodded weakly. "I'm glad."

"And you saved Flood City from being nuked with your ridiculous plan."

"Oh?"

Yala nodded, looking prouder than Max had ever seen her. "You did good, little bro."

Max smiled and then realized that there was a huge armored dinosaur-type monster standing discreetly off to the side. "What the—?" he yelled, scooching up.

"Relax, Captain Awesome. It's Osen. The tarashid I told you about?"

"Oh." Max tried to study the creature without being all obvious about staring, but it didn't work. The thing didn't seem to mind all the uproar; it just bowed its big armored head and stood there emanating a peacefulness that was startling for such a bugged-out-looking alien.

"He healed you, Max. All those scars that the iguanagull Baron lashed across your back when you were fighting? They're barely even noticeable."

"He . . . he did?" Max turned to the tarashid again and summoned up his humblest voice. "Thank you, Mr. Osen, for healing me."

Again the great creature bowed slightly.

"Where are we?"

"The roof of our building. Mom thought you might want some fresh air. Plus people keep coming by to visit and talk to you and bring flowers and things and they wouldn't take the hint that you need your rest."

"I guess I do since I've been unconscious for . . . how long?"

"Just a day, more or less. They checked you out at the hospital and said you'd be okay. But everyone's talking about you and Djinna and Ato and the iguanagulls fighting that Baron creature . . . it's amazing!"

"There he is." Biaque glided across the rooftop toward them, a big grin plastered across his face. Tinibu fluttered up past him and perched on Max's shoulder. "The hero of Flood City."

"Stop," Max said. "I didn't do anything alone. And Tinibu saved Yala's life!"

The hunterfly made a chirpy noise and adjusted his footing on Max's shoulder.

"Max!" Ato and Djinna came running across the roof.

"You guys okay?" Max asked.

"Are *we* okay? Of course we are!" Djinna said, her hands on her hips. "You're the one that almost got ate by a giant transforming Baron monster! Are *you* okay?"

"I do believe I am," Max said, and when Djinna smiled he knew it was true.

Ato still looked worried. "We didn't know what happened to you for a little while there. You just disappeared into the clouds and then went radio silent."

"I know. It was messy. Mephim?"

"Became one with the Electric Ghost Yard, far as we can tell," Biaque said.

"What happens now?"

The vapor put a thoughtful expression on. "Truth be told: We don't know yet. The Star Guard is gone, so Flood City is without any real food source and completely unprotected from the Barons for the first time since the original rebellion."

"Are people scared?"

"Of course," Yala said. "But they're excited too. It's something completely new, and even though it's dire, everyone seems to believe, against all odds, that we'll find a way to survive. We've come this far."

Max thought about it. He felt the same way. By any reasoning, there was no hope whatsoever, but that had been true when the first floodwaters splashed across Earth, and still, Cortinas and the others had made it through. *There must've been thousands of bleak, seemingly impossible moments in all the years of Flood City history, but still, we live on*, Max thought. There was no other choice, really. "What's the plan?"

"We captured Ato's brother and the other Barons," Yala said, smiling triumphantly. "And . . . do you wanna tell him, Ato?"

Ato stepped forward. He looked slightly queasy and thoroughly excited. "I'm going back up."

"What?" An unexpected sadness fell over Max. He'd thought his new best friend would be around for a long time.

"We figured they know that I defied ArchBaron Mephim and went AWOL, but they don't know what happened after that. And they don't know . . ."

"That we captured your brother!" Max finished.

"Exactly," Yala said.

"So you're going in disguise." It sounded dangerous. Would he ever see Ato again?

Ato nodded. "Who better to impersonate the angry young ArchBaron-to-be than his own twin? Anyway, it'll be a chance to learn some more about all this strange magic my people have been using, which seems a lot more powerful than I ever realized. We sent a coded message to the base fleet and told them to rendezvous with Get on the nearest satellite station. And then . . . we'll see. Somehow, I hope to be able to at least hold off the attack long enough to give you guys time to prepare."

Max didn't know what to say. *Thank you. Goodbye.* They would all sound inadequate coming out of his mouth at a time like this, so he just nodded and tried to convey everything in that one motion. Ato nodded back and seemed to understand. "Did you tell everyone about the soil?"

"He did," Biaque said. "And we're preparing to take a team to find where it came from."

Yala grinned wildly. "The Star Guard abandoned their training base in a hurry, and I happen to have been borrowing that transporter ship when they left so technically, you know . . . it's mine now."

"She's leading the mission," Biaque said, looking like a proud dad.

Max sat up. "Can I come with?"

"You need your rest, young man." It was Dr. Sarita, cutting through the crowd of Max's friends with a bowl of towelly soup and some dougies.

"Mom!"

She put the tray down and kissed Max on the top of his head. "My little hero."

"Okay, Mom. But seriously, can I go with them?"

"No promises. They're leaving as soon as the team is assembled and the route charted. If you're feeling better by then, I'll consider it."

"Don't worry," Yala said, "there'll be plenty more missions after this one."

Somewhere up in space, the Barons were plotting their next try at reclaiming Earth for good. And way out past the waves, there was land. Soil. Which meant food, which meant survival, independence, freedom.

Max looked out to where the ocean met the sky and smiled.

ABOUT THE AUTHOR

Daniel José Older is the critically acclaimed *New York Times* bestselling author of numerous books for readers of all ages: for middle grade, *Dactyl Hill Squad*, *Freedom Fire*, and *Thunder Run*; for young adults, *Shadowshaper*, *Shadowhouse Fall*, and *Shadowshaper Legacy*; and for adults, *Star Wars: Last Shot*, *The Book of Lost Saints*, and the Bone Street Rumba urban fantasy series. He has worked as a bike messenger, a waiter, and a teacher, and was a New York City paramedic for ten years. Daniel splits his time between Brooklyn and New Orleans.

You can find out more about him at danieljoseolder.net.